Everything exists, everything is true,
and the earth is only a little dust under our feet.

—W. B. YEATS

THE DEVIL'S SINKHOLE

BILL WITTLIFF

The Devil's Sinkhole

Illustrated by JOE CIARDIELLO

University of Texas Press, *Austin*

THE PUBLICATION OF THIS BOOK WAS MADE
POSSIBLE BY A GENEROUS CONTRIBUTION FROM
THE UNIVERSITY OF TEXAS PRESS ADVISORY COUNCIL.

♾ The paper used in this book meets the minimum requirements of
ANSI/NISO Z39.48-1992 (R1997) (Permanence of Paper).

LIBRARY OF CONGRESS CATALOGING-IN-PUBLICATION DATA
Names: Wittliff, William D., author. | Ciardiello, Joseph, illustrator.
Title: The Devil's Sinkhole / Bill Wittliff ; illustrated by Joe Ciardiello.
Description: First edition. | Austin : University of Texas Press, 2016.
Identifiers: LCCN 2016006693
 ISBN 978-1-4773-0974-2 (cloth : alk. paper)
 ISBN 978-1-4773-0975-9 (library e-book)
 ISBN 978-1-4773-0976-6 (non-library e-book)
Subjects: LCSH: Families—Texas—Fiction. | Texas—Fiction.
Classification: LCC PS3573.I933 D44 2016 | DDC 813/.54—dc23
LC record available at http://lccn.loc.gov/2016006693

doi:10.7560/309742

For My Grandfather

EMIL SACHTLEBEN

January 27, 1881–February 7, 1969

And For

J. FRANK DOBIE

September 26, 1888–September 18, 1964

THE DEVIL'S SINKHOLE

Who's o'Pelo Blanco,

Papa said, I ain't never heared a'him in my Life. O'Pelo Blanco, Calley said, o'White Hair. You tell him the Story Miz Choat, he said. I don't know I want this Boy to even hear it it's so Bad, Miz Choat said. If o'Pelo Blanco's a'coming he's gonna hear it soon enough any how I reckon, Mister Choat said. Yes course you are just Right as Rain bout that Mister Choat, Miz Choat said. Well it's said some thirty forty odd years ago they was this Mexkin Man and his Little Son went to stealing Horses all up and down the Country round here and one night this Bunch a'Cow Boys come up on em with they pistols out and put em to digging they own Grave for they Crime then put a Noose round they neck and set each one a'em up on a Horse to hang from a Limb but the Daddy went to Crying and a'Hollering and a'Begging for his Little Son's Life cause he said his Little Son didn't never do nothing Bad in his Life but just only what he the Daddy told him to do and all the Cow Boys cep one said Okay we gonna let the little Fella go if you was the One put him up to stealing these Horses here and the Mexkin Daddy said Oh Si Senyor I was the One then made the Sign a'the Holy Cross over his self and said Gracias for my Little Son's Life and all the Cow Boys cep one said Well we're sorry it come to this Senyor but here it is and you just gonna have to Live with it now and then that one Cow Boy said I bet you'd like to give your Little Son here a Hug and a Kiss Goodbye fore you go wouldn't you and the Daddy said Oh Si Si Si Senyor Gracias so the Cow Boy lifted the Little Son up and set him in his Daddy's lap and the Daddy put his arms round him and they was both just a'Crying and a'Carrying on and Oh it was Sad Sad Sad and then the Daddy give his Little Son a tight Hug and a Last Kiss Goodbye and when he did Why that Cow Boy of a sudden let out a Big Whoop and give the Horse a Slap with his Quirt and the Horse reared up and took off a'running and that poor o'Daddy went to kicking the air but he was still a'Hugging and a'Kissing his Little Son at the same time he was a'jumping on the end a'that rope and couldn't let go for nothing and it went on like that til at last the

ive your Little Son here a Hug
1 a Kiss Goodbye...

Daddy was Hanged Dead Dead Dead but his Little Son kep a'hanging on to his Daddy cause he loved him so much and knowed they was never gonna be no more Hugging and Kissing after this and they say that Little Son hanged on til his Hair turned total White on him then when he couldn't hang on no more he dropped to the ground but by then all them Cow Boys done already rode on off so the Little Son buried his Daddy in the Hole but first he pulled the Noose off from round his Daddy's neck and put it round his own neck and then soons he growed up Big and Strong he went to hunting down and Hanging ever one a'them Cow Boys One by One with that same xact Noose and not only them but ever Blood Kin Man born to em all up and down the line back to o'Adam his self. They Fathers and they Sons and they Grandad-dys and they Brothers and they Uncles and they Cousins and he Hanged em ever one. Yes Sir, Calley said, Hanged em ever one deadern a god dam Fence Post. All cep one, he said. I don't know what this got to do with me, Papa said, I ain't never Hanged nobody. No, Miz Choat said, but your Daddy did. Old Karl was the One quirted that Horse out from under that poor o'Daddy and his Little Son. But Old Karl is dead, Papa said. Yes Sir I know it, Calley said, but you ain't.

I GOTTA GO WARN HERMAN, Papa said, If o'Pelo Blanco's coming to get me he's a'coming to get him too ain't he. Ain't nobody gonna get you, Calley said, you don't have to worry bout that. I'll ride down there and warn Herman bout it my self, Mister Choat said, See if maybe he don't wanna move in over here with us a'while so he got him some Help if o'Pelo comes a'knocking. Miz Choat was bout to cry, Papa said, and come over and give me a hug. Seems like Old Karl just won't leave you alone will he, she said, don't matter he's a'Live or Dead neither one. Yes Ma'am I know it, Papa said. A Son shouldn't oughta have to pay for the Sins a'the Father, Miz Choat said, it's writ in the Bible. Yes Ma'am and it's writ here in my Bible too, Calley said then give his big Pistola a little pet like you might o'Fritz or some other friendly Dog. Where you reckon you and this Boy gonna go, Mister Choat said. Why to find o'Pelo Blanco that's where, Calley said. Oh good Lord I was fraid you didn't have no Good Sense when I first seen you, Miz Choat said, and now I know it.

You want this Boy hiding back behind a Rock all his Life, Calley said, You want him jumping up under the Bed ever time somebody comes a'riding up the Road on a Horse or something. Yes Sir that'd suit me fine, Miz Choat said, long as he's safe from Harm. They's all kinds a'Harm out there Ma'am, Calley said, and it's been my xperience the first place it looks when it comes a'looking for you is up under the Bed. He's right, Mister Choat said. Yes I know he is, Miz Choat said, but I don't wanna hear it. How you even gonna find o'Pelo Blanco any how, Mister Choat said, They say he got the knack to take his self clean outta View anytime he wants to and don't nobody see him til he's already there bout to Murder you. Yes Sir, Calley said, and they say he got Horns on him like some o'Pokey Dot Billy Goat too and a long Pointy Tail to boot but I don't reckon he can outrun a Lead Bullet if I was to send one out my o'Pistola here to go a'chasing him do you. You don't have Good Sense, Miz Choat said, and now you a'getting Uppity too ain't you. Now Hattie, Mister Choat said, you don't wanna lose your Sweet Manners here do you. No I don't, Miz Choat said, I take it all back. You don't have to, Calley said, I know you didn't mean it. I said I take it back, Miz Choat said, I never said I didn't mean it. You ain't gone Stupid on me now too have you Mister Pearsall. Bird wants to say something, Marcellus said, and we all looked over there to see Bird a'holding Marcellus's Finger and his eyes just a'working back and forth back behind his Lids. Sometimes Bird grabs a'holt a'Marcellus's Finger like that and then Marcellus knows what he's a'thinking, Miz Choat said. What's he a'thinking Marcellus, Mister Choat said. Bird's a'thinking they's only one way to find o'Pelo Blanco fore he finds you, Marcellus said. Yes Sir and how's that, Calley said. Well Sir, Marcellus said, Bird says Just foller the Buzzerds which ever way they fly but don't never dare to go looking up at em when you do.

*T*HAT NIGHT

I went a'walking in my Dream, Papa said, and here fore long I come up on this Dark Cave went way back in there somewheres and Why setting right there in the Door just a'Shimmering away wadn't nobody in the World but my o'three legged Coyote Friend Mister Pegleg. Oh Mister Pegleg I said, Papa said, Oh Mister Pegleg I am so glad to see you even if you are Dead and Gone and I run over there and give him a Hug and he give me a Lick back and Oh we just set there a'while being so Happy to see one another like that and then, he said, I follered Mister Pegleg on in that Dark Cave and they was Caves went off from this one in ever which direction and Oh they was neckid People in ever one of em and they was all a'Crying and a'Moaning and a'Hollering and a'Pulling they Hair out and a'Bugging they Eyes like it was the End of the World and I tell you I never seen Nobody no saddern this Bunch here in all my Life. Oh so Sad, Papa said, but Mister Pegleg went a'hobbling on pass em fast as he could go and I had to trot to keep up and Deeper Deeper Deeper we went on down in that Cave til here in a minute we come round this corner to the Bottom and Oh they was a Man a'setting there all by his self on a Flat Rock with bout a thousand Black Dominoes piled up all round his Feet and maybe two three White Ones and this Man, Papa said, had his Head way down in his Hands and Oh he was just a'Bawling like some poor Little Baby done lost his Momma and the Tears come a'pouring out tween his fingers like the River Jordan and then of a sudden Oh No I seen it was Old Karl my own Daddy was who it was a'setting there on that Flat Rock a'crying and he looked up at me and I never seen such a look a'Lostness and a'Loneness in all my Life and I said, Papa said, Daddy how come you a'feeling so Sad like this today. And then, he said, my mean o'Daddy raised up both his Hands and went to grabbing at the Air like he was trying to grab a fly or something Lost to him but No Sir it just wadn't there for him to grab no more and Oh then he just went to Crying some more and Grabbing Grabbing Grabbing at the Air and then he scrunched up his Face and he hollered LIFE. LIFE was what he hollered, Papa said. LIFE LIFE LIFE LIFE. That's what Old Karl hollered, he said, and he hollered it Over and Over and Over again LIFE LIFE LIFE LIFE LIFE. Oh LIFE LIFE LIFE he hollered and I knowed what he meant was Oncet he had him a Life but No Sir not no more and now he was gonna be down here a'setting on that Flat Rock at the Bottom a'Hell For Ever More. Oh For Ever More, Papa said, but then I seen they was somebody a'coming up back behind him out a'the Dark and they was reaching out they hand to give Old Karl a pet and Oh then I seen Why it was my very own Momma was who it was and when she put her hand out to pet him Why Old Karl jumped back like somebody just pitched a bucket a'wet Rattlesnakes at him and he started a'mouthing NO NO NO but no Sound come out Just his Mouth a'going

NO NO NO NO NO and then he covered his Eyes up with his Hands cause he didn't wanna see Momma standing there but ever time he peeked tween his fingers Why she was still standing right there a'looking back at him but not with No Hate or nothing like that for Murdering her in the First Place but Just a'standing there a'looking at him cause she was Sorry for him but Oh that was bout to drive him Loonie but they wadn't nothing he could do to get her outta his View so he took him two big Hand Fulls a'Dirt off the floor and went to pushing it in his Eyes with his Fingers til he couldn't see Her no more or Nothing Else in the World neither one and Oh he did Holler Holler Holler it hurt so bad and then Oh he went to Crying some more but all that come out his Eyes now and run down his Face was Mud but least I reckon he was glad he couldn't see Momma no more. And then I waked up, Papa said, and Oh Boy Hidy I was glad I did but the Thing surprised me most bout Hell was I didn't see no Devil down there like they say they's gonna be but was just Old Karl a'setting there on that Flat Rock a'doing all them terrible things to his self for all the Bad Things he done to Momma and all them Other People when he was up here in his Life and then it come to me, he said, that Old Karl was his own Devil and maybe Ever Body else down there is they own Devil too and that's how it works.

SO I THROWED MY MOMMA'S MEXKIN SADDLE on o'Edward that o'Plow Horse Mister Choat give me to ride on and me and Calley went a'riding on off early next morning, Papa said, and it wadn't no easy thing to do what with Miz Choat a'hugging on me for bout a year and Bird not wanting to let go a'my Finger neither and Marcellus bout to cry cause he was so scared for me to go out there in the World where o'Pelo Blanco might get me. O'Fritz didn't wanna go neither, he said, and took his self over behind a tree to where he figgured I couldn't see him but then he jumped right up on Edward that o'Plow Horse Mister Choat give me to ride on soon as I give him my heels to go. Them bout the nicest People I ever been round in my Life, Calley said, you know it. I said Yes Sir I do know it, Papa said, but I was off in that Dream I had last night. You ever think bout Hell Mister Pearsall, I said. Think about it, he said, Why listen here Amigo I live it ever day a'my Life a'being here with you. I ain't teasing, Papa said.

Well Hell ain't something I dwell on, Calley said, I figgur I already got me a First Class Blue Ribbon Ticket to there as it is. I believe you'd sooner Tease then you would Eat and Drink wouldn't you Mister Pearsall, Papa said. I'm sorry, Calley said, I'll try not to do it again. Least for a second or two he said then laughed at his new Joke, Papa said, and Fritz did too with a little Heh Heh Heh and Calley reached over and give him a little knock on his head and said Fritz if I had another hunderd or two like you to where I could make a living off it Why I'd go on the Stage and have you a'laughing all the day long. Whatta you reckon Hell is, Papa said. Well they's a big Fire down there and they won't give you a Drink a'Water to wet your Whistle, he said, That's what it is. I went down there in my Dream last night, Papa said, and they wadn't no Fire nowheres I could see. What they was, he said, was Old Karl a'setting there on a Flat Rock a'crying cause he done all them Bad Things in his Life but now he's trapped down there in this Cave and can't come back up here to patch any of em up no matter how much he wants to. So Old Karl just gonna have to set on that Flat Rock down there and cry bout it til King-dom Come huh, Calley said. Yes Sir I reckon, Papa said, and maybe even af-ter that. You sure that was Old Karl, Calley said, I never heard a'the Old Karl I know being Sorry for even one god dam Bad Thing he ever done in his Life and he got a lot to choose from too don't he. Well he was a'crying his eyes out bout something, Papa said. Calley run the whole thing over in his mine then said Yes Sir I reckon that would be about the worstest Hell they ever could be. To wanna Right a Wrong you done and not never get the Chance to do it for all Time to come Why that'd dam sure Break a Man's Heart and Stomp on it wouldn't it. Did Old Karl's I reckon, Papa said, from what I seen. Well we just gonna have to send o'Pelo Blanco down there to keep him com-pany on that Flat Rock then ain't we, Calley said, Maybe that'll cheer the o'SonofaBitch up. From what I know bout it, he said, they like two Peas in a Pod any how ain't they.

HOW WE GONNA DO THAT, Papa said. Well, o'Calley said, First Thing we gotta do is Catch him then kick his fuzzy o'Butt for hanging all them People then give him over to some body for his own Hanging and blow him a Kiss Adios Pendejo. Course, he said, I wouldn't put it pass us to go on and Hang him our self just to teach him a lesson you know it. I ain't gonna Hang no body, Papa said. You ain't huh, Calley said. No Sir, Papa said, not less they Hanged me first. You ain't gonna be in no shape to Hang some body if you already been Hanged you self you ever think about that Mister. I just don't wanna Hang nobody that's all, Papa said, I wouldn't feel right bout it. No me neither, Calley said. I reckon maybe we oughta just shoot him in sted huh. You teasing me again ain't you Mister Pearsall I said, Papa said. Maybe I am and Maybe I ain't, o'Calley said. You just gonna have to wait and see oncet we catch that o'Crimnal. Then he reached down and give his Spur a little Ching e Ching e Ching-ChingChing like he some time did when he was a'thinking bout some thing. Truth is, he said, I don't know I'm a'teasing or not my self. Then Fritz went Heh Heh Heh again and o'Calley reached over and give him another little knock on his head. You always got some thing to say bout it too ain't you Fritz, he said. I don't know what we'd do for Conversation round here if you wadn't long on the Trip.

It was bout that time, Papa said, we started seeing this big Bunch a'Buzzerds a'circling us up there in the Sky and they was still there when we went to sleep that Night and they was there when we come a'wake the next Morning too and they was still there all that whole Day long and the whole next Day too. What you reckon them Birds is a'doing up there any how Mister Pearsall I said, Papa said, and o'Calley said I reckon they up there to keep a Eye on you for o'Pelo. That's what I reckon he said. How'd he ever get em to do that, Papa said. You sure you wanna know, Calley said. Be sure now. Yes Sir I do, Papa said. The Way I heared it, Calley said, o'Pelo always leaves a little some thing Dead on the Tree for em to eat ever time he hangs Some Body and them Buzzerds been a'follering him round like Dogs ever since. Oh, Papa said, I wish you hadn't a'told me that.

*S*O WE FOLLERED THEM BUZZERDS FOR DAYS, Papa said, For Days and Days and for Weeks and Weeks and I reckon maybe even for Months and Months too but we never not even oncet seen o'Pelo Blanco nor a sign a'him neither one that we could read. Maybe he Up and Died on us and we just don't know it, I said. Yes Sir, Calley said, and maybe that's just Wishful Thinking too. You don't mind I'm gonna take me a little Snooze here a minute. Watching them Buzzerds up there gone and made me Sleepy, he said. I looked, Papa said, and sure enough they was still that Big Circle a'Buzzerds up there in the Sky but now they was more or less coming our way outta the Setting Sun and I squinted my eyes near shut to keep a good watch on em. Mister Pearsall, Papa said, that's the most Buzzerds I ever seen all together in one Bunch in my Life but he was just a'Snoring a'way over there on Firefoot and didn't hear not one word I said and then here in a minute or two o'Fritz went to Snoring too like he almost always done any how when he wadn't a'Licking on his Hiney and then next thing I was a'Snoozing a'way my self same as them and I reckon we sounded like a Little Freight Train a'going through the Country and Oh, Papa said, it was so nice and peaceful riding long like that Not a Care in the World but I didn't know all them Buzzerds was right then just a'Circling Down Down Down on us and didn't even feel nothing when they went to lighting all over me but then, he said, o'Fritz let out a little Woof and I waked up but Oh I couldn't hardly see nothing I was so covered up with Black Buzzerds. Oh Buzzerds just everwheres you looked, he said, and More and More and More a'coming down outta the Sky and lighting on me to where I couldn't even see my Hand in front a'my Face. Just nothing but Buzzerds and I went to shoo em off but Oh my Hands was a'tied up tight back behind my Back and I didn't even know it til then. Mister Pearsall I hollered, Papa said, I got Buzzerds all over me and my Hands is tied up tight back behind my Back. Yes Sir and I am in the same god dam Fix my self, Calley said, I thought you was Keeping Watch on them Buzzerds. Well I was Keeping Watch on them Buzzerds, Papa said, but I reckon it was that Keeping Watch on them Buzzerds that took me off to sleep. Then they was this big Squawk come outta one a'them o'Buzzerds a'setting on Calley and the other ones went a'flying up off a'us in a big Flap. What was that, Papa said. One a'them dam Birds put his stinky o'Foot up on my face, Calley said, and I had to bite it to get him off me. Then he said Uh Oh lookee there and I looked just when the last Buzzerd went a'flying off me, Papa said, and Oh I bout jumped out my Pants like they was on Fire cause standing right there in front a'us a'holding our Horses was this o'White Haired Man with a rotten Hang Man Noose a'hanging round his neck. Well Sir, Calley said, I reckon you are o'Pelo Blanco his self ain't you. Yes I am Pelo Blanco, o'Pelo said, and that Boy there, he said and give me a Mean Ugly Look, is on my Lista. Then, Papa said, o'Pelo led us on off in the Mesquites Thicket with all them hunderds and hunderds a'squawking Buzzerds just a'marching long behind like they was some a'Genral Lee's rowdy o'Soldier Boys a'going off to have they Suppers.

We hadn't gone but maybe a mile, Papa said, and me and Calley was already scratched up and bleeding from all them Mesquites Thorns o'Pelo was a'leading us through. I believe you are trying to hurt us ain't you, Calley said, These Mesquite Thorns is like walking through a Bob Wire Fence. Our Dear Lord Jesus Christ had to wear him a Crown of Thorns, Pelo said, I don't hear him Complaining so much do you. No Sir but I bet he didn't like it worth a Dam no moren we do, Calley said, and besides we ain't neither one a'us Jesus Christ if that's what you been a'thinking. No Senyor I wadn't never thinking that, Pelo said then led us into another thick Stand a'Mesquites. You know it ain't right to just ride round the Country Hanging People for something they didn't never do, Calley said, You ever consider that in your Travels. It's what them others and this Boy's Daddy done to my Daddy is Why I'm doing it, Pelo said, then shook his finger at me. If it'd a'been a Pistol, Papa said, Why he'd a'blowed my Head off with it right Then and There. Well the way I heared it, Calley said, your o'Papa was a Horse Thief and earned him his Hanging. No Senyor, o'Pelo said, My Papa wadn't never no Horse Thief in his Life. Yes maybe he stole him one or two for us Family to ride on and maybe a few other Ones too but No he wadn't never no Horse Thief. Well they Hanged him for Being One any how didn't they, Calley said, I ain't never heared a'Hanging some body for stealing Nothing. Here in Texas you Hang Mexkins just for being Mexkins, Pelo said, that's the only reason you need. Well me and this Boy here ain't never Hanged no Mexkins, Calley said, Ain't that right. Well I chopped one of em's toe off for him one time, Papa said, but I ain't never Hanged one in my Life. No but your Daddy he did, o'Pelo Blanco said. I know he Wishes he could take it back now that he's a'setting on a Flat Rock down in Hell, Papa said, if that matters any to you. No Nenyo it don't matter not even one little thing to me, Pelo said. And then, Papa said, o'Pelo pushed a Mesquites Limb back and of a sudden we was up under this big Secret Rock

Over Hang must a'been there since the Creation cause they was Pitchurs all over the Wall of olden Lions and Tigers and Hump Back Elephants and Little Men just a'going at em with Spears and Sticks and whatnot and then this pretty Red Head Girl bout Calley's age come out from back behind a Rock and o'Calley Pearsall took him a Look and Oh his Heart just went Bump a'Bump a'BumpBumpBump and I seen hers did too but they both turned to look way off out yonder somewheres else cause they didn't want o'Pelo to see they was already in Love with each other. I didn't know you had you a Pretty Daughter Senyor Blanco, Calley said. No I ain't got me no Pretty Daughter, o'Pelo said, This is Pela Rosa and she is going to be my Wife.

OH I SEEN THE LOOK

that come over Calley when o'Pelo said Pela Rosa was going to be his Wife, Papa said, and Oh then they was Booming Thunder and Cracking Lightning in his Eye when he seen he had her hobbled with a little Chain that run tween her ankles so she couldn't go a'running off on him when he wadn't looking. You stole that Girl off a'somebody didn't you, Calley said. No Senyor, Pelo said and give him a Look cold as Froze Ice, I saved her Life for her is what I done. Did he, Calley said, Did he save your Life for you. Pela Rosa nodded and said Yes he saved my Life from the Fire. What Fire was that, Calley said. The one that burned my Daddy up in the House, Pela Rosa said. Then Calley give me a Look like Yes Sir he knowed it all along, Papa said. Was your o'Daddy with my Daddy that time they Hanged his Daddy from that tree, Papa said. It was my Grandaddy was there, she said, not my Daddy. Calley eyed o'Pelo, Papa said, and said I reckon You was the one set that Fire burned her Daddy up in his House wadn't you and I reckon you are the Sorriest Son of a Bitch I ever did come across in my Life and I hope I don't never run across another one like you again. O'Pelo reached up and jerked o'Calley down off Firefoot to the ground, Papa said, and give him One Two Three Hard Kicks and then Oh here come all them Buzzerds a'hopping over in a big Storm and went to pecking on Calley like he was a chunk a'Meat or something but they wadn't nothing he could do bout it cause his Hands was still tied up back hind his Back and Oh Boy Hidy it scared me so bad they was gonna Eat him a'live I jumped off o'Edward and piled on but Oh

10

You stole that Girl off a'somebo
didn't you, Calley sai

them Buzzerds went to pecking on me too must a'been Ten Thousand of em but my Hands was still tied up back hind my Back too and wadn't nothing I could do to get em off me but of a sudden something jumped right down in the middle of em just a'Snarling and a'Biting like a Bob Cat Tiger and them Buzzerds went to screeching QueetQueetQueet like that and went a'Running off in ever which direction like some o'Horn Devil was after em but No it was o'Fritz was who it was. Then next thing, Papa said, here come Pela Rosa to help us get up on our feet and when she did I seen her give Calley a little squeeze round his middle then whisper to his ear Yes I knowed you was coming. Oh and then o'Pelo Blanco grabbed her away and said Don't worry Amigos these Buzzerds is going to peck your Bones clean here pretty quick any how then he sent Pela Rosa off to cook him some Suppers and put them nasty o'Birds in a big Circle round us so we couldn't run off somewheres without them a'pecking us to Death on the way.

*M*E AND CALLEY TOOK A LOOK AT ONE ANOTHER, Papa said, and Oh we was so all Pecked Up by them Buzzerds we looked like we had the Pox and our Nose and Ears was so swoll up o'Calley said If I didn't already know who you was I don't believe I'd be able to tell from looking at you now. And that wadn't all, Papa said, now all them Birds went to Pooting on they own feet then tromped round in it like they was making Mud Pies. Wooo, Papa said, them sure is some Dirty Birds ain't they. You may not know it, Calley said, but when that stuff gets Hard they each one gonna have em a Pair a'Shoes on they Feet to protect em for when they go a'walking round in all them Dead Messes they eat. All God's Creatures in the World got em they own Way don't they, he said, I don't reckon nothing surprises me much any more old as I am. Not even Poot Shoes huh, Papa said. No Sir but that ain't to say I wanna go down to the Store on Saturday Morning and buy me a Pair my self, he said, then we both looked over and here come Pela Rosa with a Bowl a'Chili and a big spoon and started feeding Calley. How'd you know we was coming, Calley whispered then Pela Rosa pointed over at the Wall with her spoon, Papa said, and when we looked we seen these Pitchurs drawed up there on the Wall a'One Big Man with his Stick up and One Little Man with his Stick a'hanging down and both of em was sending off Lightning

Strikes in ever direction and the Big Man had his Hand up in the Air and it looked to me like he was a'holding a big o'Pistola in it or might a'been it was just his Long Finger a'making that Sign the Mexkins make to say Hidy but I couldn't tell which one, Papa said. Them o'Boys can't be us, Calley said, Why somebody drawed em up there on that Wall Sixty-Seven and Two Million Years ago or more and we ain't that old yet you know it. Pela Rosa touched her Hand to her Heart and said Yes but ever night I prayed to send them Two Cow Boys here to Save me and Now Look, she said, you are Here. Yes Ma'am, Calley said, but our Hands is tied up back hind our Back and all these dam Birds is a'keeping Guard on us and I don't have no idea in the World how we gonna Save you or our self neither one. Uh Oh, Pela said and we looked over there and here come o'Pelo a'taking that Noose off from round his neck to Hang me with, Papa said. See what I mean, Calley said. The only one can Save you now is the Little Saint I been praying to, Pela said. What Little Saint is that, Calley said, I don't see no Little Saint nowheres round here. Why right over there, Pela Rosa said and pointed to a Rock over yonder with a bunch a'Candles burning on top and a'setting right there in the middle a'all them Candles was a little Mesquites Wood Saint a'wearing a o'Flop Hat and Oh I bout Fell over Dead, Papa said, cause a'all the Saints in the World that was the only one I ever knowed personal my self.

LALO. WHY THAT'S LITTLE O'SAINT LALO AIN'T IT

I said, Papa said, just when Pelo was reaching to put his Noose round my neck to Hang me with. How you know any thing bout our Blessed Saint Lalo, he said. He is the Saint a'all us Mexkins that come to Texas. Well, Papa said, that's my o'Hat he's a'wearing that I give him when we was a'riding down to Mexico so he could get him two hand fulls a'Mexkin dirt for his o'Granpa Crecencio to be buried under. Ay Ay Ay, Pela Rosa said, the Dirt. Then she made that sign they make over they selves and went to kissing my Hand and Oh I reckon that made Calley feel left out cause right away he said Well I was there too you know it. Oh, Pelo said, you must a'been that Cow Boy went in the River with all them Swirls in it. Calley bowed up and give him a nod I reckon thinking o'Pelo is bout to give him a Prize for jumping in the River and saving Lalo's Life. Yes Sir, Calley said, that was me sure enough. Oh you was lucky Saint Lalo jumped in and saved you when them Swirls started sucking you down under the water wadn't you, Pelo said. What, Calley said, I was the one doing the Saving not the Drowning you ignert SonofaBitch. But, Papa said, o'Pelo was looking at me and didn't hear not one word o'Calley was saying any how. So you was the one helped our Dear Saint Lalo bring all that Dirt back from Mexico so all us Mexkins over here in Texas can go get us some any time we want for just a few Centavos, Pelo said. Me and Calley give each other a look at that, Papa said, and then I said I didn't have no idea Lalo brung that much Dirt back with him in just his two Hands did you. Well Dirt's a funny thing, Calley said, I reckon it can multiply on you same as your o'Rabbit can you know it. No Sir, Papa said, I didn't know it. I reckon you got that little wood statue a'Saint Lalo the same place you got the Dirt huh, Calley said. Oh yes, Pela Rosa said, they got many things you can buy over there Even little jars a'water from them Swirls where all them other Saints come out the River from. Don't surprise me a'Lick, Calley said, I might like to have me a drink of that water my self some day. Oh No Senyor, Pela said, it's for your Wife so she will want to make Babies for you. Well, Calley said, people been doing pretty good at that for a long time now without no Magic Water ain't they. And then, Papa said, he give Pela Rosa a Look had a little Something Special in it and she give him that Look right back but o'Pelo Blanco seen it too and Oh when she seen he seen it Why she tried to smile like they wadn't nothing going on tween em but Pelo already seen it and she and Calley couldn't get it back. I didn't know nothing bout such things back then, Papa said, but I knowed enough to know this was Trouble Trouble Trouble a'coming. And then, he said, o'Pelo reached round back hind my Back and started undoing my Hands. I cannot Hang you Nenyo, he said, you was Little Saint Lalo's Friend when he was down here on the Earth and No I cannot Hang you. But then, Papa said, he put his Snake Eyes over on Calley and I knowed he wadn't thinking the same thing bout him.

O'PELO BLANCO UNDONE MY HANDS out from round my Back, Papa said, and said You free to go now I ain't going to Hang no Friend a'our Blessed Little Saint Lalo. Well then Mister Pearsall is Free to go too, ain't he, Papa said. No Senyor Pearsall he ain't Free to go no wheres. You go on without him, Pelo said. Well No Sir, Papa said, Mister Pearsall is my Friend and I ain't a'going off nowheres without him. Senyor Pearsall ain't never gonna be nobody's Friend ever again here in a minute, o'Pelo said, you go find you a new one. I don't want a new one, Papa said, I like the one I already got. Well you can't have him no more, Pelo said, he's mine to keep, You go on now. Oh and then I looked over at Pela Rosa and they was big tears a'coming up in her eyes. Maybe I'll get me a good Night's Sleep first, Papa said, then ride on out bright and early first thing in the morning fore the o'Rooster even crows. No you get your Horse and that little Dog you got and you ride on out Pronto right now, o'Pelo said, then picked up his Noose and said Or maybe you don't never ride out never again. Go on, Calley said, Don't worry bout me I'll catch up to you here in a day or two I reckon. But, Papa said, I knowed o'Pelo wasn't never gonna let Calley go but was gonna do him Bad Harm in sted by Hanging him and Pela Rosa knowed it too cause she was over there a'Crying in her Hands bout it. I told you to go, o'Pelo said and put his mean o'Snake Eyes on me. Yes Sir and I told you I ain't a'gonna, Papa said, and then I put my own Snake Eyes back over on him and wouldn't neither one a'us give in to the other for bout a year then Calley piped up and said No you go on now You can't do nothing for me here though I do appreciate it you give it a Try. Now just go on like the o'Son of a Bitch said, he said, and we'll meet again someday in the Sweet Bye and Bye and laugh bout these Old Times. No Sir, Papa said, I ain't a'going. Go, Pelo Blanco said. No Sir, Papa said. Go, Calley said, Go. No Sir, Papa said, I ain't a'going. Go Go Go, o'Pelo said then come at me to put his Noose back round my neck again and when he did, Papa said, I looked over there and Why I seen them Flames round Little Saint Lalo just a'flickering up and down like they was trying to jump off them Candles and go a'running off. I don't care you Hang me or not, I said, I still ain't a'going. But I will, Pela Rosa said. We was all surprised by that, Papa said. Go where, o'Pelo said. Go with You that's Where, Pela said, to be your Wife. O'Pelo bout fell down dead. My Wife, he said. My Wife. But you got to let this Cow Boy go Free, she said, that is my Bargain. O'Pelo wasn't sure he liked it. Let him go Free, he said. Yes, Pela said, and you can't never go Hang nobody else ever again neither. Pelo went to sliding his eyes this way and that and back and forth trying to decide Yes or No I reckon, Papa said, then he said Here's one more thing I want to make me Happy. You promise I won't never have to use none a'that Magic Water on you. Pela give Calley a look like she'd never ever see him again in her Life then she said to where you could just barely hear it Yes I Promise. Oh and when she said that, Papa said, Why I seen this big o'Tear come up in Calley Pearsall's Eye and go a'rolling down his Face.

O'PELO TOOK THE CHAIN OFF from around Pela's ankles, Papa said, then he said he was going over there to get Saint Lalo down off his Rock for they Trip and she better gather up all the pots and pans and whatnot right quick cause they was a'leaving Now. I'll find you, Calley said, and when I do you ain't gonna like it much. Yes you come find me o'Pelo said then went over there to get Saint Lalo off his Rock. I wish you hadn't traded your Life away for mine, Calley said, Being his Wife is worsen any Death I know of. Grab me my Pistola over there and I'll change the whole Landscape round here for you and ever body in it, he said. Pela was bout to cry, Papa said, but she just shaked her head No then threw her shoulders back like she was carrying a big Load. I give him my Word, she said, What's done is Done. Yes Ma'am I said, Papa said, Mister Pearsall is always a'saying they ain't nothing in the World more important'n keeping your Word oncet you give it Ain't that right Mister Pearsall. That was bout something else, Calley said, it don't necessarily pertain here. Look, Pela said, and we looked over there and o'Pelo was trying to get Little Saint Lalo up off his Rock but he just wouldn't budge. What's wrong, Pela said. Saint Lalo growed in this Rock or something I don't know what, Pelo said. He won't move a Lick. Maybe he just don't wanna go nowheres with you You murdering o'White-Haired SonofaBitch, Calley said. He goes where I tell him to go, o'Pelo said then give him some more shakes hard as he could, Papa said, but Saint Lalo still wouldn't budge. He's a Hard Nut to Crack ain't he I said, Papa said. Oh and that made o'Pelo so mad he grabbed Saint Lalo by his Arms and went to shaking him and Hammering on him with a Rock and cussing him at the same time. Get down off that Rock, he hollered, get down off a'that god dam Rock you little Flea of a Saint. Oh and then, Papa said, all them Buzzerds went to jumping all over the place and a'going QueetQueetQueetQueetQueet til you was bout to go Loonie from it and then Fritz went to snapping at em ever one he could and all this time, he said, o'Pelo was still over there just a'Cussing and a'Hammering on Little Saint Lalo with his Rock. Oh and then, Papa said, I seen all them fires on them Candles round Saint Lalo go to jumping up Higher Higher Higher ever time o'Pelo give Lalo a lick and then of a sudden Why them Fires jumped off them Candles and jumped right on top a'o'Pelo like a Swarm a'Bees and Oh Boy Hidy next thing they was a big Whoosh and o'Pelo's Hair was all on Fire like you was out there in the pasture somewheres and just throwed a Match on a pile a'dry Brush. Oh and then he let go a'Little Saint Lalo and went to Hollering and Jumping round like a Loonie cause his Head was all on Fire and then them Buzzerds went to Flapping they wings all over him I reckon a'trying to put the Fire out but all that come a'that, he said, was it set they Tail Feathers on Fire too and Oh now they really did go to screeching QueetQueetQueet and went a'flying off with they Hineys just a'Burning to light up the whole World in ever which direction they went.

*T*HEN ME AND PELA ROSA grabbed us up a bucket a'water and run over there right quick and put the Fire out on o'Pelo's Head, Papa said, and Oh he just set there with his Face a'smoking and giving Saint Lalo a ugly look. You know I think maybe this Little Saint here tried to burn me up on purpose don't you, he said. Turn Bout's Fair Play ain't it, Calley said from over there where his hands was still tied back hind his Back. I reckon it's what you get for burning her Daddy up in that House Fire you set. Oh it was Hard to look at o'Pelo, Papa said, his skin was all bubbled up and a'hanging down off his face like one a'Miz Choat's curtains on the Winder and they wadn't enough hairs left to run a comb through on top a'his head. Where is my Amigos the Buzzerds, o'Pelo said. They left the Country with they Pants on Fire, Papa said, and it don't look like they ever coming back neither. O'Pelo went to crying then, he said, then went to crying some more ever time one a'his tears run down cross his burned off face it hurt so Bad and Pela went to dabbing em away with her shirt soon as they come out his eyes to save him the Hurt. I hope yall ain't forgot bout me over here while yall a'doctoring on that o'SonofaBitch over there, Calley said. He sounded irritated bout it too, Papa said, so I run over

17

there and undone his hands for him quick as I could. Good to see you again Amigo, Calley said, My Goodness you bout all growed up since I last seen you ain't you. O'Pelo's bout all burned up over there too I said, Papa said, I ain't never seen nothing like it. Well it don't Break my Heart any, Calley said. Generally speaking a Man pretty much gets back what ever it is he put out there in the World so I reckon he had it coming. Well, Papa said, o'Pelo must a'done something Good in his Life too cause Look over yonder at how Pela's trying to make him feel better now. It was true, he said, she was over there a'doctoring his face with big Dabs a'Bee Honey she got outta a little pot with her Finger. I believe I'd a'just let him sizzle til they wadn't nothing left but a little Crispy Thing, Calley said. I don't know how he ever earned him a Tender Touch. I give o'Calley a Look then, Papa said, and Oh his eyes was just two little slits and his Jaw Bone was clomped down tight. Mister Pearsall I said, Papa said, I believe you a'growing you a Mean Streak here lately ain't you. Oh I growed me a Mean Streak long time ago, Calley said. I just try not to let it get out its Cage no moren I have to. But If and When it does, he said, Why then you and me both better run find us a place to hide quick as we can cause you don't never know what it's liable to do.

FIRST THING

Calley said when he went over there and seen o'Pelo's burned up Face, Papa said, was Well you wadn't nothing Pretty to look at in the First Place was you. We got to save him, Pela said, he needs our Help. Don't matter we save him or not, Calley said, they gonna Hang him any how. You ask me they oughta do it with his own Noose too. Ain't Nobody going to Hang me you just wait and see, o'Pelo said. Yes Sir well you just might be surprised bout that, Calley said. Then this big Sadness come over o'Pelo, Papa said, and he said I already been Hanged oncet, Me and my Daddy both at the same time. I admit that's one a'the Saddest Stories I ever did hear in all my Life, Calley said, I don't know that I ever heared one no Sadder. Too bad you didn't learn a Lesson from it and go to living Right in sted a'going round the County Hanging People like you been a'doing, he said. Oh and then o'Pelo give Calley a Look wadn't nothing in it but Froze Ice. I will live to Hang you

..next thing they was a big Whoosh
and o'Pelo's Hair was all on Fire...

19

too Senyor, he said, then we will see how much you like it. Oh I already like it, Calley said, if all I got to worry bout in this World is you a'Hanging me. Oh and then o'Pelo's Eye Lids went to fluttering, Papa said, I reckon cause bout half of em was burnt off and then here in a minute he give Calley one last Ugly Look and went on off to sleep like he didn't have no Troubles in the World. I think maybe he's going to hold a Grudge on you Mister Pearsall I said, Papa said, then Calley reached over and took Pela's Hand in his own and give it a little Squeeze. And maybe one on you too, he said, cause a'you and me having this Feeling bout one another like we do. Oh and then I seen her give Calley's Hand a little Squeeze back. I know it, she said, but I can't leave him. I give him my Word on it. Yes to save me, Calley said, But that Promise ain't gonna mean nothing oncet this o'SonofaBitch gets through paying with his Life what he owes for Hanging all them other People. And then, Papa said, o'Calley put his other hand on top a'hers like they was making a Bargain on it and I won't never know for sure but I think right then I seen o'Pelo open his Eye for just a Wink or two to see Calley and Pela Rosa a'setting there right in front a'him a'holding hands like that. You better get you some Sleep now, Calley said to Pela, I reckon we got us a long ride back to Civilazation tomorrow. Then Calley give her Hand one more little Squeeze and she did his and then me and him went back over there to where o'Fritz was a'chewing on a Buzzerd Feather and put our self down to get some Sleep and Oh, Papa said, I wish we a'hadn't.

*N*EXT MORNING O'CALLEY HOLLERED WAKE UP wake up, Papa said, and me and Fritz come up wide awake both at the same time. They gone, Calley said, Lit a Shuck outta here some time in the night when we was a'sleeping I reckon. I thought o'Pelo was bout Dead, Papa said, I don't see how he could a'got off somewheres like that. He had him some Help is how, Calley said, much as I hate to say it. You think Pela helped him I said, Papa said. I ain't saying she did it On Purpose, Calley said. More Likely he forced her to it with that Promise she made. I don't reckon she'd a'just gone off on her own with him do you. I could see he was working hard not to believe it neither. No Sir I wouldn't never believe that bout her in my Life I said, Papa said. No Sir not you or me neither one, Calley said, I didn't have no idea til just this minute how much she come to mean to me in such a short time.

Then Fritz started barking from over there where they'd been, Papa said, and we went over there and Oh first thing we seen was o'Pelo'd gone and chopped poor little o'Saint Lalo up in bout a hunderd pieces fore he and Pela went off to where ever they went off to. Wooo I ain't a'that religion and not no other I know of neither, Calley said, but Bessa my Coola I don't believe I'd ever go to chopping up somebody else's Little Saint in pieces like that. No Sir, he said, that's Bad Pookie if ever I seen it. They ain't no telling what's gonna come back on o'Pelo for that you know it. Course, he said, he's gonna have to answer to me First any how and Ever Body else just gonna have to stand in line way back there behind me some wheres. Where you reckon they gone off to, Papa said. I don't have no idea Calley said and so, Papa said, we went to looking all over for a sign to what direction they took and then here in a minute Calley hollered from over there They's a Big Cave over here and me and Fritz run over there right quick to see, Papa said, and sure enough they was a Cave in the Wall big enough a Man could walk through it a'standing straight up on his own two Feet and his Horse too. Where you reckon it goes, Papa said, and Calley said I don't care so much Where it goes as I do Where it comes out and how Quick we can get there fore he takes Pela Rosa off some wheres else to where we might never find her again. And then, Papa said, he looked in his big o'Pistola to see he had plenty a'Bullets when he needed em and then stuck it way back down his Pants where it come from.

WE MADE US SOME FIRE STICKS

to light up our way, Papa said, and went on in the Cave a'leading our Horses and o'Fritz a'follering long behind. Oh it was Dark in there, Papa said, and they was Bats and little Creatures a'one kind or a'nother just a'scooting round everwheres you stepped. They ain't gonna bite us are they Mister Pearsall, I said. They might, Calley said, If I was you I'd keep my Shoes on. We went On and On in that Cave and then of a sudden it come to me I ain't seen Fritz in a good long while. You seen Fritz here lately I said, Papa said. He's over there somewheres a'licking on his Hiney I reckon, Calley said, I

21

wouldn't worry bout him. Well No Sir I am worried bout him I said, Papa said, then went to hollering loud as I could Fritz Fritz Fritz Where are you Fritz and then in a minute here he come a'Barking back at me from way off down yonder somewheres. Sounds like he found him something don't it Calley said and we started going in and out a'side Caves a'follering his Yips and Barks til of a sudden we come up on him a'Growling at some Thing a'setting over there against the Wall. Git back behind me, Calley said, then pulled his big Pistola outta his Pants and raised up his Fire Stick to have a Look and Why setting there was this Olden Man wadn't no moren Bones wearing him a Iron Suit and Hat and they was a Letter he left scratched up there on the Wall behind him for Ever Body to read if they happen to come long this way. What's it say I said, Papa said. Calley looked up at it and said, It says Hello my name is Santiago Miguel Juarez Luis Nacho Flores How are you I come here from somewheres over cross the Big Water to find Gold and Silver and Whatnot to make me rich and Now I got the Gold and Silver but o'poor me now I am Lost in this Cave where I am gonna die and I miss my Momma and my Daddy and all my Little Brothers and Sisters and my Aunts and Uncles and don't forget my o'Granma and Granpa and fore I forget it my Pet Donkey Silvester too. That's what it says, Calley said. No it don't, Papa said. Course it don't, Calley said. How in Hell would I know what it says. You think I can read ever old Antique Ancient Language some body scribbles up on a Rock Wall somewheres, he said. Why you being so Ugly to me, Papa said, I ain't done nothing. Calley put his Pistola back down his pants and said I guess I'm just Peeved at my self for letting that o'SonofaBitch get off with Pela like that and was just taking it out on You when I should a'been taking it out on Me. You ain't done nothing Bad Mister Pearsall, Papa said. What I'm a'scared of, Calley said, is I gone and made it possible for o'Pelo to do something Bad to Pela Rosa less me and you catch him fore he does. I thought he just wanted to Marry her, Papa said. Yes Sir, Calley said, that is xactly what I'm a'talking bout.

*F*RITZ WAS OVER THERE nawing on that Olden Man's leg bone, Papa said, and I said Leave go a'that o'Bone Fritz we on a Hunt for Pela Rosa and ain't got time for no Suppers.

He give it one more little Lick then follered me and Calley and our Horses in and out a'Caves all down the Way, he said, and in a minute I got scared and said Mister Pearsall you think we ever gonna find our way out a'this o'Cave a'Live. I been a'wondering bout that my self, Calley said. We wouldn't like it if we was to end up just Bones like that poor o'Fella back there would we, Papa said. No Sir not me, Calley said. Then he give me a Look and said, Course it ain't no secret we just as Lost as he ever was. Lost, Papa said, Lost. I didn't know we was Lost. Oh Yes Sir we been Lost a good long while now, Calley said, and I got some more Bad News for you too he said, Our Fire Sticks is bout to burn out and when they do it's gonna be Darkern six foot up a Possum's Butt in here. Oh and right then I heared somebody a'Crying way off back yonder somewheres EeeeEeeeEeee like that, Papa said, and I said Is that Pela Rosa a'Crying. It sounds like it don't it, Calley said, or some thing else. Well what else, Papa said. If I tell you, Calley said, you got to promise me you ain't gonna jump up and go a'running off on me. Yes Sir I promise I said, Papa said, Then here it come again but it sounded to me like it was getting Closer Closer Closer. EeeeEeeeEeee. EeeeEeeeEeee. It's getting closer ain't it, Calley said, like maybe some thing gonna jump on us here in a minute. Yes Sir it does I said, Papa said. Well tell me what is it, he said, It's like you scared to. Oh and then, he said, here it come again and this time it was just round the corner back behind us and coming on at a Run. EeeeEeeeEeeeEeee. What is it, Papa said, I'm starting to think you don't even know you self. Oh Yes Sir Mister I do know, Calley said. It's a god dam Panther is what it is he said. A Panther, Papa said. A Panther. Yes Sir a Pan- ther and he's a'looking for his Suppers and I reckon he's a'thinking you and me is it. Can I jump up and go to running now, I said, but fore o'Calley could answer me back Why I grabbed o'Fritz up in my arm and give o'Edward a slap on his Bottom and away we went fast as we could go with o'Calley a'hollering Run Run Run when he passed us by and then, he said, we run round this corner and they was Sun Light coming in at the other end a'the Cave and of a sudden we was out the Cave and didn't hear that o'Panther a'chasing us no more. Where you reckon it went I said, Papa said. What I'm a'worrying bout, Calley said, is Where you reckon it's gonna be when we come back this way with Pela Rosa. I don't have no idea, Papa said. No Sir and not me neither, Calley said, I guess that's just something we gonna have to Worry bout in our Spare Time when we get some.

$\mathcal{S}$O WE COME OUT FROM THAT CAVE in the World again, Papa said, and they wadn't nothing but Cactuses and Mesquites ever wheres you looked no matter how far. I don't see nobody, Papa said. Calley was bout to cry. No Sir, he said, they just gone is all and they ain't no Buzzerds in the Air to tell us where to neither. Calley didn't say nothing more just set down in the Dirt and went to twirling his Spur Ching e Ching e ChingChingChing sounded something like that then started saying but just to his self Pela's Gone Oh she's Gone Gone Gone and then Fritz went over there to give him a little Lick to make him feel better but Calley give him a Push to get away and said Save your Licks for your own Hiney Mister I don't want em. He don't mean nothing by it, Papa said, he's just trying to be Nice. Tell him to go be Nice somewheres else I don't want no Nice right now and maybe not Never Again neither one. Fritz get over here Mister Pearsall said he don't want no Nice right now I said, Papa said, so Fritz come over and give me some Licks in sted. You oughta think bout where that Tongue a'his been all day long fore you go to letting him Lick on you with it like that, Calley said. He's my Friend, Papa said. Yes Sir I know it but that might be taking the Friendship a little too far you ask me, Calley said. Now you being Ugly to me and Fritz both ain't you, Papa said, then Calley went to twirling his Spur again Ching e Ching e ChingChingChing and said I'm sorry. I reckon that's just my o'Broken Heart a'talking and it don't know no bettern to go and Hurt your Feelings like that. You hear what it's a'saying to me now, he said. No Sir I don't, Papa said. It's a'saying Calley Pearsall you been a'looking for that Pretty Girl all your whole Life and here you finally find her and then you dumb Pecker Wood you lose her again. Yes Sir but we gonna go find her ain't we, Papa said. Well ain't we. Oh and then Calley looked out at all them Cactuses and Mesquites a'covering up the World and said Well I ain't got no idea what Direction we oughta go to looking in do you. No Sir I ain't got no Idea neither I said, Papa said. And if that ain't Bad enough, Calley said, here's another thing even more worsen that. Say Yes we do find her, he said, But what if she won't go with me any how cause she already give her Word to o'Pelo to stay with him. What bout that. Well I don't know What bout that, Papa said, What. And then, he said, o'Calley went to twirling his Spur again Ching e Ching e ChingChingChing Ching e Ching e ChingChingChing like that and said Why it'd Break my Heart in a hunderd more places that's What. I'm sorry Mister Pearsall, Papa said, I wouldn't

24

wanna go walking round with a Broken Heart all the Time neither. Well, Calley said, I reckon its just part a'the Deal. How you ever gonna know you in Love in the First Place if you ain't got a Broken Heart to prove it. Then, Papa said, of a sudden o'Calley squinted up his Eyes like he seen some thing way out yonder in the cactuses and stood back up on his Feet.

*W*ELL LET'S GO, Calley said, Let's Go Let's Go, We ain't gonna find her a'setting here are we. I thought you didn't know what Direction to go a'looking in, Papa said, I don't see nothing out there but Cactuses and Mesquites and them thorns can sure bugger you up in a hurry you ain't careful. You don't have to be careful if you know where you a'going, Calley said, and sometimes you don't know where you a'going til you get there. Ain't nothing to it then, he said. Yes Sir but we don't know where we a'going, Papa said, do we. Well we do now, Calley said, then pointed his Finger way out Yonder at something. What you reckon that is I'm a'pointing my Finger at, he said. Why it all looks the same to me, Papa said. Look harder, Calley said, Just foller my Finger. See it, he said, Just take particular notice a'any thing that don't look like everthing else in the World and you'll see it sure as shooting. Oh and then I seen something xactly where he was a'pointing his Finger to look. I see it I said, Papa said, but I ain't got no idea what it is. It's the Best News I ever got in my Life, Calley said, that's what it is. So he give his Spur one more Ching e Ching e ChingChingChing but it was a Happy little Ching e Ching e ChingChingChing this time then jumped on o'Firefoot and run out in the Cactuses and Mesquites and me and Fritz done the best we could to catch up on o'Edward and when we got there Why o'Calley was a'reaching down to pull a little Rag off a Mesquites Thorn where it was a'hanging. I reckon you know what this is huh, Calley said. Yes Sir, Papa said, that's a piece a'Pela's Dress ain't it. Oh Calley give it a touch like it was Shining Gold and said It's moren that She's a'leaving me a Map to foller to where ever it is o'Pelo's a'taking her. And then Calley pointed his Finger way out yonder in the Cactuses and Mesquites again and said They's another one, you see it. But fore I could say Yes Sir I do see it, Papa said, o'Calley was already a'heading that way fast as he could go and me and Edward and o'Fritz went a'Bumping long to keep up and then here in a minute we come up on Calley and there he was a'rubbing another piece a'Pela's Dress on the first one he found like he was trying to conjure her up tween the two of em same as o'Jeffey might. I reckon you know what all this means don't you, he said. You mean Means moren it means a Map, Papa said. Oh Yes Sir, Calley said, Means just a whole god dam lot moren it means a Map. No Sir I don't know what else it Means moren it means a Map, Papa said, but I can tell what ever it is sure does make you Happy don't it. What it means, Calley said, is Promise or No Promise to o'Pelo she's a'sending me a Letter says Come On Cow Boy Come On.

$\mathcal{S}$O WE FOLLERED the Rags Pela left a'hanging on the Thorns to show us the way through the Cactuses and Mesquites to come find her by, Papa said, and sometimes she just bent a little Twig down double to say the same thing. Look at that, Calley said, Well Kiss a'Duck's Wet Butt if she ain't just the Smartest Girl in Town. Yes Sir I reckon she is, Papa said, long as o'Pelo don't catch her at it. Calley give me the Squint Eye for what I said and said How come you to go and say something like that You ain't a'saying she ain't the Smartest Girl in Town are you. No Sir I ain't a'saying that, Papa said, I don't even know no Girls in Town. You don't huh, Calley said. I don't believe they's been moren a Day or two in my whole Life I didn't know least three four Girls in ever Town I ever been in but that's bout twicet too many if you ask me. I got a Girl, Papa said, but she ain't in no Town. I'd like to hear bout her, Calley said, What's her name. I ain't a'telling, Papa said. I ain't gonna tell Nobody else, Calley said, if that's what's a'worrying you. No Sir I just ain't telling that's all, Papa said, you already know her name any how. Oh, Calley said, you mean Annie Oster don't you. She's your Girl huh. Well she says she is and I ain't gonna say no other, Papa said. You ain't a'scared a'her are you, Calley said. I don't know why I'd be scared a'some o'Girl, Papa said. Cause the one you talking bout there got some Red Chile Pepper in her that's Why, Calley said. But I like her for it, he said, Don't you. And then it come to me, Papa said, that Yes Sir I did Like Annie for her Red Chile Pepper too even if I hadn't been a'thinking bout her much for a long time til now. She wanted us to get married and live somewheres out there behind the House but her o'Granny

Oster said No they'd throw the both a'us way back in the Jail House for Robbing the Cradle if we was to Marry at our young age. Maybe even shoot you for it, Calley said. They ain't gonna shoot nobody for getting married, Papa said. No but you might wanna shoot you self for it, Calley said, you ever think bout that. Who said I was getting married any how, Papa said. Well you the one said you had you a Girl. Yes Sir but I didn't never say I wanted to Marry her, Papa said. Well do you or not, Calley said. She ain't gonna be able to sleep at night til she got your answer. I knowed he was just a'teasing me bout it, Papa said, but then of a sudden I seen all the way down to the Bottom a'my Heart and what I seen there was Oh Yes Sir I do wanna marry Annie Oster when the Time comes round to do it and not no Other Girl that I could think of. And in all my whole Life to come, he said, they never was not even oncet no Other One.

*W*ADN'T LONG,

Papa said, and we bout had us nough Rags to make Pela a new Dress. I hope she ain't a'walking round out here in her Birthday Suit, Calley said, course I'm gonna buy her a new Dress soon as I can I reckon she knows that don't she. Yes Sir I reckon so, Papa said, but I don't know for sure she does. Well I do, Calley said, I know for sure. Yes Sir, Papa said, Well then I reckon I do too huh. They's a'nother one, Calley said and pointed way out yonder at a Rag a'hanging off a Mesquites Limb. You see it, he said. I see it, Papa said, but I don't believe it's the same as all these other pieces we been finding off a'Pela Rosa's Dress. Why I don't know why it wouldn't be, Calley said. Cause it's Red, Papa said, and I don't recall her Dress having no Red any wheres on it. Oh and then Calley give me a Look and then he give that Rag way out yonder a'nother Look and then his Eyes went big on him and he give o'Firefoot his Heels and hollered Heeyaaaa Heeyaaaa and went a'jumping through the Cactuses and Mesquites to it and me and Fritz did too on o'Edward but we was more mindful a'the Thorns that was gonna poke us to Death if we wadn't careful so by the time we got over there Calley'd done pulled that Rag off the Mesquites Limb and was looking at it like it was the worstest thing he ever seen in his Life. That Red you seen, he said, is Pela's Blood and then, Papa said, he showed me his Finger was Red with Pela's Blood from that Rag off her Dress. It's still Wet, Calley said, They can't be a'head a'us by Far. Oh and then he pulled his big o'Pistola out his Pants and said You stay here Amigo then away he went but not so fast as a minute ago cause now he was just a'looking round careful in ever which direction for sight a'o'Pelo and what ever it was he done to Pela Rosa to make her Bleed like that. Oh I didn't know what to do, Papa said, but I knowed me and Fritz and o'Edward wadn't just gonna stay there all day long by our self like that so I give o'Edward a little shake a'the Reins to get him a'going again and off we went trying to keep Calley in view way off out yonder where he was a'going in and out a'the Cactuses and Mesquites with his Pistola there in his Hand ready for what ever Trouble might come his way I reckon. Oh and then o'Fritz a'setting up there on the saddle with me started a'growling like he knowed they was some thing up there a'head somewheres wadn't no Good at all and then here in a minute I seen Calley pull up and go to looking round like he knowed it too and so I pulled o'Edward up and we all just set there real quiet a'looking round cause Don't ask me how but we all knowed they was something Bad Bad Bad bout to happen here in just a minute and then, Papa said, Oh and then I looked way out yonder and I seen o'Pelo shove Pela out from behind a Cactuses but Pela's Hands was tied back behind her Back now and then o'Pelo raised up his gun to Aim it at Calley when he wadn't looking and didn't see o'Pelo behind him. Oh and then I just went to Hollering loud as I could MISTER PEARSALL MISTER PEARSALL LOOK OUT LOOK OUT LOOK OUT but just when Calley was turning to Look Out like I said Why they was a BIG BOOM and Smoke come a'blowing out the end a'o'Pelo's gun and Oh Calley went a'flying off o'Firefoot like he been Shot out a'Gun his self and landed somewheres down there in the Cactuses to where you couldn't even see him no more.

Next thing,

Papa said, was o'Fritz jumped off o'Edward and went a'Running and a'Barking at o'Pelo and o'Pelo seen him coming in a big Surprise and tried best he could to load up his gun to shoot him Dead but by now I was a'Hollering NO NO NO and I give o'Edward my heels hard as I could and Oh listen here we went

...Calley went a'flying off o'Firefoo
like he been Shot out a'Gun his self..

to running through them Cactuses at him and I reckon o'Pelo didn't know if we was some mean o'Bear or What and run off a'pulling Pela behind him and I seen her Face and Arms and Feets was just everwheres all scratched up and a'Bleeding and I reckon that's where that Blood come from we seen on that Rag from her Dress. Oh and then my Old Karl Blood come a'bubbling up in me, Papa said, and I could taste that Copper Taste in my mouth like always when I lost my self to Hate and Wanting to Murder some body for something or other like I did when o'Pepe and Peto was trying to kill my Friend Mister Pegleg in the Barn that night back at Home. But here was the Bad Part, he said, O'Pelo was Running off in the Cactuses with Pela Rosa in one Direction and my o'Amigo Calley Pearsall was back yonder in back a'me a'rolling round in the Dirt with a Bullet in him some wheres maybe even in his Vitals and I could go try to help him or I could go try to save Pela Rosa from o'Pelo one or the other but wadn't no way I could go do both at the same time. So, Papa said, I jumped down off o'Edward and run over there to save Calley if I could. How Bad he shoot you I said, Papa said, and Calley touched his Leg up there tween his Knee and his Pocket and said They's a big Bloody Hole a'running clean through my Leg Front to Back. I wish I had me a Bucket a'Coal Oil, Papa said, I'd pour it down that Hole for you or poke some Bees Honey down it if I had some. It ain't that what hurts me so Bad, Calley said, It's that I let that dam Pelo Blanco trick me with them pieces a'Pela's dress so he could get me out here in the Cactuses and Shoot me. I just hope Pela wadn't in on the Joke, he said. Oh I could see he was bout to cry bout it, Papa said, so I said No Sir Mister Pearsall she wouldn't never in this World a'done that. You don't think so huh, Calley said. Oh No Sir, Papa said, O'Pelo had her hands all tied back behind her Back That's how I knowed she wadn't in on the Joke cause I seen it my self. So wadn't no way Pela could a'teared off them pieces a'her Dress with her hands tied up behind her Back like that could she, Calley said. No Sir, Papa said, I don't see no way. Calley wiped his eyes and give me a little Smile. Well I'm glad to hear she wadn't in on it he said. Now Help me up I gotta go see bout saving her. Then, Papa said, he took my Hand and tried to come up on his elbow but No he couldn't do it and flopped back down again and went off to sleep like some body's little Baby Boy a'taking him a Nap.

*O*H I WAS ONE SCARED RABBIT NOW,
Papa said, and didn't have no idea in the World what to do next but First
Thing I done was go over there and grab up Calley's big o'Pistola off the
ground and stick it down my Pants and it made me feel some better to know
I had some thing to shoot o'Pelo with if he come a'creeping back in the Night
to finish the Job on Mister Pearsall. Fritz wadn't Happy bout nothing neither, he said, and come over there and set down right by me and tried to
Lick my Hand but No I said, Papa said, I ain't got no time for it now Fritz
then I went to gathering up all the Cobwebs I could find from off Cactuses
and Mesquites and then I staubed em down in Calley's Bullet Hole with
my thumb to stop the Bleeding if I could and Oh he groaned and carried
on when I was a'poking em down in him like that. But the Good Thing was
he was still a'Live and Breathing but I could tell he wadn't gonna be much
Help if I needed some to save Pela Rosa. Oh Lordy Lordy I said to my self,
Papa said, what am I gonna do and I was bout to Cry bout it my self then
Here I went to thinking bout What my o'Amigo Calley Pearsall'd do his self
if he was me and what I come up with, he said, was Why he wouldn't wait
for o'Pelo to come a'Looking for him for one minute. No Sir he'd pull his big
o'Pistola out his Pants and go to Looking for o'Pelo in sted. So, Papa said,
I pulled Calley's big o'Pistola out my Pants then give Fritz a scratch under
his chin and said Fritz you in charge a'Mister Pearsall here just like you was
Genral Robert E Lee and don't you go a'running off nowheres til I get back
with Pela Rosa safe if I can and Fritz looked up at me and said Heh Heh Heh
like he did pretty much all the time any how so I knowed what I just said
didn't mean nothing in particular to him.

Oh and then I just set there for bout a hunderd years rubbing on Calley's
big o'Pistola til the Sun gone on Down, Papa said, then I got up on my two
feets and seen the Direction o'Pelo had took through the Cactuses and Mesquites when he run off with Pela Rosa. You better Look Out there Mister
cause I'm a'coming after you, I said, but not so loud he might could hear it
and mess up the Surprise I had coming for him. And then there I went, Papa
said, just a'Tip a'Toeing one little Step at a time real quiet and it was getting
Darker Darker Darker the whole time and the Moon and the Stars come out
and some o'Coyote went to yipping way off out yonder some wheres and
that give me some Comfort I reckon cause it made me think it might be my

o'Friend Mister Pegleg a'looking out for me tonight even if he was Dead and Gone with all them Shimmery People now. Any how, he said, I just kep on a'going and a'trying not to make no Noise but then I stepped on a little stick and it went Ca-rack like that but lots louder and then everwheres I stepped was more sticks and they went Ca-rack Ca-rack Ca-rack Ca-rack sounded like some o'Bear a'walking through the Woods with his Boots on. So, he said, I just stopped still right there in my Tracks and went to trying to figgur out how I was ever gonna Surprise o'Pelo like this but bout that time, Papa said, some o'Owl went to Hooting and that o'Coyote went to Yipping again and right in the middle a'all that I heared this other Ca-rack Ca-rack Ca-rack a'somebody stepping on sticks but it wadn't me this time and then of a sudden somebody come up out a'the Dark back behind me then blowed in my Ear and said You ain't out here a'looking for me are you Moochacho.

COURSE IT WAS O'PELO BLANCO HIS SELF, Papa said, and he had a Gun on me bout yay long and it was cocked all the way back too. Where's that Cow Boy at he said. He's out yonder somewheres a'getting ready to come over here and Shoot you, Papa said, that's where he is. Pelo thought that was funny but his face was all burned up so Bad it hurt him to laugh so he just said What's he going to shoot me with then grabbed Calley's Pistola out my hand. What was you going to do with this he said. I hadn't decided yet, Papa said, but I was thinking I just might Shoot you my self. Oh he give me a Bad Look when I said that, Papa said, and said You don't know Not one dam thing bout killing nobody do you Nenyo. No Sir, Papa said, but I know what happens to you when you do. How you know any thing bout it, o'Pelo said, you don't look so smart to me. I been down there in Hell to see for my self what happened to my mean o'Daddy for Murdering my Momma and I reckon for helping them others Hang your o'Daddy from that Limb too, Papa said, that's how I come to know bout what happens. I don't believe nothing you say bout it, Pelo said, but you tell me any how then he give me a hard poke in my Belly with Calley's Pistola, Papa said, and said Tell me I said. You gonna see for you self here fore long but when you do it's gonna be way too late for you to do any thing bout it I can tell you that Mister. You telling me the Devil is going to get me huh, he said. You

32

think I am scared a'some o'Devil down there. They ain't no Devil down there that I know of, Papa said, they's just a bunch a'Neckid People all stacked up in Caves like Fence Posts and they all just a'Moaning and a'Groaning and a'Crying and a'Hollering cause now they so Sorry for all the Bad Things they done when they was up here in they Life but now they ain't nothing they can ever do to make it Right again. Who tends to the Fire if they ain't no Devil, Pelo said. No Sir they ain't no Fire to tend down there and they ain't no Devil down there neither one, Papa said, It's just all them Bad People a'setting on a Flat Rock and a'wishing they had a Chance to do some Good Things to make up for all the Bad Things they done in they Life so they wouldn't have to set down there on that Flat Rock for all Time to come but No now they won't never ever get em a'nother Chance. O'Pelo tried to laugh at that, Papa said, but when he did his o'Burned Up Lips went to bleeding on him and then in a minute they wadn't nothing to Look at but one big Red Mouth. I ain't sorry for nothing I ever done in my Life he said. Well you gonna be when you a'setting down there on that Flat Rock with nothing to do but wish you wadn't there, Papa said. I don't think I'd like that too very much, o'Pelo said. No Sir and my Daddy don't like it too very much neither, Papa said. The last time I seen him he was shoving Dirt up in his Eyes with his Fingers cause he didn't wanna see none a'the Bad Things he done in his Life. And they wadn't no Devil down there to make him do it neither huh, o'Pelo said. No Sir, Papa said, I reckon ever body just they own Devil and punishes they own self for all the Bad they done is how it works. O'Pelo put his gun down then, he said, and looked way off out yonder somewheres like he was a'getting Scared bout what I said. I don't like this one little bit, he said.

THEN WE JUST SET THERE

all night long, Papa said, o'Pelo a'asking me questions bout everthing I seen down there in Hell. Main thing was he wanted to know did I see his Daddy down there and he told me what he looked like that Day when my Daddy and all them others Hanged him. I told him No I don't recall seeing you o'Daddy but they was a bunch a'Mexkins down there and I didn't have time to go a'looking at all of em and that was true a'the White People and the

33

Black People and ever other Color a'People too cause they was all bout equal in Number far as I could tell. And then, Papa said, o'Pelo wanted to know how it was I ever come to go down there in the First Place and I told him I had me a three-legged Coyote for a Friend name a'Mister Pegleg and he took me down there one night when I was a'sleeping. Oh Yes, o'Pelo said, I knowed Coyotes was Magic People all my Life. Then I told him he was Wrong bout Calley Pearsall, Papa said, that it wadn't Saint Lalo pulled Calley out a'the Whirls in the River but was the other way round and it was o'Calley pulled Lalo out in sted and saved his Life and that's when all them Shimmery Ancestors come out the River too and now we got more Mexkins in Texas than was ever here before. Thanks to Mister Calley Pearsall I said, Papa said. O'Pelo just went to shaking his Head at that like it was the Funniest Thing he ever did hear in his Life. And I was going to Hang that Cabron you know it, he said. Yes Sir I do know it, Papa said, Only thing saved his Life was Little Saint Lalo burned your Face off fore you could do it ain't that right. Oh and then o'Pelo really went to shaking his Head and said Ay ay ay and then I went and chopped that Little Saint up in a bunch a'pieces for it. Ay ay ay, he said, Ay ay ay what am I going to do now. I don't have no idea, Papa said, but I wouldn't wanna be you when you down there a'setting on that Flat Rock with my Daddy. No me neither, Pelo said. Oh he was bout to cry, Papa said. I don't want to go down there with all them Neckid People, he said. Well from What I know, Papa said, That's where you a'going any how you don't change your Ways here while you still can and maybe not even then cause you been so Bad all you Life. Oh Poor Me o'Pelo said, Papa said, then he put his Hands up on his Face and went to Crying bout it but his Burned Up Skin come right off on his Fingers and they wadn't nothing he could do bout it but Cry some more. Oh Poor Me, he said, What am I going to do What am I going to do. I ain't got no idea What Mister Blanco, Papa said, I'd tell you if I knowed. Then o'Pelo just got up and walked on off out in the Cactuses some wheres til you couldn't even see him no more but you could still hear him a'Moaning Oh Poor Me Oh Poor Me Oh Poor Me and then in a Minute, he said, he was so far out in the Dark you couldn't even hear that no more neither.

THEN,

Papa said, I went to looking all round for Pela Rosa and a'hollering her name Loud as I could all the way PELA ROSA PELA ROSA WHERE ARE YOU PELA ROSA I hollered but No no answer come back to me then bout the time the Sun come up I seen that little rope o'Pelo'd tied her hands up with out in the Cactuses but didn't see no other sign a'her. Oh I didn't know what become a'her, he said, but what I hoped was she slipped the Knot and run on off somewheres to start her a new Life without o'Pelo to use her up. I didn't know how Calley was gonna take the news, Papa said. If he asked me Where is Pela Rosa at I got to say Well Mister Pearsall I ain't got no idea Where she is at and, Papa said, if he ask me Where is my big o'Pistola you run off with here a while ago at I got to say Why o'Pelo Blanco run off with it now Mister Pearsall but I ain't got no more idea Where he went with it than I got bout any thing else tonight. Course I didn't have no idea the way back to Calley through all them Cactuses and Mesquites neither so now I went to hollering FRITZ FRITZ FRITZ COME HERE AND GET ME FRITZ but No I didn't get no more back from him then I got back from Pela Rosa here just a minute or two ago. So now, he said, they wadn't no body in the World but just me a'standing out there in the Cactuses and Mesquites all by my self with out no Friend any wheres to help me. Course, Papa said, I been in this same Fix many the Time fore in my Life so I just set my self down by a Mesquites Tree and went to Crying bout it like always cause I didn't have no Idea a'what to do next. But then, he said, some Words come a'Falling down on me from out the sky and what they said was Don't Never Just Set There Mister and I knowed right then when I first heared it that was gonna be my Family Motto from here on out. Don't Never Just Set There Mister was what they said, Papa said, so I wiped the Tears off a'my face and got my self up on my feet and went a'walking off in the Direction I figgured I come from and Oh I walked and I walked and I walked with them o'Mesquites Thorns just a'eating me up ever step a'the way but it didn't bother me too much cause now, he said, I wadn't just setting there a'crying bout it like my Family Motto said don't never do.

*O*H YES SIR I WAS LOST, Papa said. Just Lost Lost Lost as could be and didn't have no idea What to do next or Where to go but only not to set down on it So, he said, I just kep on a'walking then bout the Time the Sun started a'going down again I seen this Blood on the ground bout where o'Pelo shot Calley off o'Firefoot and a'going off from there was these two Rows in the Dirt from Mister Pearsall's Spurs a'plowing up the ground where some body come along and dragged him off and Oh then I seen the Foot Tracks a'who it was dragged him off and Oh Listen Here Mister, Papa said, I bout come all to pieces when I did cause they was the Tracks a'that o'Panther chased us out the Cave here just yesterday. And not only that, he said, but Fritz was gone and so was Firefoot and o'Edward all just Gone Gone Gone and I knowed where to cause they tracks was all a'going in the same Direction that o'Panther was a'dragging my o'Amigo Calley Pearsall off in to eat for his suppers and may be all them others too.

I grabbed me up a Stick big as I could find to use for a Head Knocker if I had to, Papa said, and went to follering them Panther Tracks a'dragging Calley and they was Drops a'his Blood all long the way and they was ugly Yeller Fester in it too and then I knowed that Bullet Hole in his leg already gone to Poison and Oh I went to trotting fast as I could to get there fore o'Calley died a'that or that Panther eat him up one but, he said, the Cactuses and Mesquites thorned me back to a walk and it was bout all Day fore I could get up to that Cave where all them Tracks went in and Oh wadn't nothing to do, Papa said, but light me up a Fire Stick and go on in behind em.

*O*H IT WAS DARK IN THERE, Papa said, so Dark to where I couldn't hardly see nothing in front a'me even with my Fire Stick a'leading the Way then I give out a Holler MISTER PEARSALL MISTER PEARSALL MISTER PEARSALL to let o'Calley know I was a'coming to Help him if he was a'listening but No I didn't get nothing back again so now I quit a'hollering MISTER PEARSALL and went to hollering FRITZ FRITZ FRITZ in sted but No o'Fritz didn't give me no answer back neither, he said. Oh and then my Fire Stick went plum out on me and I couldn't even see my Hand front a'my Face no more and went to hollering HELP HELP HELP just louds I could HELP HELP HELP HELP HELP and took off a'running I was so scared a'that o'Panther a'getting me but didn't have no Idea where I was a'running to and run straight in the Wall ever time til I couldn't even get up off the Floor no more and just set there with Spiders and Bugs a'some kind or other a'climbing all Up and Down me and then, he said, I heared Some Body or Some Thing a'coming up behind me and Oh who ever it was just set right down there in the Dark cause I could feel em breathing on me and I said Who are you Mister and What you want with me But they didn't say nothing back so I took my Hat off and give Who Ever it was a good hard Swat with it and Oh when I did they went EeeeEeeeEeee like that and Oh Boy I knowed I'd just swatted me a Live Panther most likely the same one dragged o'Calley off some wheres to eat. You get out a'here Mister and leave me alone I said, Papa said, and give him another good Hard Swat but this time, he said, that o'Panther bit it right out my Hand and I took off a'Running fast as I could but didn't get no moren a step or two then run straight in the Wall again like before and bounced back down on my Bottom where I come from. Oh and then, he said, that o'Panther went EeeeEeeeEeee at me so I grabbed up a Rock to hit him with when he come to Bite me but No he just set out there in the Dark some wheres and I bout went Loonie a'waiting for him to come on and eat me. You better Look Out Mister I said, Papa said, I'll knock you in the Head with this Rock if I got to And I might a'done it too, he said, cep What come out a'the Dark next wadn't no Panther Bite but was a little Bony Human Hand in sted and it took a'holt a'my Hand and give it a little Pull to say Get Up Mister Get Up but No, Papa said, I pulled my Hand right back cause I didn't have no idea Who this was or What they was a'wanting with me. You go on I said, Papa said, I reckon I'm okay here where I am but No, he said, that Hand took a'holt a'my Ear and give it a Pinch and a Twist to get me up on my feet then led me off in the Dark and ever time I tried to get a'loose Why that o'Panther'd go EeeeEeeeEeee and give me a Push on my Bottom with his Nose to keep a'Going and Oh Yes Sir that done the Job ever time.

*C*OURSE, Papa said, I didn't have no Idea in the World who it was a'leading me off in the Dark by my Ear or what they was gonna do with me oncet they got me there neither. All I could think bout, he said, was Where is my Friends Calley Pearsall and Fritz and Firefoot and o'Edward at and Am I ever gonna see em a'Live again in my Life. Oh I was scared to Death, Papa said, cause not only this but I seen that Yeller Fester in o'Calley's Blood too and I knowed that was Bad and most likely a'getting Badder and Badder all the Time. Where yall a'taking me to any how I said, Papa said. I ain't got no Time for walking round in the Dark like this you know it. But No, he said, they didn't pay no Mine and On and On and On we went, that o'Bony Hand just a'leading me a'Long and that o'Panther a'giving me little Pushes on my behind. And then, Papa said, why of a sudden we come round this Corner and Oh they was Fire Light a'flickering out a Side Cave way up yonder and not only that, he said, but Oh there was my little o'Amigo Fritz a'standing there just a'crying his Heart out bout some thing or other so I slapped my Ear a'loose from that o'Bony Hand and run on up there quick as I could to see what was Wrong for him to be a'crying like this and what I seen was a Camp Fire out in the middle a'this big o'Cave Room where Firefoot and o'Edward was a'eating some Grass Some Body piled up on the Floor for em and Oh then I looked over and seen Mister Pearsall a'laying over there on his Back just a'Moaning and a'Groaning and a'Shaking like a Leaf from a Fever that got a'holt on him and wouldn't let go but he raised his self up on a Elbow when he seen me coming, he said, and said Where's Pela Rosa at and I had to say No Sir I don't have no idea Where she's at and then he said Where is my Big o'Pistola at. I don't have no Idea bout that neither Mister Pearsall, I said, o'Pelo run off with it some wheres in the Night. And another thing, he said, is who the Hell put me here. No Sir I don't know, Papa said. Well Dam if you ain't a'Cold Splash a'Water here first thing in the Morning, Calley said, ain't you. Yes Sir I know it, I said, and I don't feel very Good bout it my self neither. Well you was right to give me the Bad News first thing. Do Right and Risk the Consequences, he said, You ever heared that. No Sir I never, Papa said. O'Samuel Houston was the one said it, Calley said, I reckon you heared a'him huh. Yes Sir he was that Fella helped my Grandaddy Andrew and his Daddy John whup the Mexkins over yonder some wheres or other. San Hacinto, Calley said. Then I give him the little rope I found out in the Cactuses and said I reckon Pela Rosa ain't got her Hands tied up back behind her Back no more huh. She's out there some wheres then, Calley said, She's out there somewheres just a'waiting on me to come and Save her. Now help me up Amigo,

...seen Mister Pearsall a'laying over there on his Back just a'Moaning and a'Groaning..

he said, and let's be away fore who ever it is brought me here comes back to eat me up or something worse'n that. But No, Papa said, Mister Pearsall was too Big and too Hurt and I was too Little and Scrawny to where I couldn't do no moren just Squirrel him round in the Dirt on his Bottom a'little. Oh Calley tried and tried to get up on his Feet, Papa said, but he just couldn't do it. Maybe I oughta take me a'little Siesta and give it another Try here in a minute or two he said then reached up and give me a little Knock on my Head. I want you to know I admire it you tried to save Pela for me when I wadn't up to the Job my self he said then went on off to Sleep even if he was still a'shaking so Bad it made his spurs go Ching e Ching e ChingChingChing without him a'doing it with his own Finger like before.

OH I DIDN'T HAVE NO IDEA what to do, Papa said, but I knowed if I didn't get o'Calley some Doctoring here pretty quick I was gonna lose him to the Fevers or to the Festers one. Mister Pearsall I said, he said, we gotta get you up to Miz Choat so she can bring you back to Health or I reckon you just gonna up and Die here in a Day or two but I don't believe you can count on much moren that. What you think bout that Mister Pearsall I said, Papa said, but o'Calley just curled up in a Ball and went to Shivvering so Bad I thought he was gonna roll on off some wheres. And then in a minute he went to Shaking so Bad he shaked his self a'wake again. Where you been he said I been a'looking ever wheres for you. I been right here with you the whole Time Mister Pearsall, I said. I wouldn't never just run off and leave you in a Fix like this. Oh I'm gonna make it now Amigo, he said, soons we get out a'this Ugly o'Swamp. We ain't in no Ugly o'Swamp Mister Pearsall, Papa said, you just got the Fevers is all and they a'making you see things ain't there. This ain't no Swamp we in he said, and I said, No Sir they ain't no Swamp no wheres round here. They's just the Fevers. The Fevers, Calley said, Hell I ain't a'scared a'no Fevers. A Fevers don't scare me no moren a Fly scares me, he said. Yes Sir, Papa said, but a Fevers can kill you Dead where some o'Fly just gonna pester you some. Well No Sir that ain't always Right, he said, They's some Flies get together and Gang up on you and then here in a minute some of em is a'eating your Ears off and some others is trying to get up in your Nose and down in your

Pants and then, Papa said, he just went total Loonie on me and went to swatting all over his self at Make Believe Flies and I don't know what all else. Mister Pearsall I said you gonna swat you self to Death here in a minute you don't quit doing that you know it. And Oh, Papa said, Then he give me a Look and said Who you any how I ain't never seen you fore in my Life. Oh Yes Sir you have too I'm your o'Amigo, I said, That's Who I am. He give me a'nother Look tween Swats and Shakes and I could tell he still didn't have no idea in the World who I was. No you ain't, he said. Well Yes Sir I am too I said back, Papa said, we been Amigos here a Long time now don't you remember it. If you my o'Amigo, he said, Why you a'letting these Flies here eat me up like this. They ain't really no Flies here a'eating you up Mister Pearsall, I said, that's just your o'Head a'playing Tricks on you cause you got the Fevers from o'Pelo a'shooting you in the Leg is all. What, he said, O'Pelo shot me in the leg. Where is that mean o'Son of a Bitch then o'Calley Squinted his Eyes and pulled a Make Believe Pistola out his Pants and Cocked it back then went to pointing it all round ever which a'way and I had to duck to keep from a'getting Make Believe hit. You see him, he said. Just show me where he is. No Sir I don't see him, I said. Well I don't know why not, Calley said, he's a'setting right over yonder on that little Jackass a'combing his hair. No Sir, I said, that's just o'Fritz a'licking on his Hiney is all Don't you remember him. Who, he said. Fritz my Dog I said, Papa said, Oh and now Calley bugged his Eyes out to get a better Look and said Oh you mean the one in the Wagon there. I don't see no Wagon Mister Pearsall, I said, that's just some big o'Rock you a'looking at. Yes Sir but my Pela Rosa is a'cooking my Suppers for me back behind it ain't she, he said. No Sir, Papa said, they ain't no Pela Rosa no wheres round here that I know of. They ain't, Calley said. No Sir they ain't, Papa said. Well where is she at then, Calley said, She was here just a minute ago. I don't have no idea Where she's at, Papa said, She either run off with o'Pelo Blanco on her own or he made her do it one or the other. You mean she don't Love me no more, he said. Oh he was bout to break down and cry bout it, Papa said, So I said No Sir I wouldn't go so Far to say she don't Love you no more No Sir I wouldn't never say that. But here's something you might wanna think bout you self, I said. She might not wanna trade o'Pelo off for some Crazy o'Loonie thinks a bunch a'Flies is trying to eat him up when they ain't None there. It took o'Calley bout a year, Papa said, but then he pulled his self back together in one piece again

41

much as he could tween Shakes and said I'm okay now Amigo. Them Flies is gone back to where they come from ain't they. Then he made sure the Hammer wadn't cocked back no more and put his big o'Make Believe Pistola back down his Pants and went on off to sleep again. And then so did me and o'Fritz, Papa said.

*O*H AND THEN I COME A'WAKE with that o'Panther a'eating on my Face, Papa said, but No it was my o'Amigo Fritz giving me a Lick in sted. Fritz you bout made me Jump up and Run I said then looked over there and seen poor o'Calley still bout shaking his self to Death with the Fevers. How you doing Mister Pearsall I said, Papa said, but I knowed he wadn't doing no Good cause I could see in the Fire Light that Bullet Hole in his Leg was a'Oozing big ugly Yeller Fester out it And I knowed one more thing too, he said. I knowed I wadn't never gonna get him back to Miz Choat in time to Save his Life and they was only Me to Save It if I could. So, Papa said, I pulled me a Fire Stick out the Fire to light my way and went a'looking round in there to see what I could find might Heal him but No I didn't have no Luck just seen where Water come a'dripping down out the ceiling in a good size Puddle there on the floor to where me and the Creatures could get us a Drink a'Water anytime we wanted one. Oh and then I seen something else too, Papa said, but I didn't give it much Thought at the time cause I was so busy trying to find something might save Mister Pearsall's Life and that was they was Pitchurs somebody'd drawed all up and down the Wall with a sharp Stick or something and one a'them Pitchurs showed a bunch a'People a'Horseback with Guns and Pitch Forks and Ropes a'chasing some Poor Girl had a Little Baby there in her Arms. But right then, he said, o'Calley give out a Holler and when I looked back over there to where he was Why I seen in the Fire Light they was a Little o'Wrinkled Up Black Man a'Pushing a long Stick all the way down through that Bullet Hole in o'Calley's Leg and then on out the other side and not only that but he was a'wearing my o'Hat too, Papa said.

I HOLLERED STOP IT STOP IT,
Papa said, and run over there to Stop Who Ever it was a'poking that Stick
down through Mister Pearsall's Leg like that but fore I got there Why that
o'Panther raised up out the Dark in front a'me and Oh it scared me so Bad I
just set right down there on the Floor and now we was Eye Ball to Eye Ball
our Nose just bout touching each other and then I seen his Eye Balls was
just white as Egg Shells and he was Blind as a Bat. And, he said, he didn't
hardly have no Teeth in his head neither. Oh and then, Papa said, I seen that
Little Man a'wearing my Hat wasn't no Little Man neither but was a Little
o'Wrinkled Up Bare Foot Black Lady in sted must a'been a'hunderd and ten
years old and Snaggle Toothed bout the same as that o'Panther. Oh and now
she went to wrapping a Long Rag round and round that Stick then poked it
all the way back through that Hole in Calley's Leg again to the other side like
before but this time she give that Stick a little Twist fore she pulled it out
and when she did, he said, Why that o'Rag was still a'running through the
Hole. And then she grabbed a'holt a'each end a'that Rag and went to sawing it Back and Forth down through that o'Festered Up Bullet Hole in his
Leg and Oh then here come Gobs a'that o'Ugly Yeller Fester a'spurting out
both ends bout made you Sick just to see it. And then, he said, she grabbed
up this Honey Comb she had and ever time that Rag come out her end Why
she squeezed some Bee Honey on it and sawed it Back and Forth on down in
the Hole again and Oh she went at it like that just a'Sawing Back and Forth
and a'Squeezing Honey on til they wadn't no more Yeller Fester a'coming
out neither end the Hole no more but was just Bee Honey a'Going In and
Bee Honey a'Coming Out both, Papa said. And all this time, he said, I been
scared I wadn't never gonna find a Doctor in time to save o'Calley's Life but
they was already One just a'waiting for us right here in this Dark o'Cave
and that made me think a'what o'Calley said one time and that was What
ever you a'looking for in this o'World is out there somewheres in the World
a'looking for you too. That's the Great Secret a'Every Thing they is, he said.
And Yes Sir it sure was this time wadn't it, Papa said.

*W*HEN SHE WAS ALL DONE WITH IT,
Papa said, that Little o'Wrinkled Up Lady throwed that Rag had all the Fes-

ter on it in the Fire and Oh they come up a Smoke from it bout blinded you and when I Looked again Why she and her o'Blind Panther was both gone and I got to thinking Well maybe She and Him both is some a'them Shimmery People I been a'Seeing here off and on my Whole Life, he said, but I didn't have no idea Was she or not and I had Other Fish to Fry any how and that was to take Good Care a'my o'Amigo Calley Pearsall til he either come back a'live all the Way or Died from the Fevers one. So, Papa said, I went over there and pulled the Saddle Blankets off a'Firefoot and o'Edward and wrapped o'Calley up in em best I could to keep him warm but the Fevers still had him and Oh he was a'shaking so Bad I thought his Bones was gonna jump out his body and go to running off somewheres in the Dark so I put my self down on top a'him like I was another Saddle Blanket and o'Fritz did too but o'Calley went to shaking moren ever now and I thought Well he is gonna throw us off like some o'Bucking Horse out in the Pasture ain't he but we helt on like that all Day or all Night which ever one it was til, Papa said, Mister Pearsall went total Still under us and then I looked over there and Why here come Mister Pegleg and three four Shimmery People from out the Dark somewheres and they clustered round o'Calley and I seen No he wadn't even breathing no more and, he said, I thought Well I reckon my o'Amigo just up and Died didn't he and went to crying bout it even if I was there in a Dream. And Oh I reckon he had Died too, Papa said, cause now here come this Other Calley a'trying to Shimmer his self right out the top a'his own Head but ever time he did Why them Shimmery People'd shake they Fingers No No No at him then poke him right on back down in his Head again til he finally give it up for good and went on back in his body cause he seen they just wadn't gonna let him Die.

I PULLED THEM SADDLE BLANKETS OFF HIM, Papa said, cause now I knowed my o'Amigo was gonna Live and I was fraid them Blankets was gonna make him too hot and burn him up. After that, he said, I grabbed me up a Fire Stick and me and o'Fritz went a'looking round in there to see what all else we could see and first thing I seen was some more a'them Pitchurs drawed up there on the Wall showed that Poor Girl a'running off with that little Baby in her Arms and all them other Pitchurs

44

a'People on they Horses a'chasing her with they Ropes and Guns and Pitch Forks. And Oh, Papa said, them Pitchurs chased the Pitchur a'that Poor Girl with the Baby all up and down the Wall and through the Pitchurs a'Trees and cross the Pitchurs a'Rivers and all up and down the Pitchurs a'Hills and Gullies but that Girl just kep a'running fast as she could with that little Baby there in her Arms and wouldn't let go for nothing but then, he said, all them Pitchurs went in this Hole in the Wall and me and o'Fritz went in the Hole behind em with my Fire Stick to see what they was gonna do next and Oh they was this little Hump a'Dirt out there in the middle a'the Room had River Shells and Pretty Rocks all on it and ever Pitchur drawed up there on the Wall now was a'that Poor Girl a'kneeling down on her Knees just a'Crying her Eyes out bout some thing or other and they must a'been a hunderd Pitchurs a'her just like that drawed up there on the Wall all round that Hump a'Dirt on the Floor and Oh, Papa said, I didn't have no Idea why but Tears just come to my Eyes and went a'running down my Face cause they was just so much Sad Feelings in there you couldn't hardly wipe it off you. And me and o'Fritz might still be a'crying bout it, he said, cep bout that time o'Calley give out a Holler and we run back in there to see What was a'going on with him now.

OH, PAPA SAID, Why yonder cross the Room that Little o'Wrinkled Up Lady was a'trying to pull o'Calley's Pants off him and him just a'swatting at her with his Hat to keep her from it. And Oh then she grabbed the Hat right out his Hand and went to swatting him back with it One Two Three Four Five times like that and it surprised o'Calley so much he total give up and just set there a'looking at her til she had his Pants off him and went over there to the Puddle and put em in the water to wash the Fester out. You see that, he said, you see her take my Hat right out my Hand and go to swatting me with it. You see that, he said. Yes Sir I did see that, Papa said, She bout give you a good whupping didn't she I said then o'Calley give a big Grin like some o'Possum a'setting there and said By god she is sure nough one Spunky Little Missey ain't she. Well ain't she, he said. And Oh I could see he admired her for it. Yes Sir she is, Papa said. She sure is. And I admired her for it too, he said, same as him. Then o'Calley raised his self up best he could on his elbow and give that Bullet Hole in his Leg a Look and said Well that don't look so Bad as I xpected Where'd you find me a Doctor. No I never, Papa said, she found you then I pointed over to the Puddle where that Little Missey was still a'washing the Fester out his Pants. O'Calley give her a'nother Grin then seen all them Pitchurs up on the Wall and went to nodding his Head like he knowed it all the Time. Well that's Her sure enough ain't it, he said, Can't be no Other in the whole World I don't reckon. Her Who, Papa said. Why Her the Wild Woman a'the Navidad, Calley said. Where you been all your Life not to know bout her. Well I mostly been with you here lately Mister Pearsall, Papa said, and this is the First Time I ever heared you say one Word bout some o'Wild Woman a'the Navidad. It's a River, Calley said, The Navidad River bout two three hunderd miles or so over yonder somewheres round Jackson County. What's she doing here, Papa said. Well they was People back there a'trying to Catch her and Whup her and maybe even Hang her off a Limb, Calley said, I reckon that's Why she come a'Running up here. What'd she do to make em so Mad, Papa said. She stole a Baby and run off with it that's What, Calley said.

*W*HOSE BABY WAS IT, Papa said. Why it was her Baby, Calley said. I never heared a'no such thing in my Life, Papa said. How you gonna steal you own Baby. She was a Slave Girl, Calley said, and didn't her Baby or nothing else in this World belong to her. Shhh, Papa said, she gonna hear you talking bout her. So what if she does, Calley said, I don't reckon She speaks our Language. The way I know the Story, he said, is she come off the Slave Boat at Mada Gorda then set right down on the Dock and out come this Little Baby Boy just pretty as you please and the o'Slaver said Well look a'here I'm already a'making Money on this one ain't I. Then he give the Little Baby Boy over to some Old Woman or other to raise so the Momma could go on and start a'working out there in the Field ever day and wouldn't have to fool with it. Sounds like my mean o'Daddy don't it, Papa said. Oh listen here, Calley said, they was enough Mean in them days to go all the way round the World and come back again. They's Stories So Bad make your hairs Stand up on your head and Cry. Any how, he said, that very night when wadn't nobody a'looking that little Momma went in there where they had her Baby a'sleeping on some Rags and stole it back and went a'running off in the Woods with it cause she didn't want her Little Baby to grow up being a Slave no moren she wanted to be a Slave her self. Was a Little Boy, Calley said, and worth a'lot moren if it'd a'been a Little Girl so Yes Sir next morning they brung out they Big Mean Dogs and went a'chasing her cause they wadn't nothing in them Days make you look so Bad to your Neighbor as some dam little o'Slave Girl a'running off on you with your Property and you not able to catch her and bring her back for a good Whupping. How'd she get away I said, Papa said. I seen Miss Gusa when she first had her Baby that night and it wore her out so Bad she just up and died from it over at Fischer Hall. Well this Little Momma wadn't hardly no biggern you are now, Calley said, and she didn't get a'way with it Not that first Time she run off with her Baby and Not all them other Times she tried it neither one. Oh they dam near beat her to Death for her Sass and locked a big Iron Basket on her head to where she couldn't crawl through a Fence and they chained her to a Stump at night and I don't know what all else they done but then there she'd go again First Chance she got a'trying to run off with her Little Baby. And she finally did too huh, Papa said, even after all them Bad Things they done to her. Yes Sir she did, Calley said, She run off in the Woods with her Little Baby Son one night and course all them Slave Owners went to chasing her on they Horses and her a'holding that Little Baby Boy to her Heart and just a'Running Running Running til she bout fell down Dead with ever step she took and Oh it was Sad Sad Sad the Saddest god dam thing you ever seen in the World and it was so Sad even the Trees went to Crying bout it and big o'Tears come a'rolling off they Leaves like Rain in a Rain Storm and the Creeks come up in a big Flood but them Slavers just went on a'swinging they Loops and a'laughing and a'carrying on cause it was so much Fun to be a'chasing that Slave Girl and her Little Baby that way but it made the Trees so Mad to see such a god dam terrible thing they just went to Jumping and Shaking bout it and then here in a minute they was a'Jumping and a'Shaking so hard Why they Limbs went to falling down everwheres on top a'them Slavers and they couldn't get out from under em Quick nough and Oh Limbs come Down Down Down all over on top of em and give em Broke Arms and Broke Legs and Bloody Noses and busted they Heads like a Watermelon and here and

there took a Ear off or a Nose and they Horses went to jumping and bucking and throwed ever god dam one a'them SonsaBitches off in the Cactuses and then them that could took off a'running back Home fast as they could go cause they done had all the Fun they wanted in they whole Life and didn't want no more. Is that a True Story, Papa said. Well I won't say it's a Fact Story, Calley said, but Yes Sir I will say it is for god dam sure a True Story. I looked over there at that Little o'Wild Woman a'the Navidad by the Puddle then, Papa said, and it bout made me Cry to think a'all the things she been through in her Life to get here with her Little Son and I hoped he growed up Big and Strong and went on off some wheres to start him a new Life a'his own, Papa said. But No, he said, I knowed in my Heart that Little Baby Boy is a'sleeping under that Hump a'Dirt I seen in there a minute ago and that's what all them Pitchurs of his Momma is Crying bout.

WONDER WHAT HAPPENED

to her little Baby Boy, Papa said, to not a'growed up. Ain't no telling, Calley said, Might a'got a Cold and coughed his self to Death or maybe a Scorpyen come out from under a Rock one night and give him a Bite on his Toe. Makes me Sad to think a'all the things might a'got him But what ever it was, he said, I reckon it broke his little o'Momma's Heart don't you. Yes Sir I reckon, Papa said. Breaks mine just to think bout it. Course some time later, o'Calley said, she found that o'Panther some wheres to keep her company so she ain't been just all by her self in here her whole Life I don't reckon. That o'Panther ain't no Spring Chicken neither, Papa said, and not only that he's Blind as a Bat to boot. Well looks like he gets round all right even if he is, Calley said. But I don't know what she's gonna do when the Day comes her o'Friend can't get up on his Feet no more. That's gonna be a Hard Day for him and her both ain't it, he said. Where you reckon Panthers go when they Die, Papa said. I don't have no idea, Calley said. Maybe same place your o'Amigo Mister Pegleg went with all them Shimmery People you been a'seeing ever now and again. Well you seen em too ain't you, Papa said. No Sir never seen a'one of em in my Life, Calley said, Course I can't say I been a'looking for em neither. Well whatta you do in your Dream ever night then,

Papa said, That's when I see em. Oh I don't know, Calley said, it varies a great deal I reckon. Most times I don't even remember what my Dream was. Yes Sir but when you do, Papa said. Well here lately I been a'seeing Pela Rosa in my Dream when I remember it, he said. Was she Shimmering, Papa said. No Sir not like you mean, o'Calley said. Well How then I said, Papa said, and Calley said No Sir you too Little for me to be a'telling you things like that so let's just Hush bout it til you growed up some and even then I ain't a'gonna tell you bout it and no body else neither. It's Private just tween her and me, he said. I didn't never know you was so Private Mister Pearsall, Papa said, Seems to me like you always go on and say What Ever comes to your mine. No not always I don't, Calley said, Maybe some time I do but No not always I don't. Best to keep a few things just to you self the way I see it, he said. You might wanna remember that Might come in Handy to you some Day. Like keep What just to my self, Papa said. Well like What I'm keeping just to my self right now, o'Calley said, that's What. Yes Sir but I don't know what That is, Papa said, How'm I gonna know what kind a'things to keep just to my self if I ain't got no idea what kind a'things you a'keeping just to you self. If I was to tell you, o'Calley said, then I wouldn't be a'keeping it just to my self no more and we wouldn't have nothing to Talk bout no more would we. Then, Papa said, we looked over there to where that little Wild Woman usted to be just a minute ago but she wadn't there no more and neither was her o'Blind Panther.

*S*HE COMES AND GOES AS SHE PLEASES don't she, Calley said. Where you reckon they went I said, Papa said. Some wheres back in the Dark, Calley said, same place where they come out from I reckon. Last thing I seen, he said, was her a'looking at her self in the Puddle a'wearing your Hat and Oh just a'turning her Head this a'way and that a'way and ever other which a'way to see what she looks like in it. Course, o'Calley said, it's way too big for her and bout bends her Ears down double on her Head. Well I'm glad she likes it, Papa said. Yes Sir and it's a good thing you are, Calley said, cause you ain't never gonna get it back. And I'll tell you one more thing bout that Little Missey, he said. She don't hold a Grudge or she wouldn't a'never helped me after all them Bad Things People done to her in her Life. How'd she Fix my Leg any how. She put some Bee Honey on a Rag and run it In and Out the Hole til she run all that Yeller Fester out on the Floor, Papa said. I'd a'liked to a'seen that, Calley said. No Sir you wouldn't, Papa said, It was so ugly it bout made me Urp up. Well I reckon it's the Ugly in this o'World makes you Glad to see the Pretty when it finally comes around then huh, he said, ain't that right. I think you already told me that two three times fore Mister Pearsall, Papa said, but Yes Sir I reckon so. Course, Calley said, they's Pretty all over the place all the time any how ain't they. You just gotta be a'looking for it to see it. All I been seeing here lately is Dark, Papa said, Nothing but Dark Dark Dark all round in here. Oh Hell, o'Calley said, Ever Body sees Dark but it's what all Else you see in that Dark gonna make the Difference to you. Genrally speaking, he said, It's in the Dark where People sees the most Good if they got the sense God give a Ball Headed Possum to Look for it. Then he rolled over to take him a'nother little Nap and when he did, Papa said, Why I went to looking in the Dark like he said and First Thing I seen was Firefoot and o'Edward and then Fritz all a'sleeping over there by the Fire and Yes Sir they was Pretty to see cause they was my Friends and I was glad of it. And then, he said, I went to looking Deeper and Deeper in the Dark and then Why I seen Some Body's Shadow a'coming up on the Wall from way back behind me some wheres and they was a'hefting a Big o'Rock up to hit me on my Head with and Oh I bout Jumped and Run but then here that Big o'Rock come down on my Head but No it wadn't no Big o'Rock at all but was my Hat o'Calley said that Little Missey was gonna run off with in sted. Mister Pearsall I said, Papa said, Little Missey ain't no Hat Thief like you said she was But, he said, o'Calley was a'sleeping again and didn't wanna talk bout all the things he knowed bout Womens and Hats no more.

*T*HAT WAS THE LAST we seen a'Little Missey for a good long while, Papa said, even if she was always a'sneaking Grass in for the Horses ever Morning and a Bowl a'Some thing or Other had Bugs in it for me and Calley and o'Fritz to eat and course I don't know how she done it but they was always Wood on the Fire to keep us warm. She takes good care a'us don't she, Calley said, and I said Yes Sir she does but then her and that o'Panther goes to hiding from us too don't they. Well wouldn't you go to hiding from us, Calley said, when ever other Human Being you ever seen in your Life was always a'trying to Whup you or Work you to Death or Nail you Feet to a Log to keep you from a'Running a'way. Yes Sir I reckon I would, Papa said, and I'm sorry for what I said. I know she ain't had no Easy Life and still ain't. I know it, o'Calley said. And I don't like it she probably ain't gonna wanna go with us when we go. Why wouldn't she wanna go with us when we go, Papa said. Cause she ain't gonna wanna leave her o'Blind Amigo here just all by his self that's Why, Calley said. I reckon they been Friends bout a hunderd years by now. Well he can come a'long and go with us too when we go can't he, Papa said. He's so old he can't hardly get round on his own Feet no more as it is now, Calley said. You ever think bout that. Well you can't neither Mister Pearsall, Papa said, but you planning to go ain't you. Don't be a Smarty Pants Mister, o'Calley said and I said, Well maybe he can ride up on o'Edward with me then How bout That, and Calley said, Well here's How bout That. They's Onery People out there in the world'd shoot that poor o'Blind Bugger right off the Saddle fore you could say Bessa my Coola. And if you wanna know another Sad Thing'd make you cry, he said, Them same People'd shoot Little Missey off the Saddle even fore they would him. Well we'd shoot em back for it wouldn't we, Papa said. How we gonna do that, Calley said. I recall you a'telling me you let o'Pelo run off some wheres in the Dark with my Pistola. Yes Sir he did, Papa said. Well what you reckon we gonna shoot em with then, Calley said, our Finger or maybe a Stick. Listen here to me Mister, Calley said, you don't never wanna go to shooting no body any how. It ain't like chunking a Rock at a Pig. I wouldn't never chunk a Rock at a Pig, Papa said. Well you might, Calley said, one of em go to Snorting and Grunting and Getting in your Way when all you trying to do is Slop em. Well I reckon I might then, Papa said, they don't get out my Way when I'm trying to Slop em. Lot a'times they don't, Calley said, If you know any thing bout a Pig you know that don't you. Yes Sir I do, Papa said, Pretty much ever Pig I ever seen in my Life is that way. Course they just Hungry is Why they a'doing it, Calley said, You can't hold it against em they just Hungry Pigs can you. I didn't never hold it against em in the First Place, Papa said, You was the only one I know a'wanting to chunk a'Rock at em. Well I wadn't choosing up Sides against a Pig, Calley said, Hell I was just trying to eat up some Time a'talking bout it til we can get on out a'here and go find my Pela Rosa. When you figgur that's gonna be, Papa said. Soons I can climb back up on o'Firefoot again, he said, and Not fall off on the ground.

*T*URNED OUT wadn't but maybe three four Days, Papa said, and here o'Calley went to Hobbling round ever wheres when he wadn't bumping up gainst the Wall or a'falling in the Puddle but, he said, they just wadn't no Quit in him and he kep at it til he was bout Blue in the Face. You just a'Itching to go on and go ain't you Mister Pearsall I said, Papa said, and o'Calley said Yes Sir I am then went over there and throwed his Saddle up on o'Firefoot to go right now. What bout Little Missey, Papa said, We ain't just gonna ride off and Leave her are we. Be Glad to have her come long with us if she wants to, Calley said, but I ain't a'gonna tie her up and drag her off from her Friend if she don't. I don't reckon you would neither would you Mister, he said. No Sir I wouldn't, Papa said, Ain't neither one a'us that Mean I don't reckon are we. No Sir we ain't, Calley said, but that don't make us Happy bout it neither does it. No Sir it don't me, Papa said, then Calley come over there and give me a little Knock on my Head and said You better go on and round up o'Fritz now we gonna be a'leaving here in a minute. So I Hollered Fritz Fritz, Papa said, and he give me a little Bark back from some wheres over there in the Dark and I went over there with a Fire Stick to see where he was and Where he was, he said, was in that Room had that Hump a'Dirt out in the Middle of it. And a'setting right there with one Hand on o'Fritz and the other one on her o'Pet Panther was that little o'Wrinkled Up Wild Woman and it looked to me, Papa said, like they all three been a'Crying but that might a'been cause I was a'Crying my self cause of a sudden I seen where she'd a'drawed Pitchurs a'me and o'Calley and Fritz up there on the wall with all them other Pitchurs like we was Family too and it made me so Sad to be a'Leaving Little Missey and her o'Blind Panther like this. We gonna be a'going here in a minute I said, Papa said, I wish you'd come with us but No Ma'am I know you ain't never gonna just walk off and leave your o'Friend here no moren I would o'Fritz my self. She didn't say nothing back, he said, but I know she knowed What I said cause she give o'Fritz one more Pet then

53

give him a little Push to me but No he just set there a'Licking her Hand like he didn't never wanna leave her in his Life and then o'Calley come in with a Fire Stick of his own and squatted down right there in front a'Little Missey and give his Spur a Ching e Ching e ChingChingChing like he was a'thinking a'what to say and What he said, Papa said, was You are my Living Angel and I Thank You Thank You for my Leg and for my Life both and if they ever comes a Time in yours I can repay the favor Well by God you can count on me to be a'standing there right side you Don't matter a Lick how Deep the Water or how Hot the god dam Fire. Oh and then he reached his Hand out to give hers a little squeeze Goodbye but No that o'Panther wouldn't have it and give him a Bite on his Hand to keep away from her but it didn't Hurt much cause he didn't hardly have no Teeth left in his Head but o'Calley give him a scratch on his Chin any how for his Trouble and went on out with his Eyes just a'Shining. Come on Fritz I said, Papa said, we got to get on We got other Fish to Fry our self then me and o'Fritz went on out a'there too and, he said, I reckon my Eyes was a'shining much as Mister Pearsall's ever was.

I DON'T RECKON IT WAS MOREN A MINUTE after that, Papa said, and we was on our Horse and Ready to go and course we was both Happy and Sad bout it both at the same time. La Vida Brinca, o'Calley said, Life's bout to Jump again ain't it. Yes Sir I reckon so I said, Papa said, then we grabbed us a Fire Stick out the Fire and rode on out in the Cave. Which a'way, o'Calley said. I ain't got no Idea Which a'Way, Papa said, I was figguring you'd know. No I ain't got no Idea which a'Way neither, Calley said. Fritz, he said, Which a'Way Which a'Way and o'Fritz leaned out over the Saddle Horn and pointed his Nose That a'Way, Papa said, and we give our Horse a'touch a'our Heels and away we went just a'going in and out a'Caves long the way a'looking for Day Light. You reckon o'Fritz really knows where he's a'leading us, Calley said. Well, Papa said, He ain't never knowed it before far as I know so I reckon I'd be surprised if he knows it now. If he don't know, Calley said, we gonna be Lost here in a minute you know it. I think we already Lost Mister Pearsall, Papa said, I don't believe we can even get back to where we come from do you. Then o'Calley pulled Firefoot up and went to looking all round in the Dark. Next time we gonna have to plan our Trip better you know it, he said, We ain't gonna like Dying in here like that o'Skeleton Man we seen in the Iron Hat are we. You a'scaring me now Mister Pearsall, Papa said. Well I'm a'scaring me too, he said, if that makes you feel any better bout it. Oh and right then o'Fritz let go a Bark then jumped off o'Edward and took off a'Running in the Dark. FRITZ I hollered, Papa said, FRITZ FRITZ FRITZ but No he was just Gone Gone Gone in the Dark and my Heart just Broke in Two bout it but then Calley said LOOK LOOK and I Looked, Papa said, and Why way off yonder in the Dark Some Body was a'waving a Fire Stick to tell us This a'Way This a'Way and then we heared a'EeeeEeeeEeee and we knowed it was Little Missey a'waving that Fire Stick and her o'Panther there with her to save our Life again one more time. Well I reckon we just Lucky we hadn't a'run out a'La Vida Brincas yet huh, o'Calley said. Then, Papa said, we went to follering that Light on through the Dark.

OH WE FOLLERED AND FOLLERED THAT FIRE LIGHT all through the Cave, Papa said, then it went round this Curve and we come out under o'Pelo Blanco's big o'Rock Over Hang where we started out from but Little Missey and her o'Blind Panther was gone. Where you reckon they went I said, Papa said, and o'Calley said Back Home I reckon I don't know a'no other Place in the World they got to go back to do you. No Sir I don't, Papa said, I wish I could a'took em Home to the Choats I think they'd a'liked it there. Well Home ain't so much a Place as it is a Feeling you get when you there with Some Body you Love, Calley said, So I reckon she already Home here long as she got that o'Blind Panther she Loves with her. Where's your Home at Mister Pearsall, Papa said. You ain't never told me. Well it usted to be up yonder round Fayetteville with my Momma and Daddy and my Sister Eurica til that time my Daddy got all Drunked Up that Day in Town and run over all them People in his Wagon. Yes Sir you tolt me that Story and I don't need to hear it again, Papa said. It ain't a Pretty One. No Sir, Calley said, Don't matter how you tell it It ain't gonna be Pretty is it. But speaking a'my Sister Eurica, he said, I still need to get up there one a'these Days and tell her Her husband Jack Ivey the Third ain't in this World no more and they ain't much Chance a'him ever coming back neither what with all them Bullet Holes the Sheriff a'Comal County put in him. Course, Calley said, they ain't a Her or a Him or No Body else gonna keep me from finding my Pela Rosa now that we out a'that Dark o'Cave. You reckon we can Find her, Papa said. Well I don't know Why Not, Calley said, the World ain't big enough to keep us from it is it. Then, Papa said, he give Firefoot a little shake a'the reins cause he seen some thing over there on that Rock where all them Candles burned o'Pelo's Face off for him and wanted to go see what it was. So me and Fritz and o'Edward bumped on over there with him and when we got there, Papa said, I seen What it was on that Rock and What it was, he said, was Calley's big o'Pistola and they was that Noose o'Pelo Blanco'd been a'going round hanging People with all his Life and Why they was even that little Mesquites Wood Statue a'Little Saint Lalo o'Pelo'd chopped up in little Pieces but now was all stuck back together again with some Tree Sap or some thing. Looks like o'Pelo wants us to believe he's a'leaving his o'Bad Life behind him now and a'going off to find him a new Good One don't it, Calley said. Yes Sir I said, Papa said, it sure does look like it to me. Then Calley looked at his Pistola to make sure he still had him some Bullets in it and said, Well we gonna have to see bout that for our self ain't we.

CALLEY STUCK HIS PISTOLA DOWN HIS PANTS, Papa said, and I set o'Fritz in my lap and off we went from there and was Sad to do it cause a'Leaving Little Missey and her o'Panther like that. Where you reckon o'Pelo took Pela I said, Papa said. I don't have no idea Where, Calley said. Well Where we a'going then, Papa said. I don't have no idea bout that neither, Calley said. We just a'going that's all huh, Papa said. Yes Sir we just a'going, Calley said. Course it helps we got these Tracks down here on the ground to foller don't it, he said, and I looked down there and sure nough they was two sets a'tracks a'leading off cross the Country for us to foller. That's Him and Her ain't it, Papa said. Is now, Calley said, Won't be Him later. You mean Bad Harm on o'Pelo huh, Papa said. Yes Sir I do mean Bad Harm on him, Calley said, Yes Sir I do. What happens when you mean Bad Harm on some body, Papa said, you ain't never told me that. Why Bad Harm comes to em then, Calley said, that's What. What kinda Bad Harm, Papa said. You just gonna have to wait and see what kinda Bad Harm when the Time comes, Calley said. I don't reckon you know you self yet do you, Papa said. No Sir I don't, Calley said, but I got me bout a hunderd ideas on it. I bet you planning to Shoot him ain't you, Papa said, now that you got your big o'Pistola back down your Pants again. Well he shot me didn't he, Calley said, I don't know how I could be more Fair to him then to shoot him back same way he did me do you. Well do you, he said. No Sir I don't, Papa said. You do know how the World Works don't you Mister, Calley said, Any body in your Life ever tell you that. No Sir not that I remember, Papa said. Here's how it Works, Calley said, you a'listening. Yes Sir, Papa said, I am. Whatever you put out there in the World gonna come back on you xactly the same Way you put it out there you self. Now take o'Pelo Blanco, he said, He Shot me didn't he. Yes Sir he did, Papa said. Okay so now I'm gonna have to go Shoot him back the same way he done me ain't that Right, Calley said. See how it Works. Simple as Pie ain't it. Yes Sir, Papa said, but what if you miss Shooting him in the Leg like he done you and you Shoot him in the Arm or in the Foot or somewheres else in sted. What're you a'talking bout, Calley said. Well, Papa said, you said ever thing in the World comes back to you xactly how you put it out there you self Ain't that what you said, he said. Yes Sir some thing like that I reckon, Calley said. So if o'Pelo went and Shot you in the Leg don't that mean you got to go Shoot him in his Leg back and not in his Arm or Foot or no wheres else. I was just trying to give you the Genral Idea, Calley said, I wadn't trying to put a Fine Bead on it if that's what you a'thinking. No Sir I'm just a'saying What if you was to miss your Aim at his Leg and Blowed his Ear off for him in sted, Papa said. Don't that mean now he got to come back over here and Blow your Ear off for you. Don't that Worry you. Well, Calley said, they's two things Wrong bout that. One, he said, I don't never miss my Aim and Two even if I did and Blowed his Ear off for him I'd still owe him that other Shot in his Leg from before and I'd give him that one fore he could even raise his gun up to Blow my Ear off back. So No Sir, he said, I ain't Worried he's ever gonna Blow my Ear off or nothing else off neither. Sides that, he said, you still a'Squirt and your Job is to just listen ain't it. Yes Sir I said, Papa said. Then we just kep a'riding on but then Calley said Here's another way the World Works, he said, Some times when you put a'lot a'Bad out there in the World like o'Pelo done Why it comes back to you just a whole god dam Hell of a lot worsern it was when you put it out there in the First Place you know it. I reckon so, Papa said. Yes Sir,

Calley said, and that's xactly what's gonna happen to o'Pelo Blanco when I catch him. And then I looked back at where we come from for the Last Time, Papa said, and Why I seen Little Missey a'standing there with her o'Blind Panther a'watching us go and Oh they looked so Sad, he said, it bout broke my Heart in two so I set my Hat down on a Rock for a Good Bye Gift and waved em Adios Adios.

*B*OUT TWO DAYS LATER, Papa said, we come up on this Farm and they was a Old Farmer a'setting out on his Porch a'having him a sip out a Jug at the end a'the Day. How do, Calley said. I do pretty Good long as I got this Jug here and it don't go empty on me, the Old Farmer said, that's how I do. Been getting any Rain, Calley said. Oh Yes Sir it rains all day and all night round here, the Old Farmer said, bout oncet ever five six hunderd years and we're due another one here in Oh say bout sixty years or so. Last one we had I seen o'Noah and his Animals come a'floating by in his Big Boat right out yonder in the Pasture, he said. I like a good Joke, Calley said, but we a'looking for some body and ain't got time for Laughing right now. Maybe when we come a'riding back by this way here some time in the Future. I reckon you'll still have a Joke or two on you then won't you, he said. That's all I got now, the Old Farmer said, but I already used the one up on you bout o'Noah floating by didn't I. Yes Sir and it was a good one, Calley said, wadn't it. Yes Sir I said, Papa said, it was. Some a'the Jokes I got wouldn't do to tell a Boy, he said, so don't ask me for that kind. No Sir we won't, Calley said, but what we a'looking for is two People. One of em is a Pretty Red Head Girl, he said, and the other one is a Fella got his Face all burned off in a Fire. Oh Yes Sir seen em both, the Old Farmer said, they come by here just the other day that o'Red Face Man a'wanting to know was they any thing Good he could do for me. Good, Calley said. Yes Sir but course I didn't have no idea what he was a'talking bout, the Old Farmer said, so I just said Well if you wanna do some thing Good needs to be done round here my poor o'rusty Chain out yonder in the Barn ain't been polished since fore o'Saint Patrick went to chasing Snakes. Course that was just another one a'my Jokes, he said, But next morning when I got out there to milk the Cow why that o'Chain was polished to where you'd a'thought it was

58   *...I seen Little Missey a'standing there with he*
       o'Blind Panther a'watching us go.

made a'Silver. What you figgur bout that, he said. You know who that was polished your Chain for you, Calley said. No Sir ain't got no idea who it was, the Old Farmer said, some body likes to polish Chains I reckon. It was o'Pelo Blanco was who it was, Calley said. You ever heared a'him. Who ain't, the Old Farmer said, but No Sir wadn't him. O'Pelo Blanco likes to Hang People off a Tree where this o'Red Face Man I'm talking bout here just wanted to do me some thing Good. How bout this Red Head Girl was with him, Calley said, she look a'scared a'him to you. No Sir she didn't look a'scared a'him to me, he said. Yes Sir, Calley said, Well that's what I was a'scared of my self.

*W*ADN'T LONG AFTER THAT, Papa said, and here we come up on this Family just a'going down the Road in they o'Wagon and a'pulling they Milk Cow long behind em on a rope. Oh they must a'been bout a hunderd little Boys and Girls both in there with the Momma and Daddy, he said. How Do, Calley said, you got you a nice big Family here ain't you Mister. Cold Nights where we come from, the Daddy said. Yes Sir and a lot of em too I reckon huh, Calley said. Where yall a'headed for any how. We wanna hear what that Fella got to say up yonder in San Antoneya, he said, That where you and your Boy there headed too. We don't know not one thing bout Who you talking bout there, Calley said. The o'Daddy looked just Surprised as could be, Papa said, and said Well you must a'been in some Dark o'Cave somewheres not to a'heared bout The o'Red Face Man. Yes Sir for a Fact we was, Calley said, and we just got out a'there too. The Momma and Daddy both had em a laugh at that, Papa said, and the Daddy said You just like that o'Fella back there a'setting on his Porch always telling a Joke. We bout fell out the Wagon at the one a'o'Noah floating by out yonder in his Pasture. Yes Sir we did too, Calley said. Now what's this o'Red Face Man you been a'talking bout got to say yall come all this way just to hear it. Well what's been told us the Man said is here a while back he took him a trip down to H-E-L-L to see his o'Daddy who wadn't never a nice man in his Life cause he wanted to see how he was a'doing down there and he come to find out his o'Daddy was just a'setting round on a Flat Rock all day and wadn't doing no good at all. Oh me and Fritz just bout went to falling off o'Edward at that, Papa said, cause it was xactly the same

60

Story I told o'Pelo bout seeing my own Mean o'Daddy a'setting down there in Hell. That don't sound so Bad to me, Calley said, just a'setting round on a Flat Rock all day. I got me a Friend or two'd say Why this is Heaven here ain't it just a'setting round on this Flat Rock all day. Yes Sir but The Red Face Man says they's a Lot more to it'n that and they ain't not one Lick a'Fun in it So he come on back up here to warn ever body else bout changing they ways fore its too Late. Well he's the Best Friend any body ever had then ain't he, Calley said. Oh I'll tell you just how good a Friend he is to ever body, the Man said, when the o'Devil seen he was coming back to warn ever body bout What he seen down there Why he burned his face off to make him look so Ugly wouldn't nobody even wanna Look at him or Listen to him neither one. I heared he got him a Pretty Red Head Girl a'travelling long with him, Calley said. They any Truth to that you know of. Oh Yes Sir, the Man said, that'd be Sister Rose. She's the one Sings and Dances and Sells the Tickets.

*W*E WAS ALREADY GONE BOUT FIVE MILES down the road, Papa said, fore o'Calley could even talk bout it. They ain't one thing in the Whole World more Saddern to Love some body and them not to Love you back is they, he said. No Sir I don't reckon they is, Papa said. Well they ain't, Calley said, No Sir they just ain't. I'm sorry I said, Papa said. You're sorry, Calley said, What you got to be sorry bout at your age. Well Mister Pearsall, Papa said, I reckon I'm just sorry Pela Rosa don't Love you no more is all. Don't Love me no more. Who told you Pela Rosa don't Love me no more, Calley said. Who told you that. Why you did here just a minute ago, Papa said. You said they wadn't nothing more Saddern in the World'n to go a'Loving some body that don't Love you back. Oh Why Hell's Bells Boy, Calley said, I wadn't talking bout me if that's what you was a'thinking. Oh No Sir I was talking bout how o'Pelo's gonna feel when Pela goes a'riding off with me on o'Firefoot and you and that little Dog there just a'follering long behind on o'Edward. Oh, Papa said. I didn't know that. I worry bout you some time, Calley said, don't pay nough attention to what's being said. Here lemme give you a xample, Calley said. That Man back yonder said o'Pelo's going round the Country telling People that same Story you told him bout you a'going down there to Hell in you Dream to see what become a'you mean o'Daddy and you didn't even Whoop bout him a'stealing that Story off you. I told him that Story same as I did you, Papa said, I don't see how he stole it off me. He ain't only a Murderer goes round Hanging People didn't never do nothing, Calley said, Now he's a god dam Story Thief to Boot ain't he. Well I don't know, Papa said, I didn't never tell him he couldn't go round telling that Story if he wanted to. You don't have to be Nice to that o'Red Face Son of a Bitch, Calley said. I don't remember him being Nice to you when he was a'reaching to put that Noose round your Neck and drop you off a Cliff or some thing. No Sir that wadn't Nice was it, Papa said. O'Pelo wants to talk bout Hell, Calley said, by god I'll give him all the Hell he's ever gonna wanna talk bout in his Life. And then some more just like it on top a'that, he said.

FIRST THING O'CALLEY SAID when we come a'riding into San Antoneya, Papa said, was First Thing we gotta do is get you a Bath and a new Hat. I don't need no Bath, Papa said, but I reckon I could use me a new Hat all right cause I ain't got none at all right now. No Sir you need em both, Calley said. You wanna look nice when Pela Rosa sees you. You the one needs to look nice when she sees some body, Papa said, She don't care nothing bout seeing me. I already had my Bath here just the other day, Calley said, Don't you remember Little Missey give me one then went over there and warshed my Pants out for me too. I still don't want no Bath, Papa said. Listen to me now, Calley said, they got what they call a Bath House in San Antoneya where they's People give you your Bath for you. Ain't no body gonna give me my Bath, Papa said, No Sir. They scrub you with a Brush and Soap then dry you off with these big Towels they got and Why then you come out a'looking Bran Spanking New. I don't wanna come out a'looking Bran Spanking New, Papa said, They ain't no body gonna scrub me with no Brush. How bout we just chunk you in the River then, Calley said. Why you could give you your own Bath then and wouldn't have no body a'rubbing round on you with a Brush or nothing else if that's what got you so Worried. How bout I just warsh my Face off, Papa said, how bout that. That's all Pela or any body else ever gonna see a'me any how ain't it, Papa said. But o'Calley wadn't bout to let it go. I know just where the River runs through Town, he said, Grab a'good holt on o'Fritz there I don't reckon he's gonna want him a Bath no moren you do when we get there.

Oh they was people all up and down in the River, Papa said, some of em a'warshing they little neckid Babies and Childrens and others a'warshing they own neckid self and they clothes and whatnot and they wadn't no body I could see worried bout doing it in front a'ever body else like that neither, he said, Even one Old Man a'warshing his big o'fat Hiney with a rag over there by the Bank. The main thing I didn't like bout it, Papa said, was it made me think a'that Happy Time when me and my Momma and my Brother Herman was out there in the Creek with the Little Bay Mare that my mean o'Daddy went and shot Dead that night and then my Momma run off from Home the next morning after that and I never did see her again cep in my Dreams. It was just bout then, he said, when o'Fritz come a'swimming up His feets just a'going and I grabbed him up in my arms and give him a Hug cause right then, Papa said, I needed to be a'thinking bout the Good Things in my Life and o'Fritz was sure nough one a'em.

*O*H AND THEN THE NEXT THING, Papa said, was here come two Men a'carrying a Sign with a Big Red Face on it and ever body went to jumping out the River to go see, even that Old Man a'warshing his big fat Hiney but his Wife hollered at him to get on back in the River and stay there til she said so. Why that's a pitchur a'o'Pelo Blanco ain't it I said, Papa said, after he got his Face all burned off in the Fire. Yes Sir it is, Calley said, cep now the o'Thief wants ever body to believe it was the Devil his self Who burned it off for him when he was down there in Hell and he come all this way back up here so he could warn ever body else in the World bout it as a Favor. That's what the sign says huh, Papa said. Says that, Calley said, and says he's gonna tell us how to save our own Soul from the Red Hot Fiery Burning Flames down there in Hell fore its too late. They ain't no Flames down there that I seen when I was there, Papa said, just ever body a'setting round on a Flat Rock and a'Crying bout it. Yes Sir, Calley said, but getting a Red Butt a'setting round on a Flat Rock all day long ain't near so exciting to People as getting it burned off in the Fires by the o'Devil his self is it. No Sir, Papa said, it ain't. So which way you reckon he's gonna tell

63

the Story, Calley said. Yes Sir he's gonna Whoop it up bout the o'Devil ain't he, Papa said. Yes Sir, Calley said, And we gonna be there when he does.

Then when we got our Horse out the River and went to saddling em up to go, Papa said, Why we looked over there and seen one a'the Men a'carrying that Sign reach over with his Boot and give o'Fritz a kick when he passed. You ever do that again Mister, Calley said, and you gonna lose you that Boot and Foot both. The Man just laughed, Papa said, and said I ain't a'scared a'no Little Toot of a Dog like this one here. No Sir, Calley said, But I ain't a'talking bout no Little Toot of a Dog like that one there and you better god dam well know it while you still can. Oh and then the Man seen the Look in Calley's Eye and said Yes Sir Well I know it now. Well then, Calley said, maybe you oughta just tell that Little Toot of a Dog there you Sorry for that Kick you give him. Yes Sir I am Sorry the Man said, Papa said, but Calley said No don't tell me you Sorry I ain't the Dog you kicked. So, Papa said, the Man turned to Fritz and said I'm Sorry I kicked you Dog but Fritz was a'licking on his self and wadn't paying no attention. He ain't a'listening, the Man said. Tell him again, Calley said, You ain't a'going off no wheres til he knows you Sorry for kicking him. I'm sorry Dog, the Man said, I'm Sorry I'm Sorry I'm Sorry but, Papa said, o'Fritz didn't even look up at him from his a'licking on his self. That little Dog ain't a'listening, the Man said. Well maybe you better tell him again then, Calley said. Hey Dog I'm a'talking to you the Man said then reached out with his Foot and give o'Fritz another kick to get him off his Hiney and pay attention and Oh when he did, Papa said, Why of a sudden o'Fritz come a'Live and reached his Teeth out in a big Surprise and took him a Bite on that Man's Foot and Oh the Man hollered and run off fast as he could go and, he said, we ain't seen him since. Fritz you Little Toot of a Dog, Calley said, you was just a'playing Possum on that Man wadn't you. I don't know he was or not, Papa said, but when Calley said that Why o'Fritz just grinned and went Heh Heh Heh like he always does some time.

*W*E STILL GOTTA BUY YOU A NEW HAT Mister Pearsall said. So, Papa said, we rode on into Town and when we got over there to the Plaza Why they was Pigs a'rooting round all over the Place in front a'this o'Building they had with a pretty Winder in it and the Street in front was made a'Mesquites Blocks. You know What that is I reckon don't you, Calley said, then took his hat off and put it on his Heart. It's Some Body's Church I reckon, Papa said. I ain't never been here fore to know. Well, Calley said, you're more Right than Not. It's kind a'ever Texan's Church now I reckon, he said, cause it's where one Texas died that Mexico usted to own but at the same time it died Another Texas was borned in its place that didn't Mexico or no body else in the World own cep itself. Course o'Sammy Houston had to whup o'Sanny Anny over at San Hacinto to do it. Yes Sir, Papa said, my Grandaddy Andrew and his Daddy John was along on that trip. Yes Sir I know it, Calley said, I remember you a'telling me that Story one time. After we get you a new Hat here in a few minutes, he said, you always remember to take it off and hold it to your Heart when you come a'riding by here cause the Alamo is a Holy Place and you want It to know you know It is. Yes Sir I will, Papa said, but how you know It's gonna know I know It's a Holy Place when I do. Well that's what a Holy Place is, Calley said. It's a Place knows ever thing they is to know in the World and it'll help you tell you self things you wadn't able to tell you self just on your own. But to get the Right Answer, he said, you got to have your Question just Right in your mine first. Is that why we come a'riding this way, Papa said, so you can ask the Alamo here a question you can't answer just on your own. No Sir, Calley said, we come a'riding this way cause just down the street right over yonder is the Joske Brothers Store and that's where we gonna get you a new Hat and me a new pair a'Pants that ain't got a Bullet Hole in the Leg. And maybe if she's lucky, he said, we just might find a little Treat for Pela Rosa too while we at it.

I NEVER SEEN SO MANY PEOPLE

a'going In and Out a'store in all my Life as I seen a'going In and Out the Joske Store that day, Papa said. But I reckon what surprised me most, he said, was they was selling Saddles and Spurs and whatnot right there when you first come in the Front Door and back behind that they had em a Wall didn't have nothing on it but Hats Hats Hats. I ain't never had a Store Bought Hat in my Life, Papa said. Well you gonna have you one today, Calley said, even if

we got to go down to the Creek and shave some o'Beaver's Butt to make it. Bout that time the Store Man come out from back behind the Counter, Papa said, and said What can I do for you Gentlemens here today. First thing, Calley said, is this Young Man here needs him a good Hat and not one a'them silly things some stores sell to the Greenhorns off the Train neither. Why certainly not, the Store Man said, then reached up and took a Hat off the Hat Wall had a round top and a big wide flat brim on it and just set it right down on top my Head and Why it was so light, Papa said, I wadn't even sure it was up there or not til I looked in the mirra and seen Yes it was. And Oh Yes Sir, he said, I did like what I looked like in that Hat. John B Stetson Hat like that gonna last you a Life Time, the Store Man said, then you can pass it on down to your own Son just fore you go in the Box. Oh Calley and me give each other a Smile at him a'thinking we was Daddy and Son, Papa said, but I reckon by now we come to Think pretty much the same way our self. I reckon I'm gonna need me one a'them John Bs too, Calley said, One just like that One there if you got it but my size. Boss of the Plains Old Man Stetson calls it, the Store Man said. I wouldn't have no other my self and I ain't surprised you wouldn't neither Mister. If I was you, he said, I'd go upstairs and get my Pitchur made in them John Bs soons you Settle Up for em here.

And that's xactly what we done, Papa said, and Oh the Pitchur come out on a piece a'tin just Pretty as you please with Calley a'setting in this big Chair they had made out a'Texas Long Horns and Rawhide and me a'standing back behind him with my hand on his shoulder the way Daddys and Sons do in Pitchurs I reckon. And if that wadn't enough, he said, Why then o'Calley went over there and got em to put it in a Silver Locket with a chain to hang round Pela's neck. Hard to tell if this is a Pitchur a'us or a Pitchur a'our John Bs they so much prettiern we are ain't they, Calley said. Then, Papa said, we went in that other Room where they was selling Pants and Calley told the Man he needed him a new pair didn't have no Bullet Hole in the Leg and One More Thing, he said, They got to be loose nough round the middle sos I can stick my big o'Pistola down there in the pocket for when I might need it. Yes Sir the Man said, Papa said, and fixed him right up.

*F*RITZ WAS A'SETTING UP ON O'EDWARD in front a'the Joske Store a'grinning at all the People a'passing by when we come out, Papa said, and it give em so much Pleasure to see him I wish I'd a'had bout a hunderd more of him. Fritz you been a'behaving you self I said, Papa said, then looked over there where Calley was admiring the Locket with us a'wearing our John Bs in it. You reckon she's gonna like it, he said. I don't see why not, Papa said, pretty as we are in our John Bs. Well look a'here, Calley said, I got him to make one for you too when you wadn't looking and then, Papa said, Why o'Calley come out his pocket with a'nother Pitchur a'us just like that other one and give it to me to keep and Oh I was glad to have it. The only other Pitchur I ever had took a'me was with o'Arlon over yonder in Kendalia, Papa said, just fore he Murdered that Man with Mister Armke's little Cook Knife and got his self sent off to Gatesville Boy Prison for it. Thank you for the Pitchur I said, Papa said. I'd a'put it in a Locket for you, Calley said, cep I was scared it'd make you look so pretty some body might try to give you a Kiss. I'm glad to have it any way you wanna give it to me, Papa said. Well, Calley said, I reckon it's some thing you can look at in your Old Age when you a'setting out there on your Front Porch with bout sixty-seven Granchildrens a'squirming round in your lap. Pela's gonna like it too ain't she, Papa said, but I seen they was some thing bout it bothering him cause he couldn't look me in the Eye when I said it. You ain't scared she ain't gonna like it are you I said, Papa said. I ain't a'scared a'nothing in this World, Calley said, cep maybe starving to Death.

So, Papa said, we went on down the Street and had us a Bowl a'Chili at Senyora Garza's Place but fore we got there, he said, we come a'walking pass this Poor o'Beggar a'setting out there on the Board Walk had him these Fins with little short Fingers on em where his arms oughta been and he didn't have no Toes neither then Calley reached over and give him some coins cause a'what he looked like and told him he admired him moren just bout any body he ever seen in his Life cep maybe just One or Two cause it takes a'lot a'Courage to Beg. And when Calley said that, Papa said, Why I looked at that poor o'Loonie to see if he was gonna say any thing back but No he just set there with his o'twisted up Face and give a little Smile like he was thinking bout some thing Funny didn't no body else in the World know.

BY THE TIME WE GOT DOWN THERE
to the opre house, Papa said, Why they was hunderds a'People a'crowding in
to hear what o'Pelo got to say bout the Devil burning his Face off for him and
we had to find us a place to set way back in the Back. You ain't gonna shoot
him from way back here are you, Papa said. Oh No, Calley said, I wanna hear
what he got to say first. Oh and then here come Pela Rosa out on the Stage,
Papa said, and She went to singing Amazing Grace How Sweet is the Sound
and me and Calley and ever body else in there just went to singing right long
with her cause that was ever body's Favorite and still is, he said, and o'Calley
was so took by the Sight a'her after all this time Why he had to wipe his Eyes
dry with his Bandana to get over it and after that, Papa said, he wrapped
that Silver Locket up in it good and tight and give a Boy a nickle to run down
there and put it on the Floor to where Pela could see it was a Present for her
from Some body or other and then some Man a'setting behind us hollered
Hey Lady I thought you was gonna Dance I thought you was gonna Dance
and Calley give the Man a Look back over his Back and said You the one gonna be Dancing here in a minute Mister you don't Hush and be Quiet. I don't
know what makes you think you the Big Boss round here the Man said, Papa
said, and when he said that Why o'Calley just reached round back there and
pinched the Man's Nose so hard he Tooted and both his Feets come up off
the Floor. Think you can behave you self now Mister, Calley said, and the
Man nodded so he let the Man's Nose go and turned back round just in Time
to see Pela Rosa pick up her Present from off the Floor and go set down in
a chair with it. Oh and then here come o'Red Face out on the Stage, Papa
said, and all the People O-ed and Ah-ed then drawed back in they Seats and
covered they Eyes up cause they ain't never seen Nobody look this Ugly in
all they Life and wadn't likely to ever again neither. Get ready, Calley said,
that Ugly o'Red Face Son of a Bitch is bout to tell these People that Story he
stole off a'you. But, Papa said, what o'Pelo tole em in sted was I wanna tell
yall a Story I got off a Boy who went down to Hell one Night in his Dream to
see what become a'his mean o'Daddy and it changed my Life to hear what
he said and I believe it's a'gonna change Your Life too when I tell it to you
here in just a minute.

WELL WHAT YOU THINK BOUT THAT

Mister Pearsall, Papa said, I bet you didn't never xpect him to own up like that did you. No Sir I didn't, Calley said, but let's just set tight and see where he goes with it from here fore we go to making him a Angel or some thing. Next thing, Papa said, was o'Pelo said Of all the Things that Boy tole me bout Hell that night the Thing scared Me most was Oncet you down there don't matter a Lick how much you want to Right a Wrong you done when you was up here Why you just wadn't able to come back and do it. No Sir you just down there til Kingdom Come a'setting on that Flat Rock and even if now you Sorry Sorry Sorry for ever one a'the Bad Things you ever done in your Life you just can't come back up here and make em Right again like some other People can who wadn't near Bad as you was and that's Hell ain't it Mister, he said. Yes Sir, o'Pelo said, That's Hell with the Lid off ain't it. And Oh, Papa said, when he said that Why this big o'Wave a'Fear come a'washing up over ever body in there like a Flood cause ever body went to counting up all the Bad Things they done in they Life and now they was fraid they wadn't never gonna have nough Time left in they Life to make em Right again fore they up and Died. Then, Papa said, o'Pelo told em bout all the Bad Things he done in his own Life ever since my Daddy and them other Cow Boys Hanged his Daddy off a limb that night and how he went round Hanging People after that to get Even for it but now here lately he just been a'going round trying to do Good while he was still here in this World cause oncet you down there in Hell Mister, he said, you just ain't got another Chance do you. And then, Papa said, he said Another reason he was a'going round trying to do Good now was cause he figgured if he done enough Good Why then maybe they might knock off enough a'the Bad Things he done in his Life to where he wouldn't have to stay down there in Hell no moren just a year or two at the most and then they just might give him another Chance to come on back up here and do Better next Time. And then o'Pelo told em they might wanna consider going round doing Good they self fore it was Too Late Too Late Too Late but he wadn't gonna make no Promises even if they did. And bout the time o'Pelo said that, Papa said, I seen Pela open up Calley's Bandana and come out with that Silver Locket had the Pitchur a'me and o'Calley a'wearing our new John B Stetson Hats in it. Oh and when she seen who it was in the Pitchur, Papa said, Why her Face become the Saddest Face you ever did see in your Life and she went to looking for us everwheres out there with the People but No Sir we was too far back in the Back to see and she couldn't do it but she smiled a Tear and blowed out two Kisses any how, he said, One for o'Calley and the other One for me I reckon. And then ever body Whooped and come up on they Feets when o'Pelo finished what he had to say and when they set back down again to where you could see, Papa said, Why Pela Rosa just wadn't there no wheres to be Seen but Calley said he bet she was gonna come find us in the Crowd now and we oughta just set tight here a few minutes. So we just set tight there til they wadn't nobody left in the Place cep Me and o'Calley and bout ten Helpers a'sweeping the Cigars and whatnot up off the Floor, Papa said, but Pela didn't never come round at all. I recall you a'saying you was feeling Sorry for me here a'while ago, Calley said, You rememeber a'saying that. Yes Sir I do remember a'saying that I said, Papa said. Well o'Calley said, I reckon you can Feel Sorry for me now if you still want to.

POOR O'CALLEY WAS OH SO SAD bout losing Pela again, Papa said, that me and him and o'Fritz went over there and set back down on that Bench in front a'the Alamo again to Buck him up some. You kep a'trying to remind me she already give her Word to o'Pelo not to leave him if he spared my Life that day, Calley said, but No I just wouldn't listen to you would I. No Sir Mister Pearsall, Papa said, you was just Hard Headed like some o'Dutchman bout it wadn't you. Ever Time you open your mouth they ain't nothing but Sunshine and Flowers comes out, Calley said, ain't that right. What'd I say to make you say that, Papa said, But my o'Amigo was a'looking way off down the street like he was just Lost as Losted could be. I reckon they's one good thing bout it though, he said. I don't know I'd wanna hang my Hat on the wall with some Woman went round the Country going back on her Word all the time any how would you. You mean you wish she hadn't a'never saved your Life that day, Papa said, That what you mean. Let's talk bout some thing else here a'while, Calley said, you always a'Boxing me in cause you ain't old enough to understand things yet.

So we just set there a good long while not saying nothing, Papa said, but they was People all round setting on other Benches and they was all a'talking bout how they was gonna change they Life now cause a'what that o'Red Face Man tolt em bout not never being able to Right they Wrongs oncet they was down there in Hell a'setting on that Flat Rock. They liked what o'Pelo said didn't they I said, Papa said. Well it's a good Story he told em ain't it, Calley said, Hell it oughta be It was mostly all yours any how wadn't it. Cep for that Part bout How some People get to come back and take em another Shot at it. That wadn't in your Story was it, he said. No Sir, Papa said, I don't even know what it means. Means Dead ain't necessarily Dead, o'Calley said, That's What it means. Who says so I said, Papa said, Ain't no body ever told me that. Same One says You Choose I reckon that's Who says it, o'Calley said then went to twirling his Spur Ching e Ching e ChingChingChing and said You remember me a'telling you this Place here is a Holy Place and helps you tell you self things you ain't able to tell you self just on you own. You remember me a'telling you that, he said. Yes Sir, Papa said, Least some of it I reckon. Well, Calley said, it just come to me maybe that Story o'Pelo stole off you is a Holy Story same way this is a Holy Place cause a'how it's making all these People a'setting round here think bout what Direction they Life is a'going in. And you too huh Mister Pearsall, Papa said. Oh No Sir not me, o'Calley said, I'm always doing just fine in that Department by my self.

*N*EXT MORNING, Papa said, we went on back down to the River to get us and our Horse a'drink a'water and Calley said Why here we are a'setting Horseback out in the San Antoneya River and you ain't even give o'John B a'drink a'water yet have you. I don't have no idea what you a'talking bout Mister Pearsall, Papa said. Well here lemme show you, o'Calley said then reached over and grabbed my new John B Stetson Hat right off the top a'my Head and sailed it way out yonder in the River like he was skipping a Skinny Rock cross the Creek. Hey what you doing I said, Papa said, But then he grabbed his own John B off his own head and sailed it way on out there in the River right next to mine. Keep a Good Eye on em, he said, We don't want o'John B to drown this early in the Morning do we. Oh and then, Papa said, just when mine was bout to Float off why o'Fritz jumped off o'Edward and paddled out there and brung it back for me but o'Calley had to go get his own. I don't know Why you threw my new Hat out there in the River, Papa said, I ain't done nothing to you this morning. They's some thing you might not know bout o'John B, Calley said, He always likes him a good drink a'water fore he lets you shape him to your liking. Then, Papa said, Why o'Calley went to working on the brim a'his Hat and putting dents in the top and fitting it on his head just right and then at the last, he said, he give it a little pull to get it down over one Eye like he was one a'them Fancy Mans or some thing then give me a Wink and wiggled his Eyebrow up and down. Don't never hurt to Bait your Hook does it, he said, Even if they's only one Fish in the Ocean you really trying to catch.

*T*HEN THE SUN COME OUT BRIGHT AND STRONG, Papa said, and wadn't long our John Bs was dried to the Shape we give em and was like a second head a'hair growed on your head. That's a pretty good trick, I said, Last time I threw my Hat in the River it just come all a'part on me. That's a Bad Hat for you ain't it, Calley said, Bad Boots is the same way, he said, Some Bad Friends I know too. Hats Boots Friends, Calley said, you gotta be careful picking all three of em or you gonna come up a'Hurting when things get Wet ain't you. Well I did with o'Arlon, Papa said, he bout landed me in the Jail House when he Stabbed that Man to Death over in Kendalia and I hadn't done nothing but let him ride long with me. Well that's just What you get some times ain't it, he said. Mister Armke said the o'Devil got his Hand on him and Arlon wadn't never gonna come to no Good. Well Life's a Funny o'Dog, Calley said, and I reckon you just can't never tell bout Some Body can you. I don't know what you mean by that, Papa said. Just keep a'living and you gonna see for you self here one a'these Days, o'Calley said. Your Life been a Funny o'Dog huh Mister Pearsall, Papa said. Yes Sir but that don't mean I been a'riding round Laughing bout it all this time, he said. You know what makes me Laugh, Papa said. No Sir I don't believe I do, Calley said. Tell me when you got time. When you threw my Hat out there in the San Antoneya River and said you was giving o'John B a'drink a'water, Papa said, that made me Laugh. It was just a'way a'talking, Calley said, I wadn't trying to be Funny. Well you was Funny any how, Papa said. I think maybe you that Funny o'Dog you been a'talking bout you self Mister Pearsall. Well it don't bother me to be some Funny o'Dog, he said. I reckon I like that bettern being some Funny o'Cow Pie a'wearing a John B Stetson Hat here. Oh I got a Pitchur a'that in my Head, Papa said, and just went to Laughing. And then o'Calley did too and then me and him both just set there on our Horse a'Laughing bout it and now o'Fritz started going Heh Heh Heh and couldn't none a'us stop it But Oh, Papa said, right then here come some big o'Mean Pack a'Dogs just a'Barking and a'Growling and a'Snarling at some body or other back up yonder in Town and you could hear bout a hunderd and seven Boys a'Egging em on with they Whoops and Laughs and Sic Ems and then, he said, Why o'Fritz jumped down off o'Edward and took off a'Running to go see what was a'going on. Curiosity killed the Cat, Calley said, I don't reckon o'Fritz ever heared that one huh and we was just bout to Laugh bout that too long with ever thing else we been a'laughing at when Oh here come this EeeeEeeeEeee EeeeEeeeEeee EeeeEeeeEeee from up there in the middle a'all them Dogs and it was like a Knife a'going in our Heart, Papa said, cause we knowed xactly who it was a'Screaming like that.

O'CALLEY HOLLERED OH GOD DAM OH GOD DAM, Papa said, and Firefoot reared up and Lit a Shuck back to Town like his Pants was on Fire and me and o'Edward come a'bumping long behind fast as we could go our Hearts just a'Thumping at what we was fraid we was gonna find oncet we got up there. But Oh it was a lot worstern that, he said, Why they was Big o'Mean Dogs ever wheres you looked with they Big Teeth all bared back and a'Dripping Poison and Oh they was a'rushing in and out to get em Bites on Little Missey and her poor o'Blind Panther a'hanging onto each other out there in the Street all by they selves. Oh them Dogs was bout to Tear em all to pieces, Papa said, cep o'Calley run at em on Firefoot just a'Hollering and a'Swinging the Loop Knot on the end a'his Rope to give em Lumps on they Head and Stings on they Butt and drive em Back Back Back just a'Yipping and a'Crying it hurt so Bad. But they was just too many of em, he said, and ever time o'Calley'd send four or five or six a'running off down the street a'Yelping Ouch Ouch Ouch with they tails tween they Legs Why here'd come a'nother five ten more just a'Snarling and a'Biting like Loonie Dogs and Oh that poor o'Panther'd run at em a'Screaming EeeeEeeeEeee EeeeEeeeEeee like that and try to Bite em to keep em off Little Missey even if he didn't have no Teeth to do it with and couldn't see em to know where to Bite at any how. And not only that, Papa said, but them Town Boys was a'Whooping and a'Laughing and a'Hollering Sic Em Sic Em Sic Em and a'Throwing Rocks at em and Poking em with sharp Sticks both at the same time and me and o'Edward run over there to save em if we could but when we did, he said, Why first thing was this Big Rock come a'flying in and hit me in my Mouth and knocked bout half my Front Tooth off but Oh what scared me moren that was I looked over there and seen three four Dogs get o'Fritz down to the ground and was a'trying to roll him over on his back so they could Bite his Belly open and eat his Guts out with they sharp Teeth. But right when they was bout to do that, he said, Why o'Calley jumped off Firefoot and went to kicking them Dogs off o'Fritz then grabbed him up and went to jump back on o'Firefoot with Fritz in his Arm but them Dogs and bout twenty more run over there and started taking Bites on his Leg and wouldn't let go for nothing til he give em Knots on they Head with his big o'Pistola for it and Oh then here come Little Missey just a'Hollering and a'Swatting at em with my o'Hat and Giving em Licks with her Walking Stick cause now they was biting at her Travelling Bundle cross her back and then here come that Poor o'Blind Panther to Help if he could but them Town Dogs come a'Running in from back behind and piled on him like a Duck on a June Bug and Oh just went to Ripping him all to pieces with they Teeth and I reckon they would a'done it too, Papa said, cep o'Edward come running over and went to Kicking and Stomping em all over the Place and they drawed back just a'Howling to save they Life. Oh and then, he said, I looked over there and seen some Dogs jump up on Firefoot and was trying to bite Calley on the back a'his Neck but he whupped em off and then I looked round again best I could, Papa said, and seen Little Missey and that o'Panther was both all but wore out now and was just barely able to stand from all them Dog Bites and Rocks and Pokes but Oh Boy Hidy them mean Boys was still a'Hollering Sic Em Sic Em Sic Em at them Dogs to Get Em Get Em Get Em and Oh, he said, Oh now here come the worstest thing I ever seen in my Life and that was Men running from down the Street with they Big Guns and they was all a'Hollering PANTHER PANTHER GOD DAM O'PANTHER to

75

each other and Little Missey didn't know a Word of it but she knowed what was coming next and Oh just went to Yelling and Hollering at them Men tears just a'running down her face and then she tried to whup em back with her Walking Stick to save her Friend but No they just laughed at her and pushed her down on her Bottom in the Road and went to shooting BOOM BOOM BOOM then BOOM BOOM BOOM some more and her poor o'Blind Friend Screamed and Jumped way up high in the Air then come down Dead on the ground but tried to crawl over to her any how to say Good Bye but when he did, Papa said, Why all them Dogs run over there just a'Snarling and a'Snapping to get em a'Last Bite on him but Little Missey crawled at em on her hands and knees best she could with her Walking Stick just a'going to give em Licks and drive em off but No they just wadn't no Stopping em from getting they Bites on that poor o'Dead Panther. Oh and then, he said, I heared one a'them Men Holler You Dogs get off that god dam Panther I want his Hide for my own self then here he come with his Knife to skin that o'Panther like he said but Little Missey hit him with her Stick three four times hard as she could and then all them other Men went to Hooting and Laughing at him like Loonies and he grabbed Little Missey to skin her for it in sted a'her o'Panther but this o'Flop Eared Dog of a sudden come a'running out a'the Pack and give that Man a big Ugly Bite on his Hand to keep him from it and then that Man raised up his gun and he shot that o'Flop Eared Dog five times right there BOOM BOOM BOOM BOOM BOOM, Papa said, and them other Men went to Laughing some more cause they thought it looked like Fun to shoot Dogs so they went to shooting Dogs they self and Oh the World become nothing but Dog Blood and Dog Howls and then, he said, I heared o'Calley a'Hollering at me tween Dog Howls and BOOMS to GET LITTLE MISSEY AND GO GET LITTLE MISSEY AND GO and I looked over there and seen that little o'Wrinkled Up Woman still a'trying to Whup them mean Dogs off her poor o'Dead Friend with her Walking Stick but now they was coming at her in a Rush. Oh and then I tasted that copper Taste in my Mouth, Papa said, and run over there and went to kicking Dogs hard as I could to get em off her but No she wadn't gonna leave her Dead Friend and hit me with her Stick same as she done all them Dogs and it took me bout ever thing I had left in me to get her up on o'Edward and then me and o'Fritz on up there behind her and all this Time, he said, them Men was a'shooting Dogs and them Boys was a'Chunking Rocks and o'Calley was

...her poor o'Blind Friend Screamed and
Jumped way up high in the Air

a'Hollering at me to GIT GIT GIT GIT and Oh Boy Hidy I Got, Papa said, and didn't never stop Gitting Got til me and Fritz and Little Missey was way off on down the Road a'Long Long Way from there but you could still hear them Men a'Shooting Dogs and Laughing bout it and Oh them poor o'Dogs was just a'Howling and a'Crying til you couldn't hardly stand it no more Then I looked round, he said, but No my o'Amigo Calley Pearsall wadn't no wheres in view and Oh my Heart give a big Thump cause I was fraid they maybe got him same way they got that poor o'Blind Panther and maybe now they was both a'laying Dead out there on the Road Side some wheres with Dead Dogs a'piling up all round em.

*T*HEY WADN'T NOTHING TO DO, Papa said, cep just set there and Watch for o'Calley to come on but No he never and I was fraid that Man wadn't just only skinning Little Missey's poor o'Blind Panther now but maybe was a'skinning o'Calley too while he was at it. Oh and then, he said, Little Missey hugged her Bundle to her Heart and tried a'Running back to Town where we just come from but I grabbed her by the Arm and said No Ma'am that ain't no place for you to go back to and Oh, Papa said, she give me a Good Hard Lick with her Walking Stick to let go and Oh Yes Sir I did Let Go right quick but she knowed I was Right bout it and just set down there where she was. Oh she was Sad bout it, Papa said, Sad Sad Sad so I reached down there and tried to give her Hand a'little Squeeze to make her feel better if I could but No she drawed it back but then o'Fritz come over and give her a Lick on that same Hand and Why she put him on her Lap next to her Bundle and went to petting on both of em. Well, I said, I reckon you like o'Fritz moren you do me huh But she didn't pay me no mine then come up on her feet like she heared Some Body a'coming and I did too, Papa said, and sure nough here come Calley with that poor o'Dead Panther a'laying cross his Saddle in front a'him on Firefoot and Oh Little Missey went to Hugging on him even if he was already Dead and Gone. Gimme a hand here with this o'Boy if you would, Calley said, then me and him lifted him down off Firefoot and put him down to where she could pet on him all she wanted to. She's gonna miss her o'Friend ain't she, Papa said, I don't know how she ever gonna get over it. Yes Sir Best Friend she ever had in her Life wadn't he, Calley said, Only One too I reckon. Well Mister Pegleg'll be his Friend now over on the Other Side, Papa said, my Momma too. Yes Sir I don't doubt it, Calley said. We gonna have to dig him a Hole here in a minute. I don't want some body else a'coming up here wanting to make em a Rug like that Man up yonder in San Antoneya did. What'd he say when you run off with him, Papa said, fore he could skin him. No Sir didn't say a Word, o'Calley said, just went to shooting at me and I had a Hell of a Time a'making him stop it. Him and that other Son of a Bitch both, he said. Then, Papa said, I seen they was two Holes in o'Calley's John B one where a Bullet went in and the other where it come out again on the other side. You gonna need you a new Hat here fore long ain't you Mister Pearsall I said then o'Calley run his Finger in and out the Hole and said Well better a new Hat'n a new Head I reckon. That what happened to them other two Fellas, Papa said, But No o'Calley didn't wanna talk bout it no more and wouldn't say.

*W*E CARRIED THAT POOR O'DEAD PANTHER up the Hill a'ways and buried him there under this Big Oak Tree, Papa said, even if they wadn't much left to bury after all them Dog Bites and Bullet Holes and then, he said, that little Wild Woman come over there and give o'Calley's Hand a Squeeze I reckon to say Thank You Mister and then she did me too. Better find you Jar a'Bee Honey, Calley said, she got Dog Bites all Up and Down her you see em. Yes Sir I do, Papa said. And you ain't so Pretty you self with that Big Fat Lip you got Looks like you got a German Pork Sausage stuck in your mouth and that one Eye bout swole shut on you too ain't it, Calley said, We gonna have to Doctor on you too I reckon. Yes Sir I said and run got the Bee Honey and o'Calley went to dabbing some on Ever Body's Dog Bites and Rock Bumps cluding his own. I'm gonna put some a'this Honey on your Lip here, Calley said, but don't go to Licking it off or your Face gonna stay like this your whole Life and not even o'Robert E. Bob Lee gonna know you. Mister Lee don't know me any how, Papa said. You just being that Funny o'Dog again ain't you. I'm trying, Calley said, Yes Sir I am god dam sure trying. Then, Papa said, o'Calley give me a Look to Look over to where Little Missey was a'setting with her Travelling Bundle in her Lap and a'petting her Friend's Hump a'Dirt with the other. I bet she wishes she just stayed at Home don't you, Papa said. Her Home's with us now, Calley said. She ain't got no other Friend in the World I know of. You reckon that's why she follered us to here, Papa said. Well People need People in they Life, Calley said, and she don't have no body else in hers does she. That's sad ain't it, Papa said, not to have no Friend in Your Life. I don't know, o'Calley said, I ain't never not had no Friend in mine less you wanna count them five years they had me in that place wadn't very Friendly to start with. Where was that I said, Papa said, but o'Calley just shook his head No he wadn't gonna tell me. I reckon Mister and Miz Choat'll give Little Missey a Home same way they done me and Herman and Bird and Marcellus and ever body else comes a'Long. Well they might I reckon, Calley said. No Sir they will, Papa said, you don't have to worry bout that. No I don't worry bout that, Calley said. What I worry bout is getting her Here to There that's what I worry bout. You seen how them Boys sicced they Dogs on her didn't you. Oh Yes Sir I did, Papa said. Well we gonna have to cut cross the Country with her, he said, Stay way clear a'People such as that best we can so it don't happen again. That like to a'scared me to Death, Papa said, I didn't have no Idea what was gonna Happen. Her o'Friend is Dead, Calley said, That's what Happened and now we gotta make sure the same thing don't happen to her too. You think it might, Papa said. Well I think it might could, Calley said, if we ain't careful with her. And then he went to putting new Bullets in his big o'Pistola, Papa said, where them other Bullets he most likely shot off at them two Men tried to skin that o'Panther usted to be.

NEXT MORNING LITTLE MISSEY WAS GONE, Papa said, and so was o'Fritz but we didn't have no Idea where to. Where you reckon she went I said, and Calley said, Don't Worry she'll be back. Well I don't know how you know that, Papa said. I know it cause Lookee Here, o'Calley said then throwed his Blanket back to show me her Travelling Bundle was there under it. She sneaked it under the covers with me last night for Safe Keeping I reckon, Calley said, fore she run off. I figgur she'd a'just took it with her if she wadn't coming Back to get it don't you. Yes Sir me too, Papa said. Course that don't mean we ain't worried bout half to Death a'what she and o'Fritz might a'got into out there in the World some wheres all by they self, Calley said, ain't that right. Yes Sir I'm worried too, Papa said. Yes Sir I sure am. And that ain't all we got to worry bout neither is it Mister Pearsall, I said. Well it's enough ain't it, Calley said, I didn't know they was some thing else we need to be a'Worrying bout. Well Yes Sir they is, Papa said. You gonna tell me bout it or you just gonna keep it to you self, Calley said. I don't generally like Surprises this early in the Morning. I think they's Some Body a'follering us, Papa said. Why you think that Calley said, and I said, Cause I can see em a'sneaking in and out the Trees over yonder cross the River and they all a'pointing they Guns at us. Oh and then Calley seen em too and said Well Yes Sir that is dam sure a Surprise here so early in the Morning ain't it.

Oh and then here they come a'Spuring they Horse and a'Splashing cross the River at us. I don't know but could be me they a'looking for cause a'what I done yesterday when them Men went to shooting at me. And Oh that scared me when he said it, Papa said, and I said May be you oughta just Jump and Run like you Pants is on Fire Mister Pearsall while you still able to. No Little Missey put me in charge a'her o'Travelling Bundle here and I wouldn't never want her to think I'd slip a Duty on her when she gets back and sees me Gone.

*O*H AND THEN, Papa said, Here them Men come on cross the River and pulled they Horse up to us and the Man in Charge give me a good long Look and said We a'looking for a Boy this Morning. Well, Calley said, I got one right here but he ain't for Sale. No body give a Laugh at that, Papa said, but then the Man in Charge said My name is William Wayne Shettles and I am Superintendent up yonder at the Gatesville Correctional. Yes Sir I believe you, Calley said. You got a Voice on you biggern any Man I ever did hear in my Life cep maybe o'Preacher Seymore up in Johnson City. Had us a Boy over there at the Correctional stabbed a Guard dead with this little Hand Stabber he made out a'piece a'pointy Wire and a Broomstick handle then run off on us fore we could grab him. A Regular little Horse Turd that Boy, he said, and Thank you for the compliment to my Voice. Oh I knowed right then when he said it the Boy he was a'looking for wadn't no body but Arlon, Papa said. This Boy I'm a'talking bout here is Arlon Clavic, he said, murdered him another Man over yonder in Kendalia here a while ago and wadn't never nothing but a Sack a'Trouble his Whole Life any how. Here, he said, I got a Pitchur right here and then, Papa said, Why he pulled out a Hand Bill they made out a'that Likeness a'me and Arlon and Fritz was took on a piece a'Tin that time he was talking bout over in Kendalia just fore Arlon stabbed that Man to Death with that little Cook Knife he stole off Mister Armke. This is him right here, the Superintendent said, and pointed to Arlon in the Pitchur but course Calley seen the other Boy too and knowed it was me right off and it was Fritz there in the middle but he was licking his Hiney when the Man made the Pitchur and just come out a Smudge to where you couldn't hardly see was he a Dog or a Pig or a Possum or What. And a'course, Papa said, I was a'wearing my o'Flop Hat back in them Days and didn't look no wheres near what I looked like now with my Lip swole up like a Pork Sausage and a'wearing my new John B Stetson Hat. Who's this other Boy here in the Pitchur, Calley said. No we don't have no Idear Who, the Superintendent said, but he don't look like he'd amount to much does he. Oh and that hurt my Feelings when he said it, Papa said, but then Calley said Well I've learned in my Life them that don't look like much is usually the Ones you gotta look out for cause some times they the Most they ever was. Then he looked at me, Papa said, and said Now ain't that right Mister. Well some times it is and some times it ain't I reckon I said, Papa said. You're both Right and I believe you bout it, the Superintendent said, but that ain't the One we a'looking for any how. No Sir, Calley said, I reckon we was just having us a Conversation here wadn't we. They's just this one more thing the Superintendent Shettles said, Papa said, and then he give o'Calley this long look like he was seeing some thing else bout him he hadn't never seen here just a minute ago. By the way, he said, you ain't the Fella whupped them two Men back in San Antoneya to a Fare-thee-Well over a Dead Panther are you, he said. Well I ain't a'saying I am and I ain't a'saying I ain't, Calley said. Well Sir what are you a'saying then, Superintendent Shettles said, and o'Calley give him a little Smile and said Well I reckon I'm a'saying if I was you Mister I just wouldn't Ask. Oh and then the Superintendent give Calley a Look to size him up and said Well No Sir I wouldn't never. The only reason I even brought it up is to mention them Two Men is a'getting ready to go a'looking for Who Ever it Was whupped em and Who Ever it Was whupped em might wanna know bout it. Yes Sir Good to know, Calley said, and I thank you for warning o'Who Ever it Was if I ever run cross him to tell him. They's just one more thing Mister Shettles said, Papa said. Yes Sir what's that, Calley said, we're late for some thing and got to get on down the Road here in a minute. I was just wondering Was it down at the Joske Store yall got them John Bs. Yes Sir it was down at the Joske Store for a Fact, Calley said, you oughta go down there and get you one you self. I'd have to rob me a Bank or two to do it, the Superintendent said, they ain't giving em away today are they. Didn't these two here, Calley said. Yall go hear What that o'Red Face Man had to say for his self bout the Devil burning his Face off for him last night. Was you there too, Calley said. Yes Sir I was, Superintendent Shettles said, and it sure got me to thinking bout my own Faults. Well we all gotta do better if we can I reckon, Calley said, fore its too late. Already too late for this Bad Boy we a'hunting here, the Superintendent said, First Thing that come to my mine when I looked him in the Face back at the Correctional was Why here I am a'looking in the Eye a'the o'Devil his self ain't I and listen here Mister the Shivvers just went to running all up and down my Leg and in and out my Boot like a bunch a'god dam Poison Snakes bout to bite me Dead.

I RECKON THAT WAS YOUR FRIEND he was a'talking bout wadn't it, Calley said when Superintedent Shettles and his Men rode on off. Arlon wadn't really never no Friend a'mine, Papa said, but Yes Sir that's who he was a'talking bout I reckon. Want my advice, Calley said. Stay way a'way from that little Pecker Wood Son of a Bitch. It's a wonder you ain't already tainted just by being in that Pitchur with him. I thought that o'Superintendent was gonna see it was me there for sure didn't you, Papa said. I reckon this Fat Lip's what saved me. No Sir it's that John B what saved you, Calley said. Wouldn't nobody in the World think a Boy wearing him a John B Stetson Hat like that could ever be no body but a good Citizen. Where'd you get the Money for em any how, Papa said. Oh I'm still spending Money that come out a'o'Jug Ears Saddle Bags way back there when he was bout to do you and Little Lalo Bad Harm and I had to shoot him for it remember. I still got some Money come out a'his Saddle Bag my self, Papa said. I could a'bought my own John B you know it. I know it, Calley said, but I wanted your First Good Hat in your Life to be my Treat. The Man at the Joske Store said it was gonna last me a Lifetime, Papa said. Might be a little early in your Life to go a'saying that, Calley said, All depends on how you Live it I reckon. I ain't scared a'dying, Papa said, cause I know they ain't no body ever really Dies any how. Well you're way a'head a'me on that one, Calley said, I don't know it. You ain't never seen the Shimmery People huh, Papa said. Oh I reckon I seen one or two Shimmery People in my Life, Calley said, but these wadn't the same Shimmery People you a'talking bout here. Who was they, Papa said. Well one of em was this Fella I was having this Fight with bout some thing or other, Calley said. and he hit me cross my Head with a wagon rench and bout took my Ear off and then ever time I looked at him for a Day or two after that he was just a'Shimmering in his tracks. How bout the other one, Papa said. The other one, Calley said, Well the other one was this o'Gal a'trying to Spark me one night when I wadn't but a'couple a'years oldern you are now. Spark you, Papa said. It's what some People call it, Calley said. Spark you. I don't have no idea what that is, Papa said. Well that's cause you ain't never been Sparked yet, Calley said, After you been Sparked oncet or twiced is when you know what it means to get Sparked. After that you don't never forget it neither, he said, and pretty soon you just go a'riding round the Country looking to get Sparked oncet or twiced more but they ain't nothing in the World gonna ruin a Good Man quickern that less it's Whiskey, he said. Whiskey's worsen Sparking when it comes to Ruining a Good Man. Whiskey huh, Papa said. You know this o'Gal I'm a'talking bout here, Calley said. Yes Sir, Papa said. Well I thought she wanted to give me a Spark but what she really wanted was to get me down Drunk and the Sparking was just the Bait to do it with so I took me a'Drink a'her Whiskey and then another one and then some more and Oh then ever body and ever thing in the World just went to Shimmering on me like all them Shimmery People you a'talking bout but when I come a'wake next morning, he said, Why them o'Shimmery People was all gone and that o'Gal was gone and Why my Money was all gone too and all I had left on me was this big o'Head Ache kep me down on my bed for bout two days and I decided I was just gonna have to quit it for Life. The Sparking and the Whiskey both huh Mister Pearsall, Papa said. Well No, Calley said, not both.

84

OH AND THEN HERE COME O'FRITZ

just a'running out the Brush and went to barking at us to Come On Come On so we jumped Double on o'Firefoot and run after him and then here in a minute Why we seen Little Missey a'stumbling long toward us from Town with some thing so Big and Heavy in her Arm it was bout to turn her over. What is it she got there I said, Papa said, and o'Calley blocked the Sun out his Eye with his John B so he could see better and said Well Bessa my Coola if it ain't one a'them poor o'Shot Up Dogs from Town is what it is. Is it Dead, Papa said. She ain't just walking round with a Dead Dog in her Arm is she. But by then o'Calley was already off o'Firefoot, he said, and a'taking that o'Dog in his own Arm. He ain't Dead, Calley said, It's that o'Flop Eared Dog bit that Man when he went after Little Missey with his knife. Oh and it was, Papa said. And they was Bullet Holes all in him where that Man shot him and he couldn't hardly breathe neither just kinda whisper Ssss Ssss Ssss like he was trying to tell you a Secret bout some thing. You and o'Firefoot run go get the Bee Honey, Calley said, and be dam Quick bout it or we gonna be digging us a'nother Hole here in just a minute. And bring Little Missey's Bundle, he said, we don't want her worrying bout that too. So me and o'Firefoot run up there and got the Bee Honey and her Travelling Bundle both quick as we could and when we got back why o'Fritz was a'trying to Lick that o'Dog's Bullet Holes Dry and Little Missey and Mister Pearsall both was a'petting on him and she took her Bundle from me and started a'Singing that o'Dog a Little Song bout some thing or other but, Papa said, I didn't have no Idea what. How is he doing I said. I don't know he gonna Live or Not, Calley said, but I can tell you for sure his Dancing Days is over for a'while. What'd she do, Papa said, Drag him outta the Dead Dog Pile. Calley twirled his Spur Ching e Ching e ChingChingChing and said Well She lost one Friend, he said, But now Look she gone and found her a'new One ain't she. And then I looked over there, Papa said, and Little Missey was a'putting Dabs a'Honey on her Finger and a'poking it down them Bullet Holes. He don't look so Good to me, I said, I can't tell he's gonna Live or Not. Well we just gonna have to stay here with him til we see which one, Calley said. That's how I vote on it Mister. Yes Sir me too, Papa said. Course we gonna have to go find us a Bee Tree to Rob too cause a'the way we a'going through what little Honey we got left.

$\mathcal{S}$O THERE WE WAS,

Papa said, Two Dogs Two Horses Two Men and one little o'Wild Woman didn't care bout nothing in the World cep saving that Poor o'Shot Up Flop Eared Dog that here just a'little while ago was a'trying to Eat her up long with all them others. What we gonna name him if he Lives I said, Papa said, and o'Calley said Well he probably already got him a Name he just ain't tole us yet is all. How's he gonna tell us, Papa said, he ain't even hardly breathing. Well you gotta ask him nice, Calley said, and listen to what he says back to you. You a'teasing me again ain't you I said but Calley went over there and set down by Little Missey and that o'Dog and said Scuse me Little Missey your Dog got a Name that you know of but No she didn't even look up at him Just kep a'dabbing Bee Honey on. You know I don't believe neither one of em got a Name, Calley said, Ain't that the Saddest thing you ever heared in your Life. How you gonna get a'long if you ain't got a Name some body can call you by. Well we been a'calling her Little Missey, Papa said, I reckon that's a Name ain't it. Yes Sir that is a Name, Calley said then leaned down close to her and said Hidy Little Missey how you like your name. But she just went on with her Dabbing and didn't even look up at him, Papa said. I think she likes it okay, Calley said. Cause if a Woman don't like some thing Why she god dam sure gonna tell you bout it ain't she. Then, Papa said, o'Calley give that poor o'Dog a Look and said How bout you Mister you got a Name or you just want us to give you one. And then, he said, Calley reached over to give him a little Scruff on his Head to be Friendly bout it but when he did why that o'Dog we thought was bout Dead reached up with his Teeth and give him a good hard Bite on his Hand and o'Calley jumped back on his Bottom and hollered SonofaBitch SonofaBitch and then said If Little Missey didn't like him so much, I believe I'd just chunk him in the River for his Sass and he wouldn't need no Name. But right then, Papa said, Why that o'Dog lifted his Head up and give Ever Body this Sad I'm Sorry Look like that was the First Friendly Hand ever reached out to him in his Life and Now he was Sorry bout Biting it and bout ever thing else Bad he ever done in his Life too. And then, he said, o'Fritz give him a Lick and then Little Missey give him a Pet and then I did too and all that o'Dog done was close his Eyes down for a Nap. Give him a Pet Mister Pearsall I said, Papa said, he ain't gonna Bite you now that he's a'sleeping I don't reckon. No Sir Thank you, Calley said, I like just setting here a'keeping my Hand to my self

Little Missey was a'putting Dabs a'Honey on her   87
nger and a'poking it down them Bullet Holes...

in case he's playing Possum on me again. So we named him Possum, Papa said, cause we couldn't think a'nothing better.

THEN ME AND O'CALLEY walked the Creatures down to the River to get em a Drink a'Water fore Dark, Papa said, but Mister Pearsall kep his hand on his Pistola and his Eye back on Little Missey and Possum the whole time they was drinking. I think o'Possum's gonna Live don't you I said, Papa said. Yes Sir I believe o'Possum's too sneaky to Die ain't he, Calley said then made a ugly face at that Dog Bite on his hand. Ever time we turn round, Papa said, Why here comes Some Body else. First it was Little Missey showed up and now it's o'Possum. It's like we a'growing us a Family here ever step we take ain't it Mister Pearsall. Yes Sir cep they's still one a'missing to make it whole for me. Oh I could see how Sad he looked, Papa said, and I knowed why too. You talking bout Pela Rosa ain't you Mister Pearsall I said. It's either Her you a'talking bout or your Sister Eurica one ain't it. Speaking a'my Sister Eurica, Calley said, I still ain't rode up there and told her the Sheriff a'Comal County done shot and killed her Husband and she better go on and find her a new one fore she gets too old, he said, I told you long time ago that was some other Fish I got to Fry didn't I. Don't you reckon some body else already gone and told her by now, Papa said. They's that, Calley said, and it's Possible she just got tired a'waiting for him to come back Home and went on and got her a new Husband any how. You don't talk bout her much do you, Papa said. Well, she ain't much to talk bout, Calley said, that's Why. She's your Family ain't she, Papa said, Ain't that a reason to talk bout her if you need one. They's all kinds a'Family the way I see it, Calley said, Ever Body don't always have to be Blood Kin to you like you a'thinking. You take o'Fritz there. You love him don't you. Yes Sir I do love him, Papa said. You love him moren you do your own god dam mean o'Daddy ain't that right, he said. I had to think bout that a minute, Papa said, then I said Well maybe I do and maybe I don't. I don't know. Even after all them mean things you o'Daddy done to you and your Momma and your Sorry o'Brother Herman in his Life and you still don't know, Calley said. Well he's down there in Hell a'setting on that Flat Rock for it, Papa said. I reckon I just feel a little Sorry for him is all. Ain't been but a minute, Calley said, and here we already got off on Old Karl when I was trying to say some thing to you bout they being all kinds a'Family not just By Blood Family okay. Yes Sir okay, Papa said. Here's Family to me, Calley said, Ever body and Ever thing you Ever Loved Don't matter if it's your Momma or your Daddy or your Dog or your Horse or your o'Amigo or just that o'Cow you been a'milking all you Life or even that big o'Oak Tree out yonder in the Pasture you usted to climb up in to see the World when you was just a Little Boy, he said, Why they ever god dam one a'em your Family if you Love em ain't they. You see what I'm a'saying here, he said. Yes Sir, Papa said, You a'saying you and me is Family too long with all these others you been a'talking bout ain't that Right Mister Pears-all. Why Yes Sir it just couldn't be no more Righter'n that he said and Oh, Papa said, him a'saying that just filled me up to the Top.

NEXT MORNING

I asked o'Calley had he dabbed some a'that Bee Honey on his new Dog Bite from o'Possum, Papa said, and he said No we need that Bee Honey for you and Little Missey there and for all the Creatures even o'Possum before I need any. Well I said, Papa said, that ain't Right you need some Bee Honey on that Dog Bite you got too so it don't Fester and you lose that Hand like you bout did you Leg Mister Pearsall. Well they's three ways I know a'getting Bee Honey, Calley said, You can go find you a Bee Tree and Rob you some or you can go knock on some o'Farmer's Door and ask him if he won't sell you some or you can ride on back to San Antoneya and they's usually some Mexkin or other a'selling some on the Plaza in Jugs and you can get you some there. No Sir I'll go find a Bee Tree, Papa said, I don't wanna go back to San Antoneya with this swole up Lip I got. It don't look so Bad, Calley said. I reckon you can get you a job in the Circus for good Pay with it but you better Look Out if you go to climbing a Bee Tree, he said, Cause them little SonsaBitches'll sting you all up and down and ain't you or no body else got nough Hands to swat em all off oncet they get after you. I'll just go find me some o'Farmer then, Papa said, they always got some Bee Honey on em I reckon. I'd go with you, Calley said, but I don't wanna leave Little Missey and o'Possum here just all by they self. No Sir me neither, Papa said. They's some thing else been a'bothering me too, Calley said, you know it. No Sir I don't know it, Papa said. O'Possum over there, he said, Why in Hell you reckon he don't like me. Ever Dog I ever knowed in my Life always likes me. Well maybe he just had him a Hard Day is all, Papa said. Why Hell we all had us a Hard Day the other Day, he said, but didn't no body see you and me go to Biting some body for it did they. No Sir but I might'a if I could'a, Papa said, I was so Mad at them Town Boys when they was a'hitting me and ever body else with all them Rocks and a'poking us with they Sticks I could taste that Copper Taste come up in my mouth. When I get Mad, Calley said, I just empty out all the Mean I got in me at who ever it is a'standing there I'm Mad at and Hooo Look Out then Mister Look Out. Like them o'Dogs you was a'Popping with you Rope when they was trying to bite Little Missey and her o'Panther huh, Papa said. That what you talking bout. You a'saying that just give me a Thought, Calley said, you don't reckon o'Possum was one a'them Dogs I give a good Lick to and that's why he give me a Bite back for it first chancet he got. I'm kind a'that way my self, he said, I don't Never forget a Offense some time not even for a Day. You talking bout o'Pelo Blanco now ain't you Mister Pearsall, Papa said, I know you still Mad at him even if he is a'changing his Ways. A Skunk don't never lose his Stink Mister, Calley said, you might remember that in you Travels if you ever catch you self a'thinking Otherwise, he said.

Then I went over there, Papa said, and give o'Possum a Pet to say Good-bye and get Better if he could fore it was too Late and tole Little Missey I'd be back fore long with some more Bee Honey for ever body's Dog Bites and Not to Worry bout it no moren she had to. Keep you Eye on which a'way you a'going so you'll know which a'way to get back when the Time comes, Calley said then he give me a little Tip a'his John B like he was o'Genral Lee his self and I was his Best Soldier a'going off to Capture the Fort. Yes Sir I will I said, Papa said, and me and Fritz and o'Edward went on off from there to go find us a Farmer had some Bee Honey on him.

*W*ADN'T MAYBE BUT A DAY OR TWO when we come up on this Farm House and they was a Lady a'Churning But-ter out there under the Tree in the Shade. How you this morning Ma'am I

said, Papa said, and tipped my John B to her like Miz Choat told me always
to do. I could use some Help a'Churning this Butter, she said, I'm bout all
wore out from it. Don't you have no Chilrens a'you own to Help you, Papa
said. That's what my Momma always done when she needed some Churning. My Boy run off some wheres yester day I think it was and I ain't seen
him since the Lady said and Oh then, Papa said, I seen Tear Trails down her
Face and knowed she been a'crying bout it all day long. Why'd he go and run
off, Papa said, you didn't make him Mad bout some thing or other did you.
No and my Husband didn't neither she said. He just run off is all. You want
me to go see if I can't find him for you Ma'am, Papa said. It ain't no Trouble.
Oh she really went to Churning then and said I'm Scared to Death some
thing Bad might a'happened to him ain't you. Well I don't even know him,
Papa said, but Yes Ma'am I reckon I am a little Scared too. How you gonna
find him any how, she said, if you don't even know him. Well you just tell
me which a'way he went and I'll go Look and see if he ain't there. He might
a'gone off some wheres with his Daddy you know it the Lady said. No Ma'am
I didn't know it, Papa said, you ain't never said Nothing bout no Daddy til
just now. I think he's out there in the Barn doing some thing, she said. He
been out there all morning long may be even longern that. Oh and then I
heared some body a'hammering on some thing with a Hammer out there in
the Barn behind the House. Well maybe I oughta go see I said, Papa said, but
she was a'Churning the Butter so Hard and Fast now she couldn't a'heared
it Thunder and then Oh I seen they wadn't nothing in the Churn to Churn
and that poor o'Woman was Loonier'n six Snakes in a Basket.

I WENT OUT TO THE BARN THEN,

Papa said, and knocked on the Door where some body on the other side
was just a'hammering a'way on some thing or other. Hello in there Mister,
I said, I think you wife's gone Loonie on you out here under the Tree. Oh
and then I heared him start to crying in there his self. Who are you, he said,
And what you want. I ain't no body, Papa said, just some body a'looking to
buy em a'Jar a'Bee Honey so we can dab it on all these Dog Bites we got.
Come on in, the Man said, I got some Jars a'Bee Honey on the shelf in here
Just take you what you need and go on. So I pushed the Door open, Papa

said, and Oh I seen that Crying Man was a'making him a Wood Box to bury some body in and then I seen this Dead Boy just bout my size a'laying over there on the Hay with Stab Holes all in him. I bet I know who done that, Papa said, but the Man just went on a'Hammering and a'Crying and didn't hear not one Word I said. What happened, I said, and the Man said, They was this Boy come by here the other Day a'looking for a Bite to Eat and said he'd Trade his Work for it if I'd give him a Chance so I give him a Chance and fed him food to Eat but when it come his Turn to work why he stole my GranDaddy's Pocket Watch my Daddy give to me and run off with it and it made my Sammy Boy here so mad he went after him to get it back for me. But that was all he could say, Papa said, cause he went over there and Hugged his Sammy Boy to his self and just Cried and Cried and oh I just set there til he was all cried out bout it and then said Don't tell my Minnie bout our Boy here she don't need to know it. Yes Sir I won't, Papa said, she's already Hurt nough ain't she. She's out there just a'Churning Air ain't that right, the Man said. Yes Sir, Papa said, she don't know she ain't gonna get no Butter out a'that does she. Don't know nothing in the World, the Farmer said, and ain't never gonna know nothing else neither is she. No Sir, Papa said, I don't reckon. You got a Momma and a Daddy, the Man said. No Sir not no more, Papa said, but I usted to have. We gonna be a'needing us a new Boy like this one here, the Farmer said. You wanna be it. You can keep your little Dog if you want to but I'd probably wanna trade that o'Nag off you got there. No Sir Thank You, Papa said, but I already got me a'nother Family where I come from. What is it bout us you don't like, the Farmer said and give me the Snake Eyes, Papa said. They ain't nothing bout you I know to Like or Not Like neither one he said. I don't even know you. You'd have to do your Chores, the Farmer said, I ain't offering you no Free Ticket round here if that's what you been a'thinking. How much I owe you for that Jar a'Bee Honey I need over there on the shelf, Papa said. It ain't for Sale, the Man said. You gonna have to work it off you want it. Yes Sir be glad to work it off, Papa said, just tell me what you want me to do and I'll go do it. You sure you don't wanna be our Boy huh, the Farmer said. No Sir but Thank You for the chance, Papa said. I reckon you just afraid you gonna end up like this Dead Boy Sammy we got here is Why huh, the Farmer said and went back to his hammering.

SO I DIGGED THE HOLE

to put the dead Sammy Boy in, Papa said, and the Farmer give me a Jar a'Bee Honey for it. You change you mine bout being our New Boy just come on back, the Farmer said, and we be glad to have you even if we already got us a'nother one by then cause we might could use us Two. You gonna go Help your Wife now ain't you, Papa said. I think she needs some Help don't you. What kind a'Help you a'talking bout there, the Farmer said. You want me to drill a Hole in her Head with that o'Auger I got over there on the Bench and let all the Crazy run out is that what you a'saying. She ain't like that all the Time is she, Papa said, I figgured it just come over her here recent cause a'this Dead Sammy Boy here. No Sir she always out there a'Churning Air like that ever day, the Man said. What come over her to do that, Papa said. I ain't never heared a'such a Thing. Runs in her Family, the Farmer said. Some Body tole me they had to get a Wagon and go over there and haul her o'Momma and her Sister both off they was a'getting so Loonie they went to Biting ever body they could even they o'Cow. Mister Carson I think it was tolt me that, he said, o'Rolf people call him o'Man Rolf. Over yonder on Cypress Creek by where Old Man Borgers Lives you know him don't you, he said. No Sir I ain't ordinarily from round here and ain't never even seen Cypress Creek in my Life, Papa said. You ain't never heared a' o'Rolf. No Sir just from you here a minute ago, Papa said, I ain't never run cross him or No Body else knows him in my Life. Well they's lots a'People knows him but ain't a'one of em wants to shake his Hand I can tell you that, the Farmer said, and I'll tell you this too You ain't gonna wanna Shake it neither You wanna know Why. Yes Sir Why, Papa said. Cause his Hand Shake is so strong he just might pinch your Hand off your Arm when he shakes it and you ain't never gonna get it back again that's Why he said then raised up his Arm and said See what Happened to me but Oh they wadn't nothing there to see cep his o'empty Sleeve but not no Hand. Oh and that come as such a Surprise to me, Papa said, I jumped back from it But when I did Why he of a sudden poked his Hand out from up his sleeve where he been a'hiding it and laughed at me. Fooled you didn't I, he said. Yes Sir you did I said, Papa said. Ain't no body got a Grip on em strong nough to pinch your Hand off for you, he said, I don't know What made you think that. Well it's what you said, Papa said, I guess I just believed you when you said it is all. Well I don't believe you Smart nough to be our New Boy here any how you know it, the

Farmer said, You just gonna have to get you a Job some wheres else. No Sir I wadn't never Looking for a Job any how, Papa said. I was just a'looking for a Jar a'Bee Honey to put on some Dog Bites we got. Why Hell Boy, the o'Farmer said, you got a'Jar a'Bee Honey right there in your own god dam Hand and don't even know it. That's what I mean bout you not being Smart nough to be our New Sammy Boy. You go on now, he said, They's some body a'setting out there under that Tree in front a'the House and I gotta go see who it is and what they want fore they run off with the Place like that other Boy done with my GranDaddy's Pocket Watch and I don't know what all else.

*W*ELL THEY WAS JUST BOTH LOONIE, Papa said, the Man and the Woman both but what scared me most was it was o'Arlon that o'Farmer was a'talking bout stabbed that Sammy Boy Dead and I wanted to get on back to Camp quick as I could fore I run into him some wheres out there in the Country my self. Stop a'Licking on you self Fritz I said and Let's go so o'Fritz jumped up on o'Edward with me and a'way we did go me a'holding that Jar a'Bee Honey tight so not to drop it on the way and then, he said, after a good long Time I looked down and I seen this Pitchur a'Trees and a Bird some body or other'd painted and left on the Ground and bout the time I seen that Pitchur Why o'Fritz Hair went up on him and he scrunched back close to me as he could get like he was scared a'some thing and o'Edward didn't like some thing neither and wouldn't go no further less I whupped him to do it but No I wadn't never gonna whup my Friend to do nothing. Then, Papa said, I seen all these other Pitchurs on the Ground and they was all kicked in and busted up and some of em was Butchered ever which way with a knife and I said Well it's Time for us to go some wheres else ain't it Fritz But, he said, bout that time I heared some body just a'Hissing and a'Spitting up yonder in the Brush and I sneaked on up there by my self and pulled a Mesquites Limb back to have a Look and Oh, Papa said, Oh Oh Oh the Shivvers just went a'Running all up and down me cause what I seen next was o'Arlon just a'Snarling and a'Spitting and a'Cutting them Pitchurs up like he was one a'them Loonie o'Dogs from back in San Antoneya the other Day. Oh and then this o'Donkey come a'walking

94

out the Brush had a'Bunch more Pitchurs tied on him and he went a'going a'Hee a'Hee a'Hee HawHaw like that and o'Arlon seen him and wiped the Spit off his face on his Shirt Tail then went over there with his Knife in his Hand to do him some Meanness with it and I was just bout to holler No Sir Arlon you leave that poor o'Donkey lone He ain't never done nothing to you. But, Papa said, just when I thought he was a'making ready to stab him in his Heart Why he reached over there and give that o'Donkey a pet on his Head in sted then tried to get him to come on long with him but No that Donkey didn't want none a'him and wouldn't go a step So, he said, o'Arlon give him a Hug Good Bye then got up on his Horse and went on off back in the Brush to where I couldn't see him no more and Oh Boy Hidy, he said, that was okay with me.

OUT THEN, Papa said, here come Fritz a'setting up on o'Edward to find me and I was Glad they hadn't a'come no sooner cause Oh I seen o'Arlon was a Total Loonie now same as that o'Farmer and his Wife was back there with their Dead Sammy Boy and I didn't know but what he might a'tried to hurt em with his knife same as he done all these Pitchurs. And Oh, he said, they was Pitchurs just ever wheres you looked And not only Pitchurs but Paint Brushes and Paint Jars and they was all a'leading back in the Cactuses and Mesquites and I went to follering em and o'Fritz and Edward went to follering me then Fritz jumped off o'Edward and went a'running pass me just a'Barking at some thing or other up yonder and, Papa said, when me and o'Edward got there Why they was some little Fat Man way up a Tree a'Looking down at us. That Boy been stabbing all my Pitchurs ain't with you is he, the little Fat Man said. No Sir he ain't, Papa said, He went off in the bushes some wheres and we ain't seen him since. They's People say Things bout my Pitchurs all the time but this is the first time some body ever went at em with a Knife, he said, then climbed on down out the Tree and put out his Hand. Wasskum Yancy, he said, of Philadelphia. Philadelphia, Papa said, That's way off up yonder some wheres ain't it. Yes Sir and getting further ever day, he said. I reckon you the one painted all these Pitchurs scattered round here on the ground ain't you Mister Yancy, Papa said. Yes Sir I am, he said, when they

was still Pitchurs. I reckon it was o'Arlon run you up that Tree huh Mister Yancy, Papa said. No Sir I was already up that Tree a'Painting a Pitchur a'the World from high up like on a Cloud when that Boy come a'riding by underneath and got Mad at my Pitchurs. O'Arlon's Mad bout ever thing they is in the World, Papa said, it ain't just your Pitchurs. Mister Armke says he got the Devil's Hand on him is what. Maybe both Hands, Mister Yancy said. I'd say that'd be more like it. If I'd a'had a Rock with me, he said, I'd a throwed it down on the little Piss Ant and Knocked his Head off for what he was a'doing to my Pitchurs. Well you can always paint you self a'nother one can't you, Papa said. No they ain't no Artist can ever paint Two just xactly a'like. Cep me I reckon, he said, I'm bout the only one in the World can do it And Oh he looked so Sad when he said it, Papa said, I said Why's that Mister Yancy. Cause maybe I just only got one Pitchur in me and not no other, he said.

$\mathcal{S}$O WE WENT ROUND a'picking up all a'o'Wasskums Paints and Brushes and Scraps a'Stabbed Up Pitchurs and put em up on his o'Donkey Pete where they come off from. You Live round here, he said. No Sir, Papa said, I don't know xactly where I Live. Well where's your Momma and Daddy Live, Mister Yancy said. They don't Live no wheres, Papa said, they both gone on to the Other Side now. But I run off from my Home any how, I said. Yes I run off from my Home too, o'Wasskum said, but that was many long years ago. Oh so many, he said, Oh so very many. You ever think bout going back and saying Hidy Momma and Daddy how yall been a'doing. Well I did go Back bout twenty years ago, he said, and when Daddy seen me he said Well Wasskum tell me what all you've accomplished so far in your Life and I had to say Not one thing that I know of, Daddy. Not One, My Daddy said, Not One. My Daddy wouldn't a'never a'cared nothing bout it one way or the other, Papa said. Well may be you the Lucky One there, Wasskum said, Some times the Father's Hand on you is the one Heavier'n any other and you just gotta bow you Neck and try to get on out from under it Best you can. That's what you done huh Mister Yancy, Papa said, Just bowed you Neck and Run on out from Under it huh. Yes Sir and went out cross the World a'Looking ever wheres for my Muse but No Sir never did find her and don't reckon I ever will now with all these years a'piling up on me like Bricks. Well where's she Live, Papa said, You tell me where she Lives and I bet me and o'Calley can go find her for you. O'Wasskum give his Chest a litte Tap with his Finger then, Papa said, and said Here Right Here's where she Lives cep she ain't never Home when I go to knocking on the Door. You just trying to Tease me now ain't you Mister Yancy, Papa said, That's what you a'doing ain't it. No Sir I am not, he said. If a Artist ain't got him a Muse bout the Only Thing he can do with his Life is set over there in the Shade under a Tree and scratch his o'Ass like that little Dog a'yours is a'doing.

NEXT DAY, Papa said, me and Mister Yancy and Fritz come a'riding in on o'Edward back to camp with o'Pete a'follering long behind. Who you got here, Calley said, I didn't know you was bringing Company. Mister Yancy, Papa said, He's a Artist. Wasskum Yancy Sir, o'Wasskum said, and tipped his Hat. What kind a'Artist are you Mister Yancy o'Calley said and Wasskum said That is xactly what I do not yet know my self and give him a little Smile bout it and shaked his Hand and I could tell, Papa said, they was gonna be Friends from here on out and then, he said, o'Wasskum looked over there and seen Little Missey a'Petting on o'Possum sleeping there in her Lap. That's Little Missey and o'Possum, Papa said. She been in a Cave all her Life and o'Possum bout got his self shot to Death over in San Antoneya the other day when we was all having a Fight. Hello Ma'am, Mister Yancy said and tipped his Hat again, I hope you and Mister O Possum are having a nice day. She don't talk much, Papa said, but she draws Pitchurs up on the Wall some time to say what been going on in her Life. A Fellow Artist then, o'Wasskum said and went over there and shaked her Boney Hand bout it and she give him a Snaggle Tooth Grin back and then o'Possum give him a Lick like they always been good Friends too. He give you a Lick, Calley said, but he just give me a Bite. How you figgur that Mister Yancy, he said. You'd have to ask him, o'Wasskum said. I wouldn't know how to ask a Dog a question for you. Then, Papa said, Why o'Fritz stepped up and give o'Possum a Sniff on his Behind to see how he was a'doing and Mister Yancy said Course if I was to ask Mister O Pos-

sum a question for you I'd most likely go round to the Front End to ask it and Oh then we all had us a good Laugh even if Little Missey didn't have no idea what bout. Here's some thing ain't Funny, Papa said, o'Arlon come up on Mister Yancy out there in the Woods and cut all his Pitchurs up for him. What'd he have a'gainst you Pitchurs to go and do such a Thing, Calley said. I think he was just made that way, Wasskum said. I don't know it was any thing particular to my Pitchurs. Lucky it wadn't you he come at with his Knife Mister Yancy, Calley said, He ain't shy when it comes to stabbing People from what we hear bout him these days. Wouldn't hurt you to camp here with us a few days for your Health. I will and I thank you for the Invitation, Mister Yancy said, Soons I get back from San Antoneya with some new Canvases to paint on and maybe a new Dress for this Little Lady while I'm at it.

A PAIR A'BRITCHES AND A SHIRT

might be better, Calley said. Little Missey don't need to be going through this Country round here wearing a Dress. How bout I take this Boy long with me, o'Wasskum said. I wouldn't mind having some Company long on my Trip and it ain't but a Short One any how. You wanna go, o'Calley said, and I said, Papa said, Yes Sir I reckon I do wanna go. They's some Places in San Antoneya I wouldn't want you to take him to, Calley said, you know what I'm talking bout. Oh listen here, Mister Yancy said, They's some places in San Antoneya I wouldn't wanna take my self in. Why they's One got a woman in there'll take all her clothes off for a Nickle he said then grinned and wiggled his Eye Brow all up and down at Calley like some o'Loonie in the Booby Hatch and Oh Calley give him a Look back and said I wouldn't wanna never hear you took this Boy in a Place like that you hear me. Oh No Sir, the o'Artist said, I wouldn't never take no Boy in a Place like that or my self neither one. I wouldn't wanna have to run you off from here, Calley said, but I would. You don't have to worry bout me, Wasskum said, Oh No Sir. I know Artists got they own Views on such matters, Calley said, but when it comes Time for this Boy to see things like that I don't want it to be a'some o'Gal'd show her self to just any body comes a'walking through the door and got a Nickle on him. I'd a'never even brought it up, Wasskum said,

ne and Mister Yancy and Fritz come iding in on o'Edward back to camp...

cep I been out there in the Country all by my self too long. A man can only paint just so many Pitchurs a'Cactuses and Rocks in his Life, he said, then his mind goes to thinking bout things got two legs on em. Well he don't need to know nothing bout them things at his age, Calley said. Well he's bout the Age to hear bout em soon nough any how I reckon, Wasskum said. Not from you he ain't, o'Calley said, Then give him that Look one more time. No Sir, o'Wasskum said, not from me he ain't. No Sir, o'Calley said. No Sir, o'Wasskum said. And then later, Papa said, when o'Calley was over there a'helping me get ready to go I said What was you getting so Mad at Mister Yancy bout here a minute ago and Calley said No I wadn't getting Mad at him I was just trying to show him he didn't never want me a'getting Mad at him was all.

I LEFT FRITZ A'SETTING THERE with Little Missey a'petting on him and a'Doctoring on o'Possum both, Papa said, and me and Mister Yancy rode on off Double on o'Edward back towards San Antoneya. Keep a Good Eye as you go o'Calley hollered when we was already bout gone, Papa said, then hollered And don't Tarry a'getting on back here neither. He looks after you like a Mother Hen don't he, Mister Yancy said. He just don't want us running into Trouble is all, Papa said. He'd a'come with us cep they's Men in San Antoneya a'looking to do him Bad Harm for some thing he done the other day and he don't wanna have to fool with em right now. He don't have to worry bout Trouble, o'Wasskum said then pulled this little Two Shot Sissy Pistol out his Pants. Not long as I got this, he said. You better put that little thing a'way, Papa said, They's People round here'd shoot you and throw you in the River for even carrying some thing like that on you. You know, o'Wasskum said, when I first come down here to Texas that was xactly what I was a'looking for. What, Papa said, you mean Some Body to shoot you. Yes Sir Some Body to shoot me and I figgured Yes Sir Texas is the Best Place in the World to find Some Body to do that. You got a Sad Story back behind you ain't you Mister Yancy, Papa said. Yes I suppose I do o'Wasskum said. Well, Papa said, I hope it ain't so Sad you ain't never gonna get over it. Well I ain't got over it yet I don't reckon, o'Wasskum said, then went on and told me.

I was a'little Rich Fat Boy, he said, and ever body made Sport a'me all day long. Even my own Daddy, Wasskum said, so I went a'looking for some thing I might could do to please him. First Thing I remember, he said, was to Run and Jump but bout ever time I jumped Why I fell down and it just made him Mad me being so awkward like that so then I went to riding Horses cause my Daddy liked to ride Horses and I thought when I learn to ride good as he can Well then we just gonna go to riding Horses ever where together but I never got good enough at it to where he ever ask me to go riding with him. I don't like your o'Daddy worth a Lick, Papa said. Then I went to reading Books, Mister Yancy said, cause my Father would go in his Library after suppers ever evening and light up his Pipe and read Books and I thought Here's some thing I can do with my Daddy but if I turned a Page too loud Why he'd just run me out cause he said he couldn't think on his Reading with all that racket going on. It was bout then, he said, I remembered all these Pitchurs he had a'hanging on the Wall in our House and I thought Well Daddy might like it if his own Son could paint a Pitchur good enough to hang on the Wall like all these here. Oh I was bout to cry, Papa said, Mister Yancy's story was so Sad to me. So I told Washington to send for Brushes and Paints and whatnot, o'Wasskum said, and when they came Why I just went to painting Pitchurs of my own even if they was really just like the Pitchurs my Daddy already had up there on the Wall. But, he said, a Funny Thing happened while I was a'doing it cause Wadn't long and I was starting to like Painting Pitchurs even moren I liked to Sleep and Eat and then One Day it come to me I wadn't Painting Pitchurs to please my Daddy no more but now I was painting Pitchurs just cause I wanted to Paint Pitchurs and then it come to me I didn't care if my Daddy liked em or not no more. But course the problem was, he said, I didn't have no Idea what I liked neither so I snitched one a'my Daddy's pistols and run off from my Home and told my self I was either gonna find the Artist in me if they was One or by god I was just gonna dispatch my self to the other Realms with a Pop from this little pistol I got here in my pocket and be done with it. That's a Sad Story ain't it Mister Yancy, Papa said. Is to me, o'Wasskum said. Maybe you just ain't waited long nough yet, Papa said. How bout that. Waited long nough for what, he said. Well I said, Papa said, Mister Pearsall is always a'saying What Ever you a'looking for out there in the World is out there some wheres in the World a'looking for you too. Maybe you just ain't waited long nough for it to come find you is all. Well I'll keep my Eye open for when it does o'Wasskum said but I could tell he didn't have no belief bout it, Papa said.

FIRST THING WE SEEN when we come a'riding into San Antoneya, Papa said, was this o'Gal a'setting out on a Barrel a'Pickles and a'smoking her a Pipe in front a'this Saloon where they had a little Black Bear tied to the Hitching Rail. I reckon that o'Gal'd take her clothes off for a Nickle don't you, o'Wasskum said. I wouldn't wanna see it even if she does, Papa said. What if it was Less'n a Nickle, he said, What bout that. I thought you was needing some thing to Paint your Pitchurs on, Papa said, I didn't know you was just wanting to see some o'Gal take her clothes off. You gonna get you self in all kinds a'Trouble with Mister Pearsall you go to taking me in a Place like this after you give him your Word you wouldn't never. Oh No I ain't a'taking you in there if that's what you was thinking, o'Wasskum said, we just a'passing by ain't we. I don't see no Reason to even mention we come by here do you. Why you wanna see that o'Gal take all her clothes off any how, Papa said. I'm a Artist, the o'Artist said, It's my Job to go see Neckid Ladies and paint Pitchurs of em so ever body else can see what they look like when they ain't got they clothes on that's Why he said. What if they don't wanna see em, Papa said. Well been my xperience they wanna see Pitchurs a'Neckid Ladies moren they wanna see Pitchurs a'Trees and Birds, o'Wasskum said. I reckon that's just Human Nature if you ask me ain't it. Oh and then bout that time, Papa said, that little Bear went to crying for his Momma and it made me and o'Wasskum so Sad to hear it we went over there and undone the knot and tole him he was Free as a Bird now but right then, he said, here come this Man a'wearing him a High Hat out the saloon couldn't hardly walk him a step. I believe that Man is Drunk on some thing from in there don't you I said and o'Wasskum said Well either that or his sore leg is a'bothering him one or the other. And then, Papa said, that Man reached over and give that little Bear a Good Hard poke with his walking stick just to be mean and when he did, Papa said, Why that little Bear took a swat at him and knocked his High Hat off his Head then took off a'Running down the Street like his Pants was on Fire and then that Man and bout a hunderd and six other Men from all up and down the Street went to laughing and chasing him back in the Woods where he come from in the First Place.

YOU DIDN'T LIKE IT that Man Poking that little Bear like that did you Mister Yancy, Papa said. No Sir didn't like it, o'Wasskum said. Been Poked a few times my self that's Why. Why'd Some Body wanna go and poke you, Papa said. People just like to poke Artists I reckon, he said, I never could see no particular reason Why. You ain't gonna be a Artist you self are you. If you are I better go on and give you a Poke or two with a Stick now so you can get usted to it. No Sir, Papa said, I'm gonna be a Horn Man and play Music over in Fischer Hall for ever body to Dance to. Well we just a'like then, o'Wasskum said, cep its my Pitchurs I want ever body to Dance to not some Horn. Your Pitchurs, Papa said, Why I never heared a'no Body a'Dancing to a Pitchur. Well that's what I want, he said, Yes sir when they step up to have a Look at one a'my Pitchurs I want em to Whoop and Holler and just go to Dancing right there in they tracks they like it so much. Oh we had us a good laugh bout that, Papa said, then went on down the Street and in this Store where they had clothes for Men and Womens both and this Man come out from some wheres and said Can I help you. Yes Sir you can, Wasskum said, we a'looking for a Pretty Dress and a Pair a'Button Shoes for a Lady Friend a'ours. What size is your Friend the Man said, Papa said, and Mister Yancy said Well she's just bout the size a'this Boy here but maybe just a tad smaller I'm not sure and then the Man give me a Good Look all up and down and said well we'll just have to try some Dresses on him and see what Fits. I ain't a'wearing no Dress, Papa said. No Sir not me. You don't have to wear it, Wasskum said, you just got to try it on so we can get the right size fits Little Missey. I ain't asking you to parade down the Street in it on Saturday morning if that's what got you worried. I ain't wearing no Dress even if you close all the Winders and Double Lock the Doors, Papa said, No Sir I ain't. I have an Assistant bout the same size as this Boy here, the Man said, I think you'll find her satisfactory then he hollered Annie Annie and went off in the back some wheres to fetch her and when he did Why o'Wasskum went to grabbing Dresses right and left and a'piling em up on me like I was some o'Donkey or some thing.

103

Just say when you see one you like he said, Papa said, then here come the Man back and he said They's a Trying On Room back there in the Back just take all them Dresses in there and Annie'll try em on for you to see. So, Papa said, Wasskum throwed another one or two on me and I went on back there couldn't hardly see for all the Dresses piled up on me and then I pushed the Curtain back to the Trying On Room and Oh, he said, Oh they was a Girl in there a'taking her clothes off had her Back to me and I said Oh. And when I said Oh Why that Girl turned round to look at me and she said Oh too and then I said Oh again, he said, cause it wadn't no body in this World cep Annie Oster from that time me and o'Calley lived in her Daddy's Barn after the Hail Storm and Oh Oh Oh she was a'standing there Neckid as a Jay Bird and Oh Boy Hidy, Papa said, I wadn't never just a Little Boy ever again after I seen that.

*D*ID YOU EVER FIND YOUR MOMMA Annie said and I said yes Annie I did find my Momma, Papa said, but by the time I did my mean o'Daddy'd already gone and Murdered her. I lost my Daddy too since we last met, Annie said, did you know that. No I been all over the Country since then Annie and didn't have no way to know, Papa said. Well I did lose him, she said, Life just got too hard for him after what them two Men done to my Momma and he just went on out of it soons he could manage. They's terrible things all round in this Life ain't they Annie, Papa said, I reckon you and me know that bout much as Any Body don't we. Yes Annie said, Papa said, then here we just couldn't help it and give each other a Hug with her not hardly wearing a stitch a'Clothes on her but No the Hug wadn't bout nothing like that. I don't know why you'd be in here a'buying a Dress for some body else Annie said and I had to tell her all I could bout Little Missey and after I did, Papa said, Why she picked the Prettiest Dress in the Bunch she could find and put it on for all us to see. That's the One, o'Wasskum said. Just makes you smile to see it don't it. Granny's gonna be mad if you don't come see her now that you in town, Annie said and Mister Yancy said, Yes go on and have you a Visit while I'm a'shopping for Canvases down at the Wagon Yard and the Man said, Yes go on Annie if it ain't for all Day.

So me and Annie went on down the Street with her a'trying to hold my Hand ever step a'the way. You come back to Marry me didn't you, Annie said, like you said you was some day. Well I remember You a'saying it I said, Papa said, but I don't xactly remember Me a'saying it. You can't hold me to some thing I don't remember I said or not, he said. No and I wouldn't, Annie said, but you did say it Mister. They ain't never gonna be No Body else for me in my Life cep you Annie, Papa said, I just don't know it's Now or Later. You already seen me without no clothes on, she said, Don't that count for nothing. I just barely looked, Papa said, I don't know that I even seen any thing or not. I think you did, Annie said, cause I seen your Eyes Bug out on you like some o'Frog. No you didn't neither, Papa said, my Eyes don't Bug out. They do when they see me neckid Annie said and Oh, Papa said, we just went on down the street a'laughing bout it til we come to this little House where Annie and her o'Granny Oster was a'living there in San Antoneya.

G̲RANNY OSTER WAS OUT BACK A'THE HOUSE a'warshing some body's Dirty Clothes for em cause that was a'nother way they was a'making they Living now, Papa said, but fore she could even say Hello to me Why Annie said He come in the Store and seen me without no clothes on Don't that mean we gotta go on and get Married now. No, Granny Oster said, it means I'm gonna have to tie you to a Fence Post some-wheres if you don't start behaving you self Young Lady then, Papa said, she give me a Look too and said And you shouldn't been a'looking at some thing ain't none a'your Business any how. Annie thought that was the funniest thing she ever did hear in her Life and said He's turning Red as a Beet bout it ain't he Granny but all she said was How's your o'Amigo Calley Pearsall a'doing these days. He's a'doing Good, Papa said, I don't see how he could be doing no Better. You must be a'doing pretty Good you self, she said, to be a'wearing a John B Stetson Hat like that one there on you Head. Mister Pearsall give it to me for a Gift, Papa said. I Lost my Son did you know that, Granny Oster said, here just a'couple months or so ago. Annie told me, Papa said. I was sorry to hear it. He went down in his Head after what them two Men done to his Wife, she said, and just couldn't never get it back up again. I know it, Papa said. I was sorry to hear bout that too. Well I reckon it just shows how much he Loved her with all his Heart don't it. Yes Ma'am it does to me, Papa said. I wouldn't want you and Annie to go a'getting Married til you can say to each other I Love You with all my Heart and mean it much as my Son did his own Wife fore he Hanged his self off that Tree down yonder by the Creek. You remember it, she said. Yes Ma'am, Papa said, that big o'Oak Tree just up from the bank a'ways. Yes Sir that one, Granny Oster said, Yes Sir.

LATER WE FOUND US A BENCH TO SET ON out there in front a'the Alamo, Papa said, cause I remembered o'Calley a'saying it was a Holy Place and just a'being there could help you say things you needed to say but couldn't say just all on you own. I got some things I need to say to you Annie, I said, and she said Yes I know you do and I got some things I need to say to you too but You First. I didn't know I could do it or not, Papa said, but I drawed back and said Annie they ain't never gonna be No Body else in the whole World for me but You. But I don't know I'm ready to Hang my self off a Tree for You just yet. And then, he said, Why Annie took my Hand and a Tear come out and she said No I can't say it neither much as I thought I could. And Oh Boy Hidy, Papa said, that did Hurt my Feelings after all her Talk bout wanting us to get Married ever time I even seen her. You sure I said, Papa said. Yes I reckon I am sure, she said. So I reckon it don't mean nothing to you that I seen you without no clothes on like that huh, Papa said. You said you didn't see nothing any how, Annie said. You wadn't just Storying to me bout it was you. Maybe I was and maybe I wadn't, Papa said, you just gonna have to go on worrying bout it all your Life. I ain't gonna worry bout it for one minute, Annie said, you wouldn't know what you was a'looking at even if you did see some thing. Oh Yes I would too, Papa said, it ain't nothing for me to see some o'Gal a'walking round neckid all the time. Oh you never, Annie said, you just a'saying that to make me feel Bad. No I ain't, Papa said, they's one o'Gal down the Street'll take all her clothes off for a Nickle. I heared all bout her, Annie said. You ain't telling me you give her a Nickle to see some thing are you. No I ain't a'telling you that, Papa said. No I didn't think you was, she said. I don't reckon you even got a Nickle any how do you. No I don't I said,

Papa said, So she just went on and showed me ever thing for Free cause she liked me so much and couldn't help it. And Oh when I said that, he said, Why Annie give me a slap cross my face knocked my John B Stetson Hat off my Head then she run on back Home just a'crying all the way.

I SET THERE A LONG TIME
feeling Bad for what I said to Annie Oster, Papa said, and I reckon I was hoping she was feeling the Same for what she said to me. And if that wadn't Bad enough, he said, then here come o'Wasskum on o'Edward with his canvases and that Pretty Dress and a Pair a'Britches and a Shirt for Little Missey and he said Where you been Jesus the Christ I been a'looking all over for you. I been a'setting right here, Papa said. I don't see nothing wrong with it. Here's what's wrong with it Mister, Mister Yancy said, then come out his Pocket with a big o'piece a'paper had that Pitchur a'me and o'Arlon on it was made that time over yonder in Kendalia. These are nailed up all over Town you know what it says, Mister Yancy said. Some of it I reckon, Papa said, I seen that Paper before. It says they a'looking for Arlon Clavic for four Murders and maybe some more and they a'willing to pay good Money for some body to help em catch him. Yes Sir that's what I thought it says too, Papa said, but then o'Wasskum said But what they don't tell you is which one a'these Boys in the Pitchur here is Arlon Clavic and which one is just some body else they don't care nothing bout. Yes Sir and that one is Me ain't it, Papa said. Yes Sir it is, o'Wasskum said, but how's any body gonna know which One is you if they don't tell you. Oh I got the Squirms when he said that, Papa said, cause I seen then what he was talking bout. Well you'd tell em I ain't the One they a'looking for wouldn't you I said, Papa said. Yes I most certainly would, Wasskum said, but who's gonna believe a Artist over getting some Reward Money in they Pocket to spend You ever think bout that. Oh, Papa said, I looked all round to see if they was any body a'looking at me then pulled my John B down on my Head so far it bent both my Ears down double. I'd wear it like that the rest a'my Life if I was you, Wasskum said, They think you Murdered some body round here Why they'll Hang you for it and won't be nothing you can do bout it when you up there a'swinging off a Sickemore Limb. Did I just paint a Pitchur for you, he said. Yes Sir you did, Papa said.

Well then, Mister Yancy said, you get on up here on o'Edward with me and we just gonna slip on outta Town like we wadn't never even here. And then, Papa said, o'Wasskum pulled out his little Two Shot Sissy Pistol and put it down tween his legs to where couldn't No Body see it less he was a'pulling it out to shoot em.

SO I CLIMBED ON UP, Papa said, and off we went a'riding Double through San Antoneya to get shed a'it quicks we could. You see any body a'Looking at us, o'Wasskum said. No Sir not a' one, Papa said. Keep a Good Eye, he said, I don't want no Surprises you hear. Yes Sir me neither I said, Papa said, but didn't No Body even look up when we went a'riding by. Maybe they all just gone Blind to-day, Wasskum said, you'd think least one of em'd wanna know who that Boy is a'riding by here and who all did he Murder. Let's not talk bout it no more I said, Papa said, let's just keep a'going but o'Wasskum couldn't stand it that hadn't No Body noticed the Boy a'riding right by em was One a'the Boys in the Pitchur nailed up everwheres all round Town. How they ever gonna catch a Murderer if they won't even look up at you when you go by, Wasskum said. Let's just keep a'going, Papa said, I don't need no body a'looking at me but o'Wasskum was getting Huffy bout it and said what kind a'Citizenry is this any how I don't believe they'd know o'Robert E. Lee his self if he was to come a'riding down the street on a Jack Ass with a Sign round his neck would they. It don't matter, Papa said, let's just go. But Mister Yancy looked over there to where four Men was playing at a Game a'Dominoes on a table set out there on the Board Walk tween em. Looks like yall got a good Game a'going, o'Wasskum said, but I ain't so sure I'd wanna set out here like this with that Boy a'running loose and a'Murdering People all over the place ever chance he gets. But they didn't even look up, Papa said, So I said Let's just us go on now but the o'Artist just couldn't stand it they didn't say nothing back so he said How yall ever gonna catch a Criminal round here if you got your o'Nose stuck so far way up your Butt like this. And Oh, Papa said, when o'Wasskum said that Why all them Men looked up and Oh One of em had a Black Eye and a Broke Nose and both his Ears was all puffed up like a Piller off the bed. I know you, the Man said, you the Friend a'that Son of a

Bitch Pistol Whupped me and o'Curley ain't you and then he reached down his Pants for his Pistol but by then I already give o'Edward my Heels and we was a'running on off down the Street, Papa said, cause I knowed him too. He was that Man that come at Little Missey's poor o'Blind Panther with his Knife to skin him and then o'Calley'd gone back and whupped him and this other Man a'setting there to a Frazzle for it. Oh and then I looked back, he said, and now them Men was getting on they Horse and a'chasing us. Maybe I ought not to said any thing, o'Wasskum said.

*O*H WE RUN AND WE RUN, Papa said, them Men right after us and a'catching up fast with they Pistols in the Air. Run Run, o'Wasskum said, Run Run Run and o'Edward he did Run Run all he could but I knowed it wadn't nough and them Men was gonna get us for sure but then, he said, bout that time we come a'Running in to Mexkin Town and I seen two Men a'selling little Mesquite Saint Lalos off a table set out there on the Plaza and Oh I knowed em both, Papa said, They was my o'Amigos Pepe and Peto and then they seen us a'coming and then they seen them Men a'chasing us and they give me a wave to say Come On Over Here Come On Come On Come On and Oh we did fast as we could then jumped off o'Edward and Pepe and Peto pushed us under they Table with all them Little Saint Lalos on top then got bout six thousand and four Mexkins to crowd round to where couldn't no body see us under the Table. Then, he said, here come them Men a'charging in on they Horse and the one with the Face o'Calley beat up on said Where you Mexkins a'hiding em from us but Pepe and Peto and all them other Mexkins just give em a Look like they just only been borned that Morning and didn't know nothing bout nothing in the World. Yall ain't fooling me, the o'Beat Up Man said and climbed off his Horse but when he did, Papa said, o'Pepe reached down and chunked a little Saint Lalo at him and put another Knot on his Head for him and Oh when Pepe done that Why Peto and all them other Mexkins started grabbing Little Saint Lalos and went to chunking em too and Oh them Men just Hollered and Jumped cause it hurt so Bad them Little Mesquite Lalos a'hitting em like that and then that o'Beat Up Man got him a Lalo right in his mouth and it put him down on the ground but now, Papa said, he could

see me a'hiding there under the Table with o'Wasskum and Oh his Eyes went big as some o'Supper Plate and he said Why you little Son of a Bitch I got you now ain't I and brung his Pistol round to shoot me and Oh he would a'done it too, he said, cep right then o'Wasskum reared back on his Bottom and give him a Kick right in his Ear that rolled him back out from under the Table and then next thing was o'Pepe and Peto and all them other Mexkins went to stepping on him like he was in they way and they just couldn't help it. Oh and then, Papa said, Pepe looked down under the Table at me and o'Wasskum and said You know I think it is Time for you two to go. So we crawled back out from under that Table and sneaked over and climbed up on o'Edward a'standing there and Oh Listen Here, he said, o'Edward went a'running on off down the Street with us just a'barely hanging on he was a'going so Fast. And then, Papa said, bout the time we run pass the Alamo I looked back behind us and Oh here come Annie a'Running down the street after us and just a'Waving her arms and a'Hollering at me to Stop Stop Stop but No they wadn't no Stopping o'Edward now that he got his Feet a'going like that and, Papa said, I wouldn't know for a long time after that what it was Annie was a'wanting to tell me so Bad.

*W*E DIDN'T GET BACK TO CAMP

til bout Dark, Papa said, and Why here come o'Fritz and Possum a'trotting out to say Hidy. I believe that Bee Honey is a'doing its Job on o'Possum ain't it, I said, he's up on his feet and getting round pretty good now ain't he. But o'Wasskum had his Eye on Little Missey over there a'putting all them stabbed Up pieces a'his Pitchurs back together again but just not in the same place they come from. Why they was Cactuses up in the Sky and Clouds down under a Rock and the Creek run round in a Circle like a Snake biting his Tail. We got us a'nother Artist here ain't we, Calley said, I bet you ain't never seen the World like this. Then he give Little Missey a big Smile for what she was doing But, Papa said, o'Wasskum didn't like it worth a Lick and went to hollering No Ma'am No Ma'am No Ma'am and run over there and started putting things back where they belonged. Yes Sir, he said, they's always Some Body knows more bout a pitchur than the Artist who painted it in the First Place does ain't that Right. Oh, Papa said, Calley didn't like it him a'talking to Little Missey that a'way and give him a Look and said If I was you Mister I don't believe I'd go to getting Huffy with Little Missey like that. Well I never seen the All Mighty put Cactuses up in the Sky that's why, o'Wasskum said. Well He had his Turn to put it any wheres he wanted to put it and so did you Mister, o'Calley said. Now its Little Missey's Turn and she can put it any god dam wheres she wants to put it and ain't you or Him neither one got any thing to say bout it now. Oh it wouldn't a'surprised me a Lick but what a Bolt a'Lightning come down out a'the Sky and knocked o'Calley's John B Stetson Hat right off the top a'his Head for talking that way, Papa said. But No the All Mighty just set there and didn't let out a Peep. And o'Wasskum Yancy didn't neither, he said, cause now o'Wasskum was down on his knees just a'watching Little Missey remake the World to suit her self but he couldn't stand it she had that Cloud down under a Rock and pulled it out and put it back up in the Sky where it come from but No, Papa said, Little Missey put it right back down under that Rock again then scooched over to set on it so he couldn't move it again. She got Some Brass don't she, o'Wasskum said, May be she is a Artist after all huh. Then he just set there a'watching her and a'petting o'Possum and Fritz both and I went on and told Mister Pearsall bout them two Men he Pistol Whupped over Little Missey's poor o'Dead Panther and how they bout got us cause they was still so Mad bout it. They foller you to here, he said, and I said No Sir I don't believe they did but I don't know they did or not for sure. And Oh right then, Papa said, we heared some Riders a'coming fast through the Brush at us and o'Calley pulled his big o'Pistola out his Pants and hollered at Little Missey and o'Wasskum to get over here behind him right now but to go Run and Hide some wheres else when the Shooting starts.

*B*UT NO, Papa said, wadn't them Men from San Antoneya but was o'Superintendent Shettles from the other Day and all his Men. How do, Calley said, I don't see you got that Boy you been a'looking for yet do you. Got more reason to put him in Chains now'n ever, the Superintendent said. Just yesterday bout Supper Time he come up on this Family a'Mexkins a'working out there in they Field and put em all down with a Pistol he stole even they poor o'Skinny Dog but not quite So we had to go on and put him down all the way our self. That's a mean little SonofaBitch you after there for sure ain't it, Calley said. Mean little Son of a Bitch and a'getting meaner ever dam Day, Superintendent Shettles said, I'd stay me Total Clear a'him if I was you. We already a'leaving this part a' the Country any how, Calley said, Taking this Little Lady here to a new Home up yonder round Pleasant Valley on the Blanco River if you know it there close to Fischer Hall where ever body goes to Dance when they got a Band a'playing some Music. Why ain't she Picking Cotten some wheres, one of the Superintendent's Men said then pointed at Little Missey and spit on the ground like he had some thing in his mouth didn't taste good. Cause she's a'standing here with me, Calley said, What'd you do Mister run off and leave your Spectacles in the Shit House. My Daddy's old enough he could a'owned her and all her Family too, the Man said then heeled his Horse up close to Calley and climbed off Eye to Eye. And they wouldn't a'been a god dam thing you or no body else could a'done bout it neither, he said. But when he said that, Papa said, Why Little Missey took a shine to his Hat and just reached right round me and made him a Trade Hers for His and Oh, he said, all them other Men just went to Whooping and Laughing at him like a bunch a'Loonies and one of em said Why I do believe you look Prettier wearing her Hat then you do a'wearing your own Medcalf but then Calley reached over and traded they hats back again and said Yall better go on We ain't got no more time for Fun. Yes Sir, Superintendent Shettles said, we ain't got no more time for Fun neither less it comes from putting the Budge on that Murdering little Son of a Bitch we a'looking for. I wouldn't worry bout it so much, the Superintendent's Man Medcalf said, Hell it was just a'bunch a'Mexkins he shot and they's a lot more where them come from if you scared we gonna run out a'Mexkins round here. Oh and then bout Half of em laughed, Papa said, and the other Half didn't and Calley said Always a Pleasure to see you Boys then, Papa said, him and me and o'Wasskum tipped our Hats Adios and then Little Missey I reckon wanting to be like us tipped hers Adios too and they rode on off from there in the Direction I reckon they already been a'going in any how.

113

WHAT YOU RECKON

they gonna do to o'Arlon oncet they catch him, Papa said. I know xactly what they gonna do to o'Arlon oncet they catch him, Calley said. They gonna Hang him off a limb by his neck til his Eyes bug out on him. But it ain't o'Arlon that got me worried. What got me worried, he said, is Little Missey here. That was funny her putting that Man's Hat on her head and giving him hers in the trade wasn't it, Papa said. Funny like that round here can get you Dead and dropped down a deep Hole somewheres quickern you can say Bessa my Coola, Calley said, and we can't have no more of it. She was just Funning, Papa said. Lot worsen that, Calley said, she was being Human and they's more People in this o'World'n you can shake a stick at don't like the idea a'Black People being Human. But you and me do don't we, Papa said, ain't that right. Well I admit I go Back and Forth on it some time, Calley said, same way I go Back and Forth on some White People I know and on some Mexkins People I know and on some o'Hard Headed German Farmers I know too. Yes Sir, he said, I pretty much go Back and Forth on ever body til I see if they gonna be a Man or a Mouse or a god dam Bob Tail Rat and I learned over my Life Time you can't tell which one just by how they Look but only by they Deeds. I'm that way too ain't I, Papa said. I would say Yes Sir you are, Calley said, I ain't never seen you no other. I think Little Missey is the same way too don't you, Papa said. I think so, Calley said, but the thing you got to remember bout her is she ain't been in the World long enough to get Tested yet and til she does, he said, we can't be for Total sure what she is. The only thing I ever seen her do is steal my Hat, Papa said, but she give it right back. She's a Woman, Calley said, and you can't hold it against the Womens they wanna look Pretty and it's our Job to just be glad of it. How you reckon she's gonna get tested, Papa said, is that our Job too. No Sir that ain't our Job, Calley said, That'd be the World's Job and it wouldn't surprise me if it went on and give Me and You a little Test or two while It's at it.

FIRST THING ME AND O'FRITZ SEEN

next morning when we waked up, Papa said, was o'Wasskum and Possum a'setting over there side by side a'looking at Little Missey's Pitchur a'how she remade the World. You look at it long nough, Mister Yancy said, it starts to making Sense to you don't it. I looked over to where Little Missey was a'hugging her Travelling Bundle in her sleep to make sure she couldn't hear me and said Well I ain't so sure bout that Mister Yancy. They just ain't nothing in they Right Place. No, o'Wasskum said, I think maybe she just saying they ain't nothing got a Right Place in the World cause Ever Thing just a Part a'Ever Thing else. It's all just one Big One Together, he said, Don't you see that. I said I thought I did even if I didn't, Papa said, then found me two Smooth Rocks and went on out in the Bushes to do my Morning Bidness and then I heared Mister Pearsall over there some wheres in the Bushes a'doing his too and I hollered Morning Mister Pearsall. Morning, o'Calley hollered back. Soons we finish here we need to pack up and get on out this Country fore we run cross them Men from San Antoneya a'looking to shoot me or that dam Boy going round Murdering People and maybe us too if we ain't careful. Yes Sir, Papa said, I'm ready to go right now Mister Pearsall. So, Papa said, we went back and o'Calley put Little Missey and her Travelling Bundle up on Firefoot with him and o'Wasskum got up behind me on o'Edward but fore that he picked up all the pieces a'Little Missey's Pitchur so he could put em back together again like she had em some wheres else and see her Pitchur any o'time he wanted to. They's some People might look at that Pitchur and say yall both gone Loonie, o'Calley said, The World don't look nothing like that. Well it does to Little Missey, o'Wasskum said, and I'd be a'Lying if I didn't admit its starting to Look a little bit like that to me too. Oh and then bout that time o'Possum went to howling at the Moon even if it was still Day and they wadn't one and next thing we heared a Shot from a Gun somewheres way off then another one. That's Trouble for some body, o'Calley said and come over and set Little Missey down triple on o'Edward with me and o'Wasskum then hollered Yeeha Yeeha Yeeha and run on off on o'Firefoot to go see what all the shooting was bout and so did o'Possum right behind him, Papa said, but poor o'Possum had to limp to do it. O'Possum's a'Tough o'Bird ain't he, Mister Yancy said. I can't help but admire him for it. I reckon you a Tough o'Bird you self ain't you Mister Yancy, Papa said, the way you kicked that Man in his Ear when he come at us under the Table back yonder in San Antoneya. Well I wadn't never Tough in my Life til I come to Texas, he said. I reckon that's just what happens to you when you do huh. I don't know it does or not, Papa said. I always just been here my self. Then, he said, we bumped on off to catch up with o'Calley.

to where Calley went, Papa said, and first thing we seen was the Superintendent's Man Medcalf who sassed Calley a'setting there in the Road a'holding his Belly and Oh Blood just a'running ever wheres and o'Possum a'trying to Lick it up fore it run down in the ground and course, he said, I knowed right off who done it to him without no body a'having to tell me. That Bad Boy yall a'looking for shot you huh, Calley said. I reckon he killed me Mister Medcalf said, Papa said, and Oh when he said that Why Blood just come a'leaking out his mouth to where you didn't hardly even wanna Look at it but Little Missey jumped off o'Edward and run over there to Heal him if she could but he give her a mean Push a'way. What's she doing, he said. Why she's trying to save your Life for you fore you die out here in the Road like this, Calley said. I don't want her dam Help, Medcalf said. She made a Laughing Stock out a'me in front a'all them others. No Sir it was you done that you self, Calley said. I'd guess you been a Laughing Stock all you whole god dam Life ain't you. I'm gonna shoot you for saying that Medcalf said But, Papa said, his hand was too Blood Slick to hold his Pistol and it kep a'squirting out. Well if you gonna shoot me, Calley said, you better hurry it on up if you can cause I don't believe you got moren a few minutes left in you to do it in if you don't let this Little Missey here work a Cure on you like she done on me when o'Pelo Blanco shot me. You just a'trying to Trick me into letting her touch me ain't you, Mister Medcalf said. No Sir I ain't, Calley said, but you sure a'Tricking you self into a Hole in the Ground if you don't change you View on such Matters here pretty Quick. And then, Papa said, Mister Medcalf said I'd rather kiss the o'Devil's Red Ass then let her touch her Hand to me and Calley set back on his heels and went to twirling his Spur Ching e Ching e ChingChingChing and said Well have your own god dam Ignert Way bout it then Mister. You come in this World a Laughing Stock and I reckon you gonna go out a Laughing Stock same way ain't you and then, he said, Mister Medcalf give Little Missey a Look a'Hate for being the Color she was and tried to Spit Blood at her but, Papa said, it just come a'dribbling out his mouth and run down his chin and on his shirt. We got Company, Calley said, and I looked over there and seen Superintendent Shettles come a'riding up to look down at his Man a'dying there in the Road. Medcalf, he said, are you Dead. But, Papa said, o'Mister Medcalf couldn't say nothing back no more and just give a little Whistle and went over Dead in the Road on top a'o'Possum and o'Possum went to howling bout it and Me and Little Missey and o'Wasskum all three had to go over there and pull him out from under Mister Medcalf fore it was too Late. Well if that dam Boy was gonna have to go and Murder some body else, Superintendent Shettles said, I reckon I ain't all that Sorry it was o'Shitty Medcalf here.

*I*T TOOK A LITTLE DOING, Papa said, but we roped poor o'Mister Medcalf cross his Horse and Superintendent Shettles made ready to ride him on back to his Family where ever they was. Might a'been a whole different Story, he said, if o'Medcalf here'd been a'looking for that Boy like he was supposed to be a'doing in sted a'going back to get after you for the Friendships you keep. I didn't know he was, Calley said. Well he was, Shettles said, He didn't like it worth a dam the way you talked to him and was gonna make you Pay for it. Well I reckon that's how the World works ain't it, Calley said. This Man here went a'looking to do Harm on some body else and Why that same Harm come right back on him in a Bullet and blowed a Hole in his Belly didn't it. Mister Armke said The Devil his self got his Hand on o'Arlon I said, Papa said, I reckon he's right huh. Mister Armke knows a lot a'things, Calley said, and Yes Sir I reckon that is sure nough Right ain't it. Where you Boys a'going from here, Superintendent Shettles said. We gonna get this Little Missey here on up to Safe Ground, Calley said, She don't know nough to be scared a'things when they come up on her round here. Where she been not to know, Shettles said, in a god dam Cave somewheres all her Life. Yes Sir that's xactly right, Calley said. Well I wish you Luck getting Her through the Country the Superintendent said, Papa said. They's People all round here don't like to see no Black Person less they chained to a Tree and a'getting they Backs whupped to a Bloody Mess. I usted to be one a'them People my self, he said, just til the Other Day in Fact. How'd you get over it, Calley said. They was this o'Red Face Fella there in San Antone got his Face all burned off by the Devil, Superintendent Shettles said, and he painted ever body a pretty good Pitchur a'what it was gonna be like when you got sent down yonder to Hell for you Bad Deeds in

Life and had to set there on a Flat Rock for all time to come. And, he said, I decided right then and there I better pay attention to things I already didn't feel was Right to do and not never do em again. Oh, Papa said, I could tell Mister Pearsall was bout to get Mad all over a'gain at o'Pelo for a'taking Pela Rosa off some wheres. I know that Red Face Man you a'talking bout, Calley said. Ugly o'Son of a Bitch ain't he. Ain't Ugly to me, Superintendent Shettles said, not if what he said keeps me off that god dam Flat Rock. That's the way I feel bout it my self, Papa said. Yes Sir but you still Young and ain't thought bout it nough yet have you, Calley said. Here's what I'd like to see, Superintendent Shettles said, I'd like to see that Bad Boy we a'hunting set down with o'Red Face and let him tell him bout that Flat Rock he's gonna be a'setting on if he don't stop a'Murdering People like this. Course, he said, if I get the chance I'm the one gonna send that little Son of a Bitch down there to set on that Flat Rock my self ain't I. Then, Papa said, Little Missey seen o'Dead Medcalf lost his Hat some wheres and went over there and put Hers on his face to keep the Sun out his Eyes on his Trip Home. No Hard Feelings huh, Shettles said, That's a Rare Woman for you now ain't it. Yes Sir ain't it o'Calley said and then, Papa said, o'Wasskum nodded and said yes Sir the Rarest kind they is on Earth.

*W*ELL THERE THEY GO, Papa said, when the Superintendent rode off with poor o'Dead Mister Medcalf then I looked over at Calley and said I reckon Little Missey gonna need her a new Hat now that she give her other one a'way to that Dead Man. Yes Sir and I reckon we gonna have to Buckle the next one on her Head too like you would a Saddle the way she's a'going through em huh, Calley said. She can wear my John B til we run cross another One somewheres I said, Papa said, then set it down on Little Missey's Head and Oh she tried it all different ways she liked it so much. You know, Calley said, if we ain't careful we gonna be riding pass people on the Road'd shoot a Black Person just for a'wearing a Good Hat like that same way that Dead Man back there'd a'shot her just for a'riding up on a Horse with a White Man. Little Missey got a Hard Life a'coming you know it, Mister Yancy said. Yes Sir, Least til we get her up yonder to the Choats where she got her a Home to be Safe in, Calley said. We just gonna have to Baby her long til then I reckon. She don't Look much like a Baby to me, Papa said. She's bout a hunderd years old ain't she. Don't matter if she's six hunderd and nine, Calley said, it's still our Job to keep her Safe you know it. Yes Sir, Papa said, I do know it but how we gonna do that with ever body in the Country a'wanting to do her Harm ever Time they see her. I been a'thinking bout that, Calley said, and first thing come to mine is We just gonna have to keep our Head down and stay off the Road, he said, so won't no body even see her How you like that Idea. Yes Sir I like it, Papa said, but we still gonna be needing to find her another Hat so I can get mine back ain't we I said then turned o'Edward to where me and Mister Yancy could keep up with Calley and Little Missey a'going out cross the Country like he said. Well you had a Hat but you give it away didn't you, Calley said. Well Little Missey give hers away too I said, Papa said, that's Why. Yes Sir but when Little Missey gives her Hat away you always a'standing there to give her another one back in its place ain't you, Calley said. But now here's the Thing, he said, Who's a'standing there to give you another one so the Sun don't burn your Head cause now you give your John B away. Ain't no body a'standing there, Papa said. No Sir ain't no body a'standing there is they, Calley said, Cep me I reckon. Then, Papa said, Why o'Calley just took his own new John B Steson Hat off his Head and set it right down on mine. Why thank you Mister Pearsall, I said and he said, You remember me a'saying how the Bad Things you do in you Life come back on you Well that's True a'the Good Things too ain't it. Yes Sir, Papa said, I reckon so. Well I'm just trying to make that Point to you since you done a Good Thing and give Little Missey your Hat when she didn't have one, he said, and now Look a new John B Stetson Hat come right back to you cause you done a Good Thing ain't that Right. Yes Sir, Papa said. So you understand how it works now don't you, he said. Yes Sir I do, Papa said. You do Bad and Bad Things comes back on you You do Good and Good Things comes back on you Ain't that how it works, Papa said. Yes Sir, Calley said, That is xactly how it works. Now that you understand it, he said, Gimme my Hat back, then reached over and grabbed it right off my Head again.

THAT NIGHT WHEN WE CAMPED, Papa said, o'Wasskum pulled out his new Canvases and went to painting like his Pants was on Fire and Little Missey and Fritz and o'Possum all three crowded round to watch and I did too he said but o'Calley set over there by the Fire and cleaned his big o'Pistola and shined his Bullets. What's this Pitchur gonna be bout Mister Yancy I said, Papa said, and o'Wasskum said I don't have no Idea What its gonna be bout I'm just gonna let it paint it self this time and see. What if it turns out it ain't bout Nothing, Papa said, What you gonna think bout that. Well if it ain't bout Nothing then they ain't Nothing I can think bout it is they, o'Wasskum said. Mister Pearsall, Papa said, Is Mister Yancy a'teasing Me over here. Yes Sir he is, Calley said, You want me to come over there and shoot him for you. Oh and we all went to laughing bout that even if Little Missey didn't have no Notion what she was laughing bout. Yall need to Hush now so I can work, o'Wasskum said. So, Papa said, we just set there and Oh Boy Hidy he went to Dabbing Paint ever which way didn't make no sense to me at all but Little Missey liked it any how and went to Nodding and Grinning her o'Snaggle Tooth Grin and a'Clapping her hands together. She likes it I hollered at Calley, Papa said, What you reckon's wrong with her. Then, he said, o'Calley come over to take a Look at it his self and scrunched up his Face when he did. What is it he said and o'Wasskum said It's just Its Self is all. That was a Stupid Question Mister. Oh now this Sassy Artist is a'teasing me too ain't he, Calley said. That's a'nother reason to go on and shoot him ain't it. But, Papa said, o'Calley just set right down there with the rest a'us to watch and ever oncet in a while o'Wasskum'd give Little Missey a Look to see what she Thought bout it and she'd study his Pitchur a minute then Nod or reach over with her Finger and Smear it a little bit here and there and then o'Wasskum'd study her Smear a minute then reach over with his own Finger and make a'nother Smear on top a'hers and Oh they went back and forth making Smears like that til they was both Happy bout it then o'Wasskum'd start painting on his Pitchur again and they wadn't no sound in the whole World cep some o'Owl a'hooting off in the Dark some wheres and then o'Fritz and Possum layed cross each other over there and went to Snoring. I still don't know what I'm a'Looking at, Papa said. It ain't what you Look at Mister, o'Wasskum said, It's only what you See. So I Looked at his Pitchur a'gain, Papa said, and this time Why I seen a Storm just a'blowing ever thing this way and that way and ever other which a'way. Well it's a Storm a'Coming ain't it, Papa said, Hooo a big one too. And then, he said, I could feel a Cold Wind a'blowing up my Shirt Tail and I reckon Little Missey could too cause she give me my Hat back then pulled the Sleeping Blanket up over her Head to get warm.

*B*UT NEXT MORNING, Papa said, they wadn't no Storm in the Sky it was all Buzzerds. Oh Buzzerds and Buzzerds and Buzzerds he said ever wheres you looked. You Reckon they a'lookin for they o'Amigo Pelo Blanco or just some thing Dead to Eat, o'Calley said. Course, he said, they gonna be one and the same if o'Pelo done any thing Bad to Pela Rosa. Who yall talking bout, o'Wasskum said so I told him Who o'Pelo was and he said Yes Sir I heared bout that o'Red Face Man and how he's a'going Up and Down the Country doing Good and trying to get Ever Body else to do Good too fore they Pass. He's a Liar and a Thief and when I catch the o'Son of a Bitch I'm gonna kick his o'Butt from Hell to Breakfast for him, Calley said, and some other Bad Things too if he ain't careful. O'Wasskum didn't have no Idea why Calley was so Mad to say that so, Papa said, I told him bout how o'Pelo run off with his Sweet Heart and wouldn't let her take her Word back so they could get Married and whatnot. So you just been walking round with a'Broken Heart all this whole time I knowed you huh, Mister Yancy said, Is that Right. I won't deny it, o'Calley said, No Sir I won't deny it. Well Womens was born to Break Hearts any how, o'Wasskum said. I reckon you know that now if you didn't already know it before huh Mister Pearsall, he said. I been walking round with a Broken Heart all my Whole Life, Calley said, This ain't nothing new to me if you want the Truth. If it wadn't for my Horse I don't know what I'd do. And my Dog too, he said, when I had one. Well I don't have a Horse or a Dog neither one, o'Wasskum said, but I know just xactly what you mean Sir. We gonna go see ain't we, Papa said. Go see what, o'Calley said. Go see what all them Buzzerds is a'doing, Papa said. Oh I bout forgot bout them Birds, Calley said. Yes Sir that's what happens ever time you go to talking bout some Woman ain't it, o'Wasskum said. Yes Sir ever time and then some. Well don't you wanna go see if o'Pelo ain't down there under them Buzzerds some wheres and Pela Rosa right there with him, Papa said. Yes Sir I do, o'Calley said. But

I already give my Word I'd get Little Missey up to the Choats safe and sound, he said, and that's what I got to do fore I do any thing else.

*W*ELL THEN, PAPA SAID, How bout I go see what all them Buzzerds is a'looking for my self then. I don't see how that'd hurt any And I can take o'Fritz and Possum long with me in case some thing tries to come up on me when I ain't Looking. Maybe I oughta go long my self, o'Wasskum said. Twos bettern One when Trouble comes a'knocking they say. Trouble don't always knock Mister, Calley said. You got to keep a Sharp Eye ever step a'the way you know it. Why don't you just come Long with us Mister Pearsall, the o'Artist said, I don't know what we gonna do for Advice if you ain't there to give it. No Sir, o'Calley said, You don't want me long on this Trip. I might have to throw you in the Cactuses for your Sass and they wouldn't be a thing you could do bout it cep just set there and Holler. Then, Papa said, o'Calley looked at me and said You be Careful out there I don't want nothing happening to you. Can you remember that, he said. Yes Sir I can, Papa said, then me and o'Wasskum went over there to give Little Missey a Goodbye and she give us each a Shiny Rock for a Gift and said some thing but we didn't have no Idea what. She's saying yall go on, Calley said, You just wasting Time. So, Papa said, I whistled up o'Fritz and Possum to go but No o'Possum just set down there side a'Little Missey and wouldn't go. What's a matter with o'Possum he don't wanna go with us, o'Wasskum said. Well for one thing, o'Calley said, he got shot full a'Holes here just the other day and ain't over it yet. Or, he said, if it ain't that Why may be he's just waiting for better Company to come long fore he goes a'walking off in the Cactuses some wheres you ever think bout that. Now yall go on and get back here quicks you can, he said, we got other Fish to Fry.

So, Papa said, o'Fritz jumped up on o'Edward front a'me and a'way we did go follering them circling Buzzerds. Where you reckon they a'leading us to, o'Wasskum said and I said Well I don't have no Idea where but then, Papa said, o'Possum started Howling back yonder with Little Missey like they was some thing Bad a'coming and he just wouldn't quit.

$\mathcal{B}$UT WE RID ON,
Papa said, and next thing we talked bout was What if o'Pelo and Pela Rosa
was up there but Pela wouldn't come back with us to Mister Pearsall cause
she give her Word to o'Pelo she wouldn't never Leave him. Well they ain't
nothing to do bout it then, o'Wasskum said. Cep just tip our Hat and go
on back and tell him I reckon. Oh and then of a sudden a Buzzerd come
a'swooping by and dropped some thing out his mouth in a Puddle and made
the water Splash up. What is that thing, o'Wasskum said. So, Papa said, I got
down on both my Hands and Knees and went to fishing round in the Mud
Hole til I found it and Oh what it was, he said, was some body's o'Ear and I
had to squeeze it tight to keep Fritz from biting it out my Hand he wanted
it so Bad. I seen a'lot a'things in Texas, o'Wasskum said, but I believe this is
the First Time I ever seen a Ear drop down out the Sky on me like that. Yes
Sir me too, Papa said. Here you want it. No you the one found it I reckon you
the one oughta keep it, o'Wasskum said. Or may be we oughta take it back to
who ever it come off of like a good Citizen. Then I put that o'Ear in my Pocket so Fritz wouldn't get it and said I got some Good News for o'Calley this
ain't Pela Rosa's Ear cause it's too Big and it ain't o'Pelo's Ear neither cause
his was bout burned off in the Fire and this one ain't even been scorched.
So who you reckon it belongs to, o'Wasskum said. I don't have no Idea, Papa
said, some o'One Eared Man I reckon. Oh and then, he said, we looked way
up yonder and they was some o'One Eared Man a'setting in the middle a'the
Road a'trying to swat bout a'hunderd Buzzerds off his Head but wadn't having much Luck a'doing it. They bout to eat him a'live ain't they, o'Wasskum
said, but No then I seen that o'One Eared Man wadn't a'live at all but was
just a'swatting and a'jumping like that cause a'the way them Buzzerds was
a'Pulling and a'Pecking on him. You know him, o'Wasskum said. I don't
know they's nough a'him left to tell, Papa said, But we bumped on over
there any how and shooed them Buzzerds off to take a Look and Oh, Papa
said, they was a'nother Man over there by a Cactuses and Oh them Nasty
o'Birds already bout Eat him down to the Bone sames this other Fella.

$\mathcal{I}$T'S THEM TWO MEN
run us under the Table the other Day ain't it, o'Wasskum said. Yes Sir I said,

Papa said, same ones was looking to get back Even with Mister Pearsall after he give em that whupping for killing Little Missey's Poor o'Panther and then shooting o'Possum to Boot. How you reckon they come to this Sad End here, o'Wasskum said and I said, I don't know but I reckon it was o'Arlon shot em like he been a'shooting ever body else round here and you and me too if we ain't careful. Well, Mister Yancy said, why don't you give this Fella his Ear back and let's go on and plant em over there some wheres out from under these Trees so we don't have to dig out the Roots. You reckon his Momma and Daddy gonna miss him, Papa said. They probably already been a'missing him a Long time, o'Wasskum said, like maybe mine been a'missing me but I don't think so. That made you Sad didn't it Mister Yancy, Papa said, to talk bout your Folks not a'missing you that way. May be a little I don't know, he said, Let's not talk bout it okay. So, Papa said, we went on and planted them Men out from under them Trees like Mister Yancy said but fore we did we seen this Pitchur fell out one of em's Pocket on the ground but they wadn't nough left to tell which one othern it was a Man and a Woman and a little Baby there tween em when they was all Young and Happy. I'd guess that was his Family when they was all Young and the Sun was still a'shining on em, o'Wasskum said. But that was a long time ago wadn't it. Wonder what happened to that Man to get him from There in the Pitchur to Here on the Ground Dead, Papa said. Life, o'Wasskum said, Life's what done it to him. That's bout what it done to me too when you found me up that Tree you know it. Didn't have no Friends didn't have no Family didn't have no Future that I could tell. Far as I could see, he said, the Sun bout give out a'Shining on me for ever and wadn't never gonna Shine on me again. Yes Sir, o'Wasskum said, if you want the Truth Mister I was bout to the End a'my Rope that day and a'sliding down fast. I'm sorry Mister Yancy, Papa said, I didn't know you was a'feeling so Low when you was up that Tree. Well I was, o'Wasskum said, and now that you know it you can just call me Wasskum sted a'Mister Yancy cause I wouldn't tell no body else that cep a Good Friend but I wouldn't want you to go telling it to No Body else if you Please. No Sir I won't Wasskum, Papa said. Okay then, Wasskum said. Okay Wasskum I said, Papa said, and Next to Mister Pearsall and o'Fritz and Mister and Miz Choat and Bird and Marcellus and o'Jeffey and o'Edward and a'course Annie and Mister and Miz Pegleg why I figgured o'Wasskum was bout the Best Friend I ever did have in my Life.

125

CALLEY AND O'POSSUM COME OUT TO SEE US
when we got back to camp, Papa said, but Little Missey was over there
a'Painting Circles and Squiggly Lines on her Travelling Bundle with
o'Wasskum's Paints on her Finger. Then, he said, we told Calley bout seeing
them two Dead Men and how it must a'been o'Arlon murdered em when
they was coming to murder him for whupping em back in San Antoneya
that day. Well I reckon o'Arlon done me a Favor then didn't he, Calley said,
even if he wadn't even trying to and didn't know nothing bout it. Least he
done one Good Thing in his Life, Papa said, and went on off to sleep.

That night, he said, I waked up and Why there was Little Missey a'setting
side me and a'holding my Hand. They some thing you wanna tell me I said,
Papa said, but No she was just setting there sound a'sleep. Then, he said,
here come Fritz and o'Possum and they made a Dog Pile on top a'me to
where you couldn't hardly even breathe. I reckon yall just been a'missing me
too huh, Papa said. But No they was already to Sleep they self and didn't say
nothing back and then I seen Mister and Miz Pegleg a'standing there and I
said Yall come on if you want to and after they climbed up on me Why then
I seen Little Missey's poor o'Blind Panther a'standing over there all by his
self in the Dark and I whistled him on over and Oh Boy Hidy here he come
even if he couldn't see a Lick. And then, Papa said, some other little scrappy
Dog come up out the Dark and set down right there in that same place and
give me a Look like he ain't had nothing to eat in a good long while so I give
him a little Whistle too and here he come and Oh then it come to me he
was Mister Pearsall's little Dog the Tonks stole out from under the Porch
that night and put in the Cook Pot for they Suppers when o'Calley was just
a Little Boy. It was bout then, Papa said, when here come some body else
and give me a big Wet Lick on my Ear and Oh I give out a Whoop cause it
was the little Bay Mare my mean o'Daddy shot and killed that night cause
she wouldn't Gentle like he wanted her to. Oh they was Dogs and Cows and
Horses and Coyotes and Foxes and Baby Rabbits and Armadillas and Pos-
sums and Coons wearing a mask and Snakes and Birds and Bugs a'piling
up on me all Night Long. Oh and then, he said, here come some Bare Foot
Black People wadn't hardly wearing Nothing and they piled on top a'me too
long with bout four hunderd and nine a'some other colors and that's when
it come to me they wadn't even a part of my Dream but splashed over on
mine from Little Missey's and the only way I could figgur it, Papa said, was

126

We all come out a'the same Big Pile in the First Place and all we was trying to do now was get on back Home together if we could.

WE LEFT NEXT MORNING, Papa said, and Oh we was glad to be a'leaving that part a'the Country what with o'Arlon a'going round a'Murdering some body or other ever time you looked. He'll get his Turn, o'Calley said. It don't run just one way forever. Then bout two miles down the Road, Papa said, why here come Pepe and Peto with a Wagon Load a'them Little Mesquite Saint Lalos. Yall must be selling them Little Lalos like Hot Cakes, o'Wasskum said, Last I seen you had a whole Table of em. We chunked em all at them Bad Men was trying to get you the other Day and had to go back Home and get some more fore we run out, Pepe said. Ever Body in San Antoneya all wants a Little Saint Lalo cause he's the One brought all the Mexkins over from Mexico to Texas in the First Place. Well No that ain't xactly Right, o'Calley said, Some maybe but not All. They's too many to be All, he said. Then, Papa said, we looked over there and Little Missey was up in they Wagon a'crying over the Little Saint Lalos. She usted to live in a Cave had a Lalo in it, Calley said, I reckon seeing these here just made her Home Sick. Oh and that made em so Sad to hear it they put they Hats to they Heart and said Tell her to pick one out she Likes and we give it to her for a Gift. She could use her a Dress too, Peto said, she ain't hardly got nothing on you know it. We bought her a Nice Dress that Day in San Antoneya, o'Wasskum said, but she don't never want to wear it. Yes Womens is funny that way, Peto said. I don't understand them too much my self. They say the Man can understand the Woman ain't even been born yet and his o'Momma and Papa is already Dead somewheres, Pepe said. Oh that one makes me laugh cause it is so True you know it, Peto said. Yes that one makes me laugh too, Pepe said. But I wouldn't never tell it to my Wife would you. No I wouldn't never tell it to my Wife neither, Peto said, then they both had em a good laugh bout it, Papa said, and so did we. Yall be careful a'that Boy Arlon Clavic going round the Country a'Murdering People, Calley said. I hear he's partial to shooting Mexkins and Murdered him a few here just the other day when they was out there a'working in they Field. Yes, Peto said, they's always some body going round shooting Mexkins in Texas ain't they. Or a'chopping they Big Toe off, he said, then give me a Look bout it, Papa said, cause I was the one chopped his Big Toe off for him long time ago when we was all a'working on the Farm for my mean o'Daddy. Maybe you oughta get your Wood Carver carved all these little Saint Lalos here to carve you out a New Toe, I said, if you a'missing your Old One so Bad. Oh and they went to laughing bout that too, Papa said, and Pepe said Yes he would do that but he didn't have no Idea how to put a Wood Toe back on to where the other one got chopped off from. Then Mister Pearsall come out his pocket with some Money and said he wanted to buy a'nother couple a'them Little Saint Lalos for a Gift to the Choats when we got there and another one to set up there on the Wagon seat with Pepe and Peto to protect em from that little Son of a Bitch Arlon Clavic a'riding round the country a'shooting Mexkins and ever body else he comes a'cross.

I COULDN'T GET ANNIE OSTER OUT MY MINE, Papa said. I'd close my Eyes and there she'd be in my mine, he said, or I'd come a'wake in the morning and Why there she'd already be a'waiting for me in my Head and then there she'd be all day long too. Some times I talked to her like she was really there, Papa said. I'd say Annie I'm sorry I storied to you bout that o'Gal Wasskum said'd take all her clothes off for a Nickle. The Truth is I never even seen that o'Gal in my Life and didn't have no Idea would she take a Nickle for it or was it more or lessn that. Then, he said, I told her all bout o'Calley and Pela Rosa and how she run off with that o'Red Face Man cause she give him her Word she would and that's what saved my o'Amigo's Life when o'Pelo was gonna Hang us both in the Cave where we got to be Friends with Little Missey. Course I was just thinking all these things in my Head, Papa said, and didn't have no idea was they getting to Annie or not so one Day me and Fritz eased o'Edward up to Calley and Little Missey there on o'Firefoot and I said Mister Pearsall where you reckon Thoughts go after you done with thinking em and he said Why they just go to floating round in the Air all over the place til they find the People them Thoughts was Thought bout. I been thinking bout Annie Oster, Papa said. Yes Sir, Calley said, you been a'thinking bout Annie Oster cause You just might be in Love with her ain't that Right. Well it might be, Papa said, I don't know.

I reckon Ever Body thinks the Thoughts a'who they are, Calley said. Big People think Big Thoughts. Little People think Little Thoughts. Bad People think Bad Thoughts. And you take some body like o'Wasskum over there Why he thinks Artist Thoughts but they ain't really no such Thing as a Artist Thought you can put your Finger on. I was just asking if these Thoughts I been a'thinking bout Annie is a'getting to her or not when I'm a'thinking em, Papa said, that's all. Yes Sir I'd say they are a'getting to her, Calley said. That's why you always got to be careful what you a'thinking cause a Thought is as much Real as a Bullet or a Kiss is and you the one responsible for Where they go and What they do to Some Body else when they get there.

OH, Papa said, we talked and Joked and laughed like that all cross the Country and didn't never get tired of it cause it was like Some Body a'traveling round with they own Family if they had one in they Life and that's what I wanted moren any thing in mine. They's another Time later on in my Life I had One but then I Lost it and Oh Listen Here it broke my Heart in Two and Me long with it. Ever body got they Good Stories and they got they Bad Stories in pretty much Equal Measure o'Calley used to say but the thing to remember he said is Not neither one of em stays round for ever. If you ain't careful, he said, The Good Ones gonna turn into Bad Ones but the Bad Ones just might turn into Good Ones too but here's the thing you always got to remember bout it Mister, Calley said, You the One in the Saddle on the Horse you a'riding in Life and you the One a'telling that Horse which Way you want it to go. So what'd I just say, he said. You just said I said, Papa said, ever body got they Good Stories and they got they Bad Stories. That's right, Calley said, so you ought not to go round feeling Special when you got a Good One a'going and at the same time you don't never wanna feel like you being Picked On when you got a Bad One a'going and now What else'd I just say, he said. Well it gets fuzzy on me after that, Papa said, I reckon you gonna have to tell me again. Well you the one in the Saddle a'riding your Horse through Life ain't you, Calley said, Don't that put you in Charge a'where you a'going. Yes Sir, Papa said, and I reckon I'd just have to climb down off that o'Horse if he wadn't a'going in the Right Direction I wanted to go in wouldn't I. No Sir, Calley said, just give him a little kick in his Fat Behind to change Direction is all. Cause it's your Job to tell your Horse which way you want it to go. Yes Sir I said, Papa said, Cause now I seen xactly what o'Calley was trying to say and that was Ever Body is a'riding they own Horse in Life and got to tell it which Direction to go and if we don't like where it's a'going Well then we just got to kick it's o'Butt and make it go somewheres else til we like Where it's a'going. Course, Calley said, you don't never want to get to liking Where it's a'going too much even if it is a'going in the Right Direction cause Things gonna go to getting Boring on you if you just a'riding round being Happy all the time and that's bout Bad as getting Shot at or Hanged.

*W*E RODE ON CROSS THE RIVER,

Papa said, then come on into Town where they had the County Court House right there on the Square and course the Town and County both was named Blanco for the River and Oh, he said, they was having a big Horse Sale that Saturday Morning when we come a'riding in and o'Calley give me a smile and said I reckon you bout due a Horse a'your own less you and o'Edward got married and didn't never tell no body. I'd have to pay you back I said, Papa said, but I don't have no idea where I'm gonna get the Money. What's that I been a'telling you bout what ever it is you a'looking for in this World, Calley said. You said, I said, Why it's a'looking for you too ain't it. Yes Sir that's right, Calley said, so I ain't a'gonna Worry bout a'getting my Money back cause I know it's out there somewheres just a'waiting to jump back in my Pocket when I ain't even Looking. Well I thank you, Papa said, I reckon Mister Choat'll be glad to get o'Edward back won't he. But fore I could finish saying that, he said, Why I looked way cross the Square and they was this Little Bay Mare a'looking back at me from over there and she looked just like the Little Bay Mare my mean o'Daddy shot and killed that Night way back all them years ago and that's why my Momma run off the next day and I didn't never see her again. You ain't gonna tell me you already see One you like are you, Calley said. That One right over yonder I said, Papa said, then pointed my Finger cross the Square to the Little Bay Mare a'standing there a'looking back at me. She's a pretty One ain't she, Papa said. Oh, Calley said, she's bout the Prettiest o'Granma I ever seen in my Life, he said, and they's some thing a'little Funny bout the way she holds her Ears up too you see it. Yes Sir she keeps em pointed up all the time, Papa said, and I reckon I know Why too. Now then you want me to do the Bargaining for you, Calley said, or you wanna do it you self. I'll do it for my self I reckon, Papa said, but Thank You any how. Okay, Calley said, Just remember you don't wanna let the Man see how much you really want that Horse cause you gonna have a hard time getting a Good Price if you do. Okay I said, Papa said, and then we all went over there together like we was some o'Inyin Tribe or some thing on the Move.

MORNING, the o'Horse Trader said, I can see yall a'looking for a Good Horse ain't you. No Sir, Calley said, we ain't got no interest in a Good Horse today We just passing through is all. Cep I'd like to buy this one here I said, Papa said, then went over there and started petting on that Little Bay Mare. Well you got the Best Eye for a Good Horse I ever seen on a Man or a Boy your age in my Life but that one is my Little Sick Daughter's Favorite Horse and I wouldn't never sell her out from under that Poor Child for nothing. Yes Sir, Papa said, Well I wouldn't wanna hurt her feelings by trying to buy her off you neither so Thank You very much any how Mister. On the other Hand, the o'Horse Trader said, they's another Horse my Little Sick Daughter likes bout much as she does this one so I might could give her that one there in sted a'this one here. Well you such a good Daddy I reckon you gonna wanna give you Little Sick Daughter both of em ain't you I said and when I said that, Papa said, Why o'Calley give me a Look and stepped back cause he seen I might could do this Horse Trade my self without no Help from Him or No Body else neither. Yes Sir, the Trader said, I was planning on doing xactly that but now my Little Daughter got so sick I got to sell one of em off to pay the Doctor Bill so the way I look at it, he said, is you'd be doing me and her both a Favor if you was to buy this Little Bay Mare off a'me so I could go on and get her some more Medicines. Well, Papa said, how much you reckon you'd want for her if I was interested in buying her but I don't believe I am. Oh, Papa said, that o'Horse Trader squinted up his eyes at me and said Well I reckon that's a Fifty Dollar Horse don't you Young Sir and Oh Calley give me a Look then to say Oh No Young Sir she ain't no Fifty Dollar Horse but I said Well I reckon Fifty Dollars is a Good Bargain for this Horse cause what I like most bout her is how she points her Ears up in the Air like that all the Time. Yes Sir Perky Ears is a sure Sign of a Good Horse ain't it, the o'Trader said, and then I walked over there to her and said, Papa said, Wonder how she keeps em up like this all Day long and then just fore he could keep me from a'doing it I run my Fingers all over her Head to feel the Thread I knowed was wrapped round her Ears to hold em up. How much a'that Fifty Dollars you reckon is the Cost a'this Thread here a'holding her Ears up, Papa said, and the Trader said I just bought this Horse off a Man from Johnson City this morning and Why Look a'here he was trying to Trick me wadn't he. So, Papa said, I give him Five Dollars a'o'Calley's money and put Momma's Mexkin Saddle on her and we all walked on off down the street. How'd you know that Trick bout wrapping thread round her Ears to make em stand up like that, Calley said. Oh, Papa said, my mean o'Daddy used to do that all the time when we was out on the Road trading Horses and he wanted to make one of em look younger'n they really was and then of a sudden, he said, o'Wasskum looked round and said Where's Little Missey at.

OH LITTLE MISSEY WAS GONE, Papa said, Gone Gone Gone but didn't none a'us have no Idea where to. Maybe Somebody just reached out and grabbed her when we wadn't looking I said, Papa said, but Calley said No Fritz and o'Possum would a'pitched a Fit if any body'd a'tried that then o'Wasskum Looked round again and said Why both them Dogs is Gone too. Oh and we was really scared then, Papa said, Scared Scared Scared. All cep o'Calley, he said, who pointed way on down the Street to where Fritz and o'Possum was a'setting there on they Hineys. I reckon they just waiting for us to come on ain't they he said so we went on down there quicks we could, Papa said, and when we got there we seen they was a Wagon Yard on the next street over where ever body put they wagon when they come to town on Saturday to buy their Necessarys and visit some. Where is she Fritz I said, Papa said, but course o'Fritz didn't have no idea in the World and just set there but o'Possum limped off a'ways then stopped in his tracks and now we seen Little Missey a'setting in a wagon way over Yonder with some Old Man ever bit old as she was and may be some older and this Old Man looked like he was sound a'sleep a'setting there even if Little Missey was a'Pushing on him and a'Jabbering in his Ear and Squeezing his Hand then Kissing on it like he was a Little Baby born just Yesterday. Is he Dead I said, Papa said. Looks to me like that Old Man is Dead and Calley said Yes Sir I think that Old Man may a'been Dead a good long while now but just don't know it. Oh and then Little Missey squeezed his Hands on her Travelling Bundle and said some thing in his Ear again but No he was so a'sleep he didn't even know it and Oh the tears just come a'Running down Little Missey's Face. Whys Little Missey so sad, Papa said. Cause that o'Man don't even know her no more thats why, Calley said and he looked like he was bout to cry too. Well how would he ever know her I said, Papa said, she been in a cave all her Life. It was fore that he knowed her, Calley said. Long time fore that. A Life Time fore that, o'Wasskum said. See them Marks on his Face and Arms there he said. Yes Sir, Papa said, I see em. I believe Them are Tribal Scars Most likely cut there when he was just a Young Man back where he come from in Africa o'Wasskum said Then Calley said and they xactly the same as all them Squiggles and Marks Little Missey painted on her Travelling Bundle the other day ain't they and then I looked, Papa said, and Yes they was xactly the same like o'Calley said. Them god dam o'Slavers got em both from the same Village I reckon, Calley said, Long long time ago when they was just young like you are now. And seeing how hard she's a'Working to bring him back to Her now, he said, they's one more thing I reckon and then o'Wasskum nodded I guess cause he reckoned it too. Yes Sir I said, Papa said, What's that. I reckon Little Missey and that Old Man was oncet Sweet Hearts in they Young Life and thats where that Little Baby she carried round in her arm all over the Country come from when they was old enough to Spark.

So WE JUST SET DOWN THERE, Papa said, and let Little Missey have all the Visit she wanted and Oh she just never let off a'Talking in his Ear the whole Time. She's telling him the Story a'her Life, o'Calley said, but he ain't hearing a word of it is he. I reckon I'd be the same way, o'Wasskum said, some o'Woman go to talking in my Ear

like that. You talk bout Little Missey like that Mister Yancy and I'm sure as Hell gonna run you off. I wadn't talking bout Little Missey in particular, o'Wasskum said. I was talking bout Womens in general. Some Time I think you just trying to pick a Fight with me Mister Pearsall. I just want you to act like a Gentleman when you round Little Missey that's all Mister Yancy, Calley said. Then, Papa said, here come the Man owned the wagon Little Missey and that Old Man was a'setting in. Well I see o'Dutch got him a Visitor, he said. First one in his Life I reckon. Well he ain't much of a Conversationalist may be that's Why, o'Calley said. We been here bout three hours and he ain't said a Single Word that we can tell. No o'Dutch never been much of a Talker, the Man said, but they was a Time he could out work any three men on the Place. Out Fight em too, he said. Oh Lord you just have to stand back and watch when he was riled. You know any thing bout him in his Young Life, o'Wasskum said. No Sir he just come a'walking up to my Daddy's Place one Day after the War and wanted some work to live on and then stayed on with me after my Momma and Daddy passed here bout six years and three months ago. Both went together one right after the other within a Day, he said, Him just fore Her. They buried out there behind the House side by side o'Dutch pulls the weeds just can't keep him from it he loved em so much in they Life I reckon cause they was pretty much the only ones was ever Nice to him. Oh listen, he said, o'Dutch got so many Whip Marks on his Back looks like a Spider Web from how he was treated fore my Momma and Daddy. I can show you, the Man said. I don't think he'd even know it was you to raise up his shirttail and Look. They ain't Brother and Sister are they, he said. No sir, Calley said, we think may be they was Sweet Hearts one time. Well why not, the Man said, my Momma and Daddy both usted say they just bout ever bit Human as you and me ever was.

OUT DARK, Papa said, Little Missey got down off that Man's wagon and come a'walking back over to us. You ready to go Little Missey, o'Calley said, but she just stood there and watched that Man go off in his wagon with that other Old Man still hadn't said a word to Her or no body else neither one. We'll ride you over to that Man's Farm here fore long and you can have you a'nother

reckon Little Missey and that Old Man
s oncet Sweet Hearts...

visit Calley said but Little Missey just stood there a'watching that wagon roll on off I reckon thinking her o'Sweet Heart was least gonna wave her a Good Bye but in a minute, Papa said, they was already all the way down the Street and gone and No he never. Didn't never say Hello didn't never say Good Bye, o'Wasskum said. I hope that Old Man grows him some Manners fore next Time then, Papa said, we all went back over there where my new Horse was a'making Friends with Firefoot and o'Edward and I went on and Named her Sister cause that was how I felt bout her and Oh when I went to looking, he said, Why they was some Beat Marks on her where some body'd been a'being mean to her but course we had us a Jar a'Honey so me and Little Missey went to rubbing some on in the right Place while o'Calley was reading her age on her Teeth. This ain't no Baby Horse you got here if that's what you was a'looking for, he said. Long way from it. Don't matter a Lick to me her age, Papa said, This was my Horse First Time I ever seen her. I might paint a Pitchur of her for you, Wasskum said, if we can get her to hold her Ears up a minute without that thread. I like her just the way she is, Papa said, Don't go trying to change her on me. Well Mister I will say this for her, Calley said, She got four Legs and a Tail just like all the Best Horses in the World got don't she. Oh and then they had em a laugh bout it while me and Little Missey give Sister a good pet all over and Fritz and o'Possum jumped up on her back like they was a'couple a'Genral Lee's Soldiers a'guarding the Fort. We still got miles to go, Calley said, less you wanna stay and buy you a Pig and a Chicken to go long with your Horse and Oh, Papa said, I had to laugh bout that one my self cause a'the Pitchur it made in my Head a'us going down the Road with a Pig and a Chicken just a'follering long behind in a Row. Yes Sir, o'Wasskum said, I'd like to paint a Pitchur a'that too. What would you call it, Calley said. You got a name yet. Well for now, he said, I reckon I'd just call it A Pig and A Chicken. A Pig and A Chicken huh I said, Papa said. Well, Wasskum said, I couldn't very well call it A Pig and A Chicken and Abraham Lincoln could I less we could get o'Abe to fall in behind. Oh we laughed and we laughed til we was almost rolling on the Ground from that one, Papa said, and here o'Calley and Mister Yancy was both full growed Men and we might a'gone on a'laughing bout it like that til Kingdom Come, he said, cep after bout five miles here come a wagon down the Road had a Dead Man in the back with a Tow Sack up over his Face and when Calley pulled it back to see who it was under there Why we bout had to cover our own Face up cause it wadn't no body but our o'Friend Superintendent Wayne Shettles from the Boy Prison over yonder in Gatesville and he had him a Bullet Hole in the middle a'his Head and some more just for Meaness in bout ever other Part too. Oh, Papa said, they was so many I didn't even wanna count em.

WHERE'D YOU FIND HIM, Calley said. Out in the Road just this side a'Saddler, the Man said. I didn't know what to do with him so I just brung him along. You know any body might want him, he said. No Sir, Calley said, but you ride him on into Blanco I reckon they's some body there'll know what to do with him. Oh and then I looked over and Little Missey was down in the wagon with poor o'Superintendent Shettles trying to help him get up Dead as he was. I don't know that Man's Family'd like that, the Man said, her a'fooling with him like that you know it. You ain't scared it's gonna kill him all over again are you, Calley said. No I'm just a'saying, the Man said. Yes Sir we know what you just a'saying Mister, Calley said, Go on with it. But fore you do, Wasskum said, it might serve you to know this Little Missey here a'trying to help a Dead Man come back to Life is our Friend and I'd just as soon skin you neckid and run you up a Tree as let you Bad Talk her for a'trying to be Nice to a Dead Person and then, Papa said, o'Wasskum come out from his Lap with that little Two Shot Sissy Pistol he had and put it on his leg to show he meant ever Word he said. Well I reckon you just a bunch a'god dam Yankee SonsaBitches ain't you, the Man said, Wadn't enough you went and Hanged o'Robert Lee now you a'picking on me too. Didn't no body Hang o'Robert Lee, Calley said, I don't know where you got that Idea. You mean o'Robert Lee ain't dead, the Man said. No Sir he ain't Dead, Calley said. Far as I know he's setting out there on his Porch somewheres a'smoking his Pipe with some body singing him Dixie. I heared they Hanged him cause he wouldn't never give up, the Man said. I don't know who you been a'talking to, Calley said, but just sos you know it Yes Sir he did give up. Surrendered his whole Army and ever Boy in it put they Gun down to the ground and went a'walking on off to Home after that. That was some years ago, he said, fore this Boy here was even borned yet. The Hell you say, the Man said. Yes Sir

137

the Hell I do say, Calley said. You must live under a Rock some wheres not to a'known that, Wasskum said. If you ain't careful Mister, the Man said, you gonna be a'riding in back a'this wagon same as this other Dead Fella here for the way you a'talking to me. Let's just leave off the Threats both a'you, Calley said, They's already enough Trouble a'lurking round here. You get a Look at Who done it, he said. Just a dam Spud, the Man said, no biggern this one here but course he wadn't wearing no John B Stetson Hat. How'd you get pass him in a wagon, Mister Yancy said, You sure he wadn't your First Cousin or some thing. Mister Yancy let's not talk that way no more you hear, Calley said. He was just standing there a'kicking this Dead Man here when I come up on him and I thought Well it's Adios Muchachos to me too ain't it but I figgur it embarrassed the Boy me a'seeing him a'crying like that over a Dead Body he just Murdered and he put his pistol back down his Pants and rode on off. You remember what Direction he took, Calley said, We ain't wanting to run into him no wheres our self. Yonder Ways the Man said, Papa said, Going South and not even looking back like he already seen all he ever wanted to see round here. That's Good News for us then ain't it, Calley said, then tipped his John B Good Bye and said Well we'll be on our way now Mister. And me on Mine the Man said then, Papa said, him and o'Wasskum give each other a Ugly Look and we never seen that Man again in our Life or poor o'Dead Superintendent Wayne Shettles from over at the Boy Prison neither one.

I DON'T LIKE IT

that Boy might still be round here in this Country somewheres, Calley said, I say Ever Body keep a Sharp Eye out. Yes Sir I got mine out, Papa said. Yes Sir me too, Wasskum said, I didn't know Evil could grow so big in a little Boy. Mister Armke said the Devil got his Hand on him that's why, Papa said. Yes Sir I've known the o'Devil to put his Hand on One or Two in my own Life, Calley said, Easiest way to tell is they already mean to Animals bout the Time they learn to foot walk. It ain't that way with Arlon, Papa said, I seen him be Nice to Animals before. Humans is Animals too, Mister Yancy said. I don't reckon he was Nice to that one we just seen full a'Bullet Holes in that wagon back there was he. They's all kind a'Evil, Calley said, it ain't just when

Some Body goes to Murdering Some Body else. Stealing a Story off a Little Boy and running off with Some Body else's Sweet Heart is another xample a'Evil the way I see it, he said then give me a Look, Papa said, and said Now ain't that right Mister. No Sir Mister Pearsall I don't think so, Papa said, it ain't like he got his Catch Rope and run off with em. Is to me, Calley said. Yall talking bout your Sweet Heart there ain't you Mister Pearsall, o'Wasskum said, ain't that right. I don't wanna hurt your Feelings Mister Yancy, Calley said, but it ain't none a'your Business what we a'talking bout. Oh Why Hell's Bells, o'Wasskum said, I've had me maybe Twenty Thirty o'Gals run off on me in my Life and after a Day or two Why I can't even remember what they looked like with they Clothes on. That's your little o'Peeny Stick a'talking to you, Calley said, that ain't the same thing we a'talking bout here. Oh so you just talkin bout being in Love with some o'Gal then ain't you, Mister Yancy said. Yes Sir I reckon may be I am, Calley said, if you wanna put it that way. Well I can tell you Ever Thing you ever gonna need to know bout being in Love with some Woman in bout two Words, he said, you wanna hear em or Not. Go on, Calley said, I know you gonna tell me any how. Run Run Run Run Run Run and then Run some more, Wasskum said, Break your Heart ever Time That's what I know bout it, he said, even if it is moren two Words. And Oh, Papa said, I could see it bout Broke o'Calley's Heart to hear it. You ever find a Cure for it in all your Travels Mister Yancy, Calley said. No Sir Not a One, he said. If yall so Sad bout it, Papa said, yall oughta go talk to Mister and Miz Choat. I never seen neither one of em a'walking round with a Broke Heart and they been a'Loving each other they Whole Life. I'd like to paint me a Pitchur a'that, o'Wasskum said, and then o'Calley said Yes Sir and I'd like to see it when you do. Oh and then, Papa said, Why o'Possum just went to Howling at the Moon even if they wadn't one you could see that time a'Day.

*T*HE MORE WE WENT, Papa said, the more Perky Sister got to where you could just bout see the Years a'falling off her she was so Happy bout ever thing. Calley seen it too and said, I never seen a Horse liked being with some body so much as that Little Bay Mare likes being with you and o'Fritz there. Yes Sir I know it, Papa said, It's like we always been Friends our Whole Life ain't it. And when I said that, he said, Why Sister throwed her Head back and give me a Smiley Look. I think shes a'listening to ever Word I say, Papa said. I don't doubt it for a minute, Calley said. Course me and o'Firefoot here been Friends so long he can tell what I'm a'thinking don't even have to use no Words. I bet me and Sister gonna get like that too here fore long, Papa said. I don't know Why Not, Calley said. I don't neither, o'Wasskum said from back yonder where he was trying to get o'Edward to catch up. Don't get Lost back there Mister, Calley said, We might have to run off and leave you. No I ain't letting yall out my sight, he said, I don't want that Boy with the Devil's Hand on him a'Shooting me. That Man said he's gone on South down the Country now, Calley said. But I say we stay on the Look Out any how. Wonder what he was a'doing up here, Mister Yancy said, last we heared a'him he was down yonder below San Antoneya somewheres shooting Mexkins wasn't he. Oh, Papa said, of a sudden I knowed xactly what he was doing up here. He was a'looking for me cause they was a Time when he wanted me to be his Friend and I wouldn't do it cause he stole Money didn't belong to him in Kendalia and Murdered a Man name a'Marvin on top a'that. I reckon he's up here in this Country just a'looking for a Friend he didn't never have in his Life I said, Papa said. You a'talking bout you self ain't you, Calley said. Yes Sir I am, Papa said. Oh and then o'Calley pulled Firefoot up to a stop and said I want you to stay close to me you hear. You and Little Missey both. That Loonie already gone from shooting People for a Reason to shooting em just for the Hell of it and I don't want yall at Risk if he comes round here a'doing it again. You scaring me with Talk like that, o'Wasskum said when he finally come a'bouncing up on o'Edward. Yes you oughta be scared Mister Yancy, Calley said, If that Boy'd shoot a Mexkin for just being a Mexkin, Why I don't know what'd he'd do to you for being a Artist.

SO ME AND O'WASSKUM CLUSTERED UP close as we could to Calley and Little Missey, Papa said, so didn't no Harm come to us from Arlon or No Body else all the Way to Buckner Store just a few Miles from where we was a'going to the Choats in Pleasant Valley. Might be Nice to get a Treat for the Choats and Ever Body else while we here,

Calley said. So, Papa said, we went on in Buckner Store and got us a sack a'Hard Candy and some Mustang Grape Juice in a Pickle Jar but fore we could get out again Why o'Wasskum reached in the Sack and got him a hand full a'Candy and a piece for Little Missey. You better show her how to suck on it or she's gonna break out what few Teeth she got left biting on it, Calley said. So, Papa said, Mister Yancy went to making a Big Show a'sucking on his Candy and Little Missey got to laughing so much at what he looked like a'doing it Why she give him her piece a'Candy to suck on too, he said, I reckon cause she didn't never want the Show to end. Here we been a'talking bout that Loonie Boy, Calley said, and all this time we already had us our own Loonie Boy right here.

Bout then, Papa said, Mister Buckner come out from behind the Counter and said They was a Boy a'looking for you in here the other Day said yall was Good Friends in the Past and he was just a'passing through this part a'the Country and wanted to give you a Hidy and shake your Hand for Old Time Sake if he could. He look like this here, Mister Yancy said, and showed him that Piece a'Paper had the Pitchur a'me and o'Arlon on it. That's him right there, Mister Buckner said and pointed at me in the Pitchur. No Sir that's me, Papa said. Oh then this is him right here Mister Buckner said and pointed at Arlon in the Pitchur. Your o'Daddy was a Bad Man, he said, I don't reckon it's much Surprise to me you turned out to be One too. He didn't, Calley said, that paper ain't talking bout him being Bad it's talking bout this other Boy here a'being Bad. I'm gonna come back in here and have a talk with you bout it if I ever hear you been going round telling other People what you just said to me. I ain't, Mister Buckner said. No Sir I know you ain't, Calley said, that's what I was just saying wadn't it. Yes Sir, Mister Buckner said, that's xactly what I heared you to say. Well then, Calley said, we gonna just be on our way now and No Bad Feeling. No Sir No Bad Feeling Mister Buckner said and then, Papa said, they shaked they Hands on it and we went on out and didn't never hear no more bout it.

OH TO RIDE THROUGH MY OWN COUNTRY AGAIN, Papa said, Why it was like I never even been gone a Day and Oh I was so Happy bout it, he said, I went to saying Hidy and some Private Things to all the Trees and Rocks and Birds and whatnot I knowed long the way but not to where No Body else could hear me but I think maybe Sister could cause she went to dancing side to side down the Road like she was in a Parade and I had to grab a'holt a'the Saddle Horn one time to keep my Seat and when I did Ever Body went to laughing at me. You ain't careful you gonna be a'walking Home on your own two Feet, Calley said. No I said, Papa said, Sister's just Happy as I am bout going Home today is all. You ain't gonna be Happy if you a'setting upside down out there in the middle a'the Road, Calley said. She wouldn't leave me there, Papa said, then reached down and give Sister a pet and then o'Fritz one too. Tell me when she's behaving her self, Calley said, and we'll let Little Missey have a Turn up there on her with you. I don't know why not right now, Papa said, You just been hogging her for you self all this time any how ain't you. Well she's better company'n you are that's why, Calley said. And bettern you too Mister Yancy, he said. You keep a'talking bout me like that, o'Wasskum said, I'm gonna take you outta my Will. And Oh, Papa said, we went to laughing bout that too like we been a'laughing bout ever thing else then of a sudden we come round this Turn and up yonder was Fischer Hall where Miss Gusa died that night when Bird was borned in the Wheel Barra but didn't no body know it at first cause they was all Dancing the Poka inside. And then bout a year later, he said, It was here in Fischer Hall they had the Bird Dance and ever body dressed up like the Bird they thought they was and come here to Dance round bout it but just when ever body was starting to have Fun here come my mean o'Daddy to hurt Little Bird there in his Nest if he could. And Oh he would a'done it too, Papa said, but of a sudden here come my Momma's Horse Precious in the Back Door and she walked right through ever thing and ever body and chomped down on my Daddy's Head like it was a Punkin and run out the Front Door with him a'flapping in her mouth and Oh it was so Sad to re-member it, he said, I had to put my Fingers to my Eyes to keep from crying. You remembering the Same Thing I'm remembering ain't you, Calley said. Yes Sir I said, Papa said, I am. I just don't know how to leave go of it. Well it's a Sad Sad Story but don't try to go hiding from it, Calley said, or that Sad Story just gonna stand there a'knocking on your Door you Whole Life a'wanting to come in. No Sir, he said, just tell it to come on in then Shake Hands with it when it does and after a'while it'll see they ain't much it can do to Hurt you no moren it already has and it'll just start a'getting Smaller and Smaller and Smaller til it ain't hardly even there no more at all then one morning just after Breakfast it'll go to sneaking out the Back Door and walk on off down the Road somewheres and you won't never hear from it again in your whole Life but maybe just a little Whisper ever now and again from somewheres way off down there to where you can't barely even hear it. You Promise me that Mister Pearsall I said, Papa said. Well No Sir, Calley said. No Sir I'm fraid I can't Promise you that.

*W*ADN'T NO SURPRISE, Papa said, that Bird was a'pointing his Finger at me when we come a'riding up to the House and Ever Body else was all standing out there in the yard just a'waiting. When'd Bird let you know we was coming Home I said, Papa said, and Miz Choat said He started pointing his finger right after we had our Bisquits and Honey this morning and he ain't quit yet so yall get on down off them Horses and come on so he can take a Rest. Oh and then, Papa said, I touched Sister and me and o'Fritz trotted right on over there and you never seen such Hugging and Crying in all you Life from Miz Choat and Bird and even Mister Choat and Marcellus too. We was fraid maybe we lost you to some Circumstance, she said. Well we come close to losing him I said, Papa said, and pointed to o'Calley when he was a'stepping down off o'Firefoot and a'reaching back to help Little Missey off. Why look a'here Marcellus, Miz Choat said, we got Company we didn't even know was coming did we. This is our Friend Little Missey, Papa said, She been a'living in a Cave most her Life with her o'Blind Panther but he's Dead now and she took up with us. And I bet you Glad of it too ain't you she said then went right over to Little Missey and give her a Hug like she was one a'the Family and then so did Marcellus and after that in a big Suprise Why Bird Foot Walked right over to Little Missey and took a'holt her Hand and put his Face down on it. He likes you, Marcellus said, you won't never get shed a'him now. She don't talk much that we know of, Papa said. Then Miz Choat went over to Calley and shaked his Hand. Mister Pearsall you took this Dear Boy off from us but now you brung him back and we Thank you for that But, she said, don't never take him off from us again or we gonna come after you next time with a Switch. And Oh, Papa said, Ever Body got a good laugh

143

out a'that then Calley said But here's some thing you ain't gonna Thank me for and then stepped back when Mister Yancy finally come a'bumping up on o'Edward and said Wasskum Yancy at your Service Ma'am. He's a Artist, Papa said. A Artist, Miz Choat said, A Artist. Then she put her Hand over her mouth to where you couldn't tell was she Happy bout it or Not, Papa said. Oh Yes Ma'am a Artist, Calley said. Why we wouldn't go no wheres at all less we had us a Artist to paint Pitchurs so we'd know what we just seen long the way. Well Mister Yancy, Miz Choat said, I reckon if we can let some o'Smarty Pants like Mister Pearsall in the House Why then it ain't a step too Far to let a Artist in too. Oh and then Wasskum took him a big Bow like he was trying to get elected to some thing and said, Why it'd be my Pleasure Ma'am. Yes we'll see that it is won't we Marcellus she said then took Little Missey by the Hand Bird wadn't already a'hanging on to and started a'leading her to the House, Papa said, and next thing she give her a little Squeeze and said Where ever did you get that Travelling Bag Hon Why I never seen nothing so pretty in all my Life as all them Pitchurs you got painted on there but Little Missey hugged it close so Miz Choat couldn't touch it and give her a Smile in sted. And then, Papa said, o'Possum stopped cause he didn't think he was gonna be allowed in the House and Miz Choat said I swear that is the Ugliest o'Flop Eared Dog I ever seen in my Life but I bet he got him a good Nature to make up for it don't he then whistled him on in long with ever body else.

FIRST THING AFTER we told em bout o'Pelo Blanco and Pela Rosa and finding the Wild Woman a'the Navidad in that Cave and getting our John B Stetson Hats in the Joske Store in San Antoneya and setting in front a'the Alamo, Papa said, Miz Choat wanted to know what Little Missey seen flying out a'Bird's little birthmark Bird there on his chest over his Heart. She ain't gonna be able to tell you which Bird even if she does see one, Calley said. Well you seen one when you looked didn't you Mister Pearsall, Miz Choat said, that proves don't no body have to be particularly Smart to do it. Oh Calley laughed out loud bout that, Papa said, and said I ain't been here but six and a half minutes and you already a'whupping me with that sharp Tongue a'yours ain't

you never seen such Hugging and Crying
all you Life from Miz Choat and Bird...

you Miz Choat. Yes Sir, Miz Choat said, I do believe I'd rather tease you'n sleep at night Mister Pearsall. Well you practice enough, Calley said and when he said that Why Miz Choat reached over there with her hand and give him a little pet on his Cheek to let him know ever thing she ever said to him like that was all just in Fun. Look she's looking, Mister Choat said, and we all looked over there and Sure enough Little Missey was down on her knees a'looking straight in Bird's little Birthmark Bird. What you see there Miss Missey, Miz Choat said, you see a Bird or some thing. Then, Papa said, Why Little Missey come up with a Smile on her Face and flapped her arms like a Bird. She sees a Bird don't she, Marcellus said. Course she sees a Bird Marcellus, Miz Choat said, you didn't think she was gonna see a Possum did you. It ain't no Bird, Mister Yancy said, No Ma'am it ain't no Bird. Oh and then we all looked over at Wasskum and he was squatting down there beside Little Missey a'looking at Bird's little Birthmark Bird too and his Eyes was just a'going back and forth like he was follering some thing moving round this way and that there on Bird's chest. Well, Miz Choat said, I reckon Artists sees things can't no body else in the World see huh. Ain't no Bird, o'Wasskum said again, No Ma'am ain't no Bird. You done said that bout a hunderd and four times, Calley said, So what is it if it ain't no Bird Mister Artist. Why it's a little Angel, o'Wasskum said, that's what it is And not only that, he said, but they's a lot moren one a'buzzing round like Honey Bees on the Hive. And then, Papa said, Little Missey reached out her Hand I reckon so one could set on it but Bird took a'holt a'her Hand and wouldn't let her do it his Eyes just a'going ever which way back behind them skinny Blue Lids. What else you see Mister Yancy, Mister Choat said. Is they any Bird there at all. I'm a'looking, Mister Yancy said, but all I see is Little Angels a'flying round Little Missey and they don't look too Happy bout it neither.

*M*IZ CHOAT KEP A'HOLT A'LITTLE MISSEY, Papa said, while the rest a'us took the Horses down to the Barn for some thing to eat and a good Scratch here and there. How'd o'Edward behave on your Trip, Mister Choat said. He wadn't a Lick a'Trouble was he o'Calley said and I said No Sir, Papa said, not one Lick a'Trouble that I ever seen. He ain't xactly a Cow Horse but he's a Good Horse ain't he Marcellus, Mister

Choat said. Yes Sir he is to me, Marcellus said. I like him. Well then, Mister Choat said, if you like him so much Why then we'll just make him Your Horse. My Horse, Marcellus said, My Horse. That don't mean he ain't gonna have to work some to earn his Keep round here you know it, Mister Choat said. O'Edward'll work all day long and then some, Marcellus said, You don't never have to worry bout him Mister Choat. Or you neither Marcellus, Mister Choat said, that's why I'm a'giving him to you. Well this is a Big Day all round ain't it, Calley said, I bet you wish some body'd give you some thing don't you Mister Yancy. Oh it's Gift enough just being here with you Mister Pearsall, o'Wasskum said. I don't know what more I could want in the World. Yes Sir I know it, Calley said. I just didn't know if you knowed it or not. Bout that time, Papa said, Mister Choat said We still got Time to set out there on the Front Porch a'while fore Suppers and smoke our Pipe if we want to.

So we went out there on the Front Porch, Papa said, and they was lighting up they Pipe when here come Miz Choat a'carrying Bird in her arm and a'holding Hands with Little Missey and o'Fritz and Possum behind em a'looking for a Place to set. You the first Artist in the World to ever set on this Porch you know it Mister Yancy, she said. No Ma'am I didn't know it, Wasskum said. Well you are, Miz Choat said, So tell us bout Art. Well what you wanna know bout Art Miz Choat, Wasskum said. Well First Thing is Where you reckon it comes from, she said. No Ma'am I don't reckon it comes from no where at all, o'Wasskum said. I reckon it's just always been here the Whole Time and it's up to us to Look for it til we Find it. How we gonna Find it if we don't even know what it is we a'looking for, Miz Choat said. Well the Way I see it, Mister Yancy said, is we already got Art in us when we First Borned but don't know it til some Artist comes long and paints a Pitchur we like and then we jump up and say YES YES YES when we see it Not cause that Pitchur is a'Telling us any thing we didn't already know but cause it's just Reminding us a'some thing we always Did Know way down deep but just forgot we did til that Pitchur come long and reminded us of it. I never thought bout Art that way in my Life, Miz Choat said. No Ma'am and not me neither, o'Wasskum said, not til just now when I first said it my self. It was Little Missey here taught me to just let things come out on they own, he said, cause they already in there any how and you don't never wanna Bottle em up.

*E*VER BODY HELPED PUT THE SUPPERS
on the table, Papa said, and then we all set down and Mister Choat said a
Blessing but he said it so Low couldn't no body hardly hear a Word of it. I
can't hear you Mister Choat, Wasskum said, I can't hear you Sir. He ain't
talking to you Mister Yancy that's why Miz Choat said then looked round
and said We a'missing Little Missey ain't we but right then, Papa said, here
come Little Missey a'wearing that Pretty Dress we got her in San Antoneya
that come all the way down pass her Feet and was a'dragging on the Floor.
And Oh, he said, Miz Choat was so took by it she clapped her Hands Hooray
and then so did ever body else but Tears was running down our Face too
cause it looked like to us Little Missey gone on and rejoined the World just
now after all them years in that Dark o'Cave. I never seen no body look no
prettier, Calley said, If I was bout ninety-two years older Why I'd ask her to
Marry me and be my Wife. I doubt she'd have you, Miz Choat said, She may
be Old but she ain't Stupid is she. Hear Hear, o'Wasskum said and had him
a Laugh bout it then Hushed soons Miz Choat give him a Look. Bout that
time, Papa said, Bird climbed down off my Lap and climbed up on Little
Missey's Bundle there in her Lap then grabbed a'holt a'her Finger and helt
on tight. They like each other don't they, Marcellus said. Why Ever Body
likes Ever Body else round here, Miz Choat said, I reckon we just Blessed
that way ain't we. You like ever body round here don't you Mister Pearsall,
she said. Well I try to Miz Choat, Calley said, But it ain't always easy. You
know what I like bout this Family, Miz Choat said, It's just a'growing all the
Time. Seems like they's some body new a'coming in through the Door ever
time you open it, she said then reached over and put a Dumplin on Little
Missey's plate for her to eat and give her a pet on the Hand. How you xplain
that Mister Artist, Miz Choat said. I ain't sure, Wasskum said. I reckon ain't
nothing ever happens but for a Reason but you don't always know what it
is til later when you least xspect it. I didn't catch a'Lick a'that Mister Yancy,
Calley said. Me neither, Papa said. No Sir, Marcellus said. Pass that Corn
Bread here please, Mister Choat said, and the Butter long with it. It's just
that ever thing connected to ever thing else in the World, Wasskum said,
Ain't nothing just goes long by itself. Yes Sir ever thing connected to ever
thing else in the World ain't it, Mister Choat said then slabbed some Butter
on his Corn Bread and licked his knife clean. For xample, he said, I heared

148

it said ever time they's a new Baby borned over there in Blanco Why they's some Man got to leave the Country in a Hurry ain't that what you mean Mister Yancy. And then, Papa said, Mister Choat went to laughing so hard at what he just said he bout spit up his Corn Bread and Miz Choat said Don't talk naughty Mister Choat or we gonna have to ask you to leave the Table for it.

MIZ CHOAT MADE A PALLET ON THE FLOOR for Little Missey, Papa said, then tucked her and her Bundle in like you would a Baby and Bird wouldn't have it no other Way but get under the Covers with her and hold her hand. Look at that. You'd almost think they was Brother and Sister wouldn't you, Miz Choat said. Oh and then, Papa said, Why Little Missey went to singing some song to Bird she must a'learned from her own Momma fore she ever even come to this Country but they wadn't no Words to it we could understand just Sounds like you was off in a Dream somewheres and didn't never wanna come back out again and Bird liked it so much his mouth just went a'working Side-to-Side Side-to-Side and then he went on off in a Dream his self. I want you to learn to sing like that Mister Yancy, Miz Choat said, make you self useful round here. Course she meant it for a Joke but o'Wasskum drawed back and Oh Listen Here he just went to singing right long with Little Missey and mixed in Pretty as you Please and then Marcellus did too and then here come Mister Choat a'joining in and then Miz Choat give o'Calley a Look over there and said What's wrong with you Mister Pearsall and so o'Calley just moreless went to hollering but trying best as he could to sound like he was singing and then me and Miz Choat did too and in a minute Why we was all a'singing some thing hadn't never been heard on this Earth before and all this Time o'Fritz and Possum was setting over there a'howling like they was singing too Then when we was all done with it, Papa said, we went to hugging each other and laughing and Miz Choat said I'm glad the Sheriff didn't come a'walking in here when we was singing or he'd a'locked ever one a'us up in the Loonie Bin and throwed away the Key.

*T*HAT NIGHT, Papa said, Me and Marcellus was out there on the Front Porch to go to sleep on our Pallet and Marcellus said What you reckon all them little Angels was doing a'buzzing round Little Missey like that for. I don't have no idea, Papa said, but I reckon your o'Granny might could tell us don't you. So, he said, me and o'Marcellus rode on over there to the Colony next morning to ask o'Jeffey and she said Lawd I don't have no idea in the World but Let's see Who all round here might can tell us then she set down in her Big Chair and closed her Eyes to See. Anybody there Granny, Marcellus said. Why ever body's here, she said, Dead People just ever wheres you look. Most a'the time they wanna talk my Ear off then go to whispering in the Hole but this morning, she said, they just setting there won't say a Word. What's wrong with yall this Morning o'Jeffey said Cat got your Tongue and then, Papa said, she just went to looking from One to a'nother even if Me and o'Marcellus couldn't see em. What's a'matter with yall, she said, yall ain't Dead are you and Oh then o'Jeffey just went to laughing at her own Joke then dried up and said they ain't laughing with me not a one. How you figgur it Granny, Marcellus said, I reckon they just supposed not to tell is all I can figgur she said. Then of a sudden she seen some body a'setting over in the corner and she went over there and bended down to get her a better look. Who you, she said, I ain't never seen you in my Life. Who is it Granny, Marcellus said, but No o'Jeffey just kep a'Looking and wouldn't tell us. What's your name Hon, she said. You got a name ain't you. Bo what, she said, Bo Mon Nee is that what you said. Bomonee. That your name huh. Bomonee. Oh that's a good name ain't it. My name's o'Jeffey I be glad to see you any time you wanna come round. How come ain't no body else talking Bomonee she said then, Papa said, what ever o'Bomonee said back give her the Chills and she put her Hands up over her Ears so she couldn't hear no more of it and shook her Head No No No. What's he saying Granny, Marcellus said, you ain't telling us nothing. But, Papa said, o'Jeffey was still a'talking to Bomonee and didn't have no time for us. You go on now Hon, she said, I know you gonna be Glad to see you Momma and she gonna be Glad to see you too ain't she. Then, Papa said, o'Jeffey reached down and give some body a pet on they Head then opened her Eyes up a'gain. Well tell us Granny, Marcellus said, ain't you gonna tell us Granny. No Sir I ain't gonna tell you, she said, cause I don't never wanna hear it again my self.

WE GOT HOME JUST FORE DARK, Papa said, and went to doing our Chores long with Ever Body else a'doing theirs out there in the Barn then Miz Choat hollered out the Back Door it was time to come on in and have some Suppers but, Papa said, Me and Marcellus hollered back we didn't want none til we give Sister and o'Edward a good Brushing first but then we'd come on in after that if it was okay with her and she hollered back Ever Body else gonna have a nice hot Suppers but yall's is gonna be cold as Froze Ice if you don't come on in now and I might not have nothing much for you two Monkeys any how. You better listen to her, Calley said, Miz Choat ain't one to fool round bout her Suppers is she. Or any thing else, Mister Choat said. Well yall can stand here and talk bout it til the River Jordan runs Dry o'Wasskum said but I'm gonna go get me some Suppers while they's still some Suppers to get and then, Papa said, he went on into the House and then so did o'Calley and Mister Choat and o'Fritz and Possum follered long behind for scraps if they was some. And then o'Marcellus got done brushing o'Edward and said Don't Worry I'll hide you some Corn Bread up under my shirt when ain't No Body looking so you don't have to starve to Death less you just want to and then he went on in the House too and so wadn't nobody left out there in the Barn but me and the Horses. But then in a minute, Papa said, Why I got this cold cold Shivver started way down in my Feet then come all the way up to the Top a'my Head and just set there like some Big o'Coiled Up Rattle Snake bout to strike. And Oh, he said, it scared me so Bad I all but Cut and Run but No I was Froze Solid in my Tracks and couldn't do it. Then, he said, I heared Some Body squeek a Board up there in the Hay Loff bove me and Oh then Next thing Some Body come a Jumping down out the Loff with a Big Laugh and landed right there in front a'me just a'grinning with a Big Long Gun in his Hand and another one a'sticking out his Pants. Well, o'Arlon said, I reckon you are one Surprised Possum to see me here after all this Time ain't you.

YOU AIN'T BEEN A'LIVING UP THERE in the Loff have you, Papa said. I live just bout any wheres I wanna Live, Arlon said, and ain't no body says nothing bout it neither. Yes Sir you got just bout ever body in the Country round here scared a'you that's Why, Papa said, the way you been a'going round Murdering People like that. Yes Sir I Murdered me a few ain't I, he said. I seen poor o'Superintendent Shettles in the wagon after you was done with him, Papa said. It looked to me like you Murdered him bout four or five times fore you was done with it. It was his own fault, Arlon said. I told that Son of a Bitch I was gonna shoot him Dead if he don't stop picking on me like he was back at the Gatesville Boy Prison. Well I sure seen where you kep your word to him on that didn't you, Papa said. Oh I'll shoot bout any body, he said, It don't matter a Lick to me who it is. Well you can't go to shooting no body round here, Papa said, you better hear me on that. Well they was gonna be my Family too wadn't they, Arlon said. You remember way back yonder when we first become Friends you said you thought it'd be Okay if I was to move in with yall one day and get me a Horse and a Bunch a'Dogs. I was talking bout when Me and my Momma and my Brother Herman got us a place a'our own, Papa said, but didn't nothing never come a'that cause Momma was already Dead by then I just didn't know it. Sides that, I said, That's bout when you went to stealing things didn't belong to you and then Murdered that Man over in Kendalia didn't never do nothing to you. You still holding a Grudge on me for it too ain't you, Arlon said. It ain't so much a Grudge I'm a'holding on you for it, Papa said, as it is I just don't want no more to do with you. Oh he give me his o'Snake Eyes then, Papa said, and pointed his Big Gun round and said Where's your Little Dog at I might have to shoot him just to see how you like it. No you ain't, Papa said, but I'd come Fix you good if you did. Arlon give it a thought and said No I wouldn't never shoot your little Dog I ain't got nothing against Dogs and Horses they a'lot bettern People to me. Well why don't you just go on and Go then, Papa said, Been good to know you I reckon. You was the only Friend I ever had, Arlon said, you know it. We knowed each other for a little Time, Papa said, but No Sir I wouldn't say we was ever really Friends. Well which ever Way we Was, Arlon said, we ain't that Way no more now are we. And then just when he turned round to go on a'way, Papa said, Why of a sudden here come Little Missey out the Back Door a'heading for the Barn with her Travelling Bundle cross her Back like always and Oh then Bird went to Hollering and Crying and a'Carrying On bout it back inside but by then, he said, it was already Too Late Too Late Too Late to ever get her back in the House again.

152

ARLON SEEN HER COMING,

Papa said, and said what's wrong with yall to let a Nigger be in the House with you. Thats Little Missey I said, Papa said, she's our Friend. You got a Nigger for a Friend but not me huh he said and I never seen such Snake Eyes in all my Life as come on him then and he put a tight holt on his Big Gun with both Hands and aimed it up and Oh I seen what he was gonna do now and Hollered Go Back Little Missey GO BACK GO BACK GO BACK but No she didn't know the Words I was Hollering and just kep a'coming so I grabbed at Arlon's Gun but Arlon said Hell No You Don't you SonofaBitch and hit me cross my Head with it and put me down and then Oh went to Kicking me and Clubbing me on my Head with his Big Gun til ever thing was all in a Cloud to me and what I seen then, Papa said, was Little Missey come a'walking through the Barn Door and Arlon said No Ma'am I don't al-low no Niggers in here and give her a HARD PUSH back out the Door and then another HARD PUSH out the Door and then he reared back his Gun and hit her cross her Back with it but it was her Travelling Bundle a'hanging there he hit and Oh when he did, Papa said, Why Little Missey went to Cry-ing Bomonee Bomonee Bomonee and Fighting with everything she had to save it from Harm but No, he said, wadn't no use cause o'Arlon just kep on a'Clubbing her and her Travelling Bundle both hard as he could with his Big Gun and Oh Little Missey was just a'Stumbling and a'Falling and a'Trying to save her Bundle fore it all come a'Part on her from all them Licks but then Oh, he said, Oh but then it did come all a'Part and what come a'Falling out now was Bones. Oh, Papa said, Bones. Bones Bones Bones, he said, Little Missey's whole Bundle wadn't nothing but Bones and they was the Bones a'her Little Baby Son Bomonee that she carried all cross the Country to get way from them Slavers til he died from some thing or other and she kep him in the Cave with her cause she Loved him so much and didn't never wanna be a'way from him no matter what. Oh and then, Papa said, Oh and then she went to crawling round trying to pick up all them Bones but o'Arlon give her a Hard Kick put her a'rolling on the ground and hollered NIGGER at her then raised up his Big Gun and shot her in her Back BOOM BOOM BOOM three times like that then BOOM one more time and Oh then ever body come a'running out the House to see what all the Shooting was bout and when they seen what it was Oh they went a'Hollering and a'Running and a'Crying to save Little Missey over yonder just a'bleeding her Life out on her

Little Son's Bones but No it was Too Late to Save Her and I seen her get up Out her Body and go a'walking off toward the Creek just a'Shimmering like all them other Shimmery People was always a'doing and then, Papa said, I come out my Body just a'Shimmering my self from all them Licks o'Arlon give me and went a'walking toward the Creek after her.

*W*ADN'T NO TIME, Papa said, and me and Little Missey come to the Creek and they was all these Other Shimmery People just a'waiting for her over there on the other side. And Oh, he said, one of em was Little Missey's o'Blind Panther but he wadn't Blind no more and standing right the side a'him was her Little Boy Bomonee and Oh Little Missey crossed on over didn't take no longern a Thought and give her Little Son a big Hug and that o'Panther one too and then all them other Shimmery People come over to pet her. But then, Papa said, I seen this Old Shimmery China Man a'looking at me from the Other Side and he give me a Wave with his Hand to come on over to where he was. So, Papa said, I crossed on over the Creek with just a thought a'doing it and then here in a minute I come to this Dark Woods and they was Seven Old Shimmery Men a'setting there round a Table and the Moon just a'shining down on em like a Lantern and it looked to me like they was getting ready to Play em a Game a'Dominoes cause they had a stack a'Black Dominoes and a stack a'White Dominoes over there in front a'this empty Chair where they wadn't no body a'setting. We been a'waiting for you this Old Inyin Man said Where you been and I said, Papa said, Well Some Body ought a'tole me yall was waiting for me and I'd a'come on a'running. Well just set you self down here in this Empty Chair Mister, the Old Shimmery Black Man said, we still got a'bunch more just like you we gotta bring on back Home tonight.

*S*o, Papa said, I went to set down in that Empty Chair and then I seen Oh I was Shimmering almost much as all them Old Shimmery Men was. Oh I said, Papa said, I reckon I'm Dead as some o'Anvil ain't I huh. But, he said, fore

...raised up his Big Gun and shot h
in her Back BOOM BOOM BOOM

they could answer me back Some Body took a'holt a'my Shirt Tail and give it a hard Pull just fore I set down in that Empty Chair and I looked to see who it was, Papa said, and Why it was my o'Amigo Mister Pegleg had my Shirt Tail in his Mouth and wadn't bout to let go and then Some Body else grabbed a'holt a'my Finger and went to pulling on it too. They's some thing wrong here, the Old Shimmery Mexkin Man said. Are you sure this One here is on our Lista. Then, Papa said, they looked at this Paper they had and the Old Shimmery China Man said Are you the One the Horse kicked in the Head when you walked by his Hind End. No Sir I said, Papa said, I'm the one o'Arlon Clavic knocked in the Head with his Big Gun. Oh that Arlon Clavic is a Bad Boy, the Old Shimmery Black Man said, I ain't never seen no Worsern him in all my Life. Yes he is Bad Bad Bad ain't he, the Old Shimmery White Man said. Then, Papa said, o'Mister Pegleg give me another Pull on my Shirt Tail and Who Ever it was I couldn't see give me another Pull on my Finger too. You know, the Old Shimmery Mexkin Man said, I don't believe this One here is on our Lista. Uh Oh Uh Oh he got to go back then, the Old Shimmery China Man said. It ain't his Time yet. I hope he ain't gonna be a Loonie all his Life from all them Licks that Bad Boy give him, the Old Shimmery White Man said. Oh that would be very Sad for him you know it. And then, Papa said, the Old Shimmery Mexkin Man squeezed his Hands on my Head and Blowed a Big Puff a'Air in my Ear and some thing blowed out the other side. And when he done that, he said, Why I seen it was Old Crecencio was who it was a'doing the blowing and right then I got another Big Pull on my Finger and Mister Pegleg give me one more Big Pull on my Shirt Tail and Oh I hollered and went to falling Down Down Down off that chair and next thing I knowed Why I was in the Bed in Miz Choat's House and Bird was a'standing there side me just a'pulling on my Finger to get me Back to where I belonged from where ever it was I been with Mister Pegleg and them Seven Old Shimmery Men.

*A*ND THEN, Papa said, I seen Mister and Miz Choat and Marcellus all a'standing there too but not Mister Pearsall and not Mister Yancy neither one but there

156

was o'Fritz over there a'Barking at me and then of a sudden it come to me Where is Little Missey at. Where is Little Missey at I said, Papa said, but then fore Miz Choat could tell me I recollected I seen her go a'Shimmering cross the Creek to where her Little Son Bomonee and her o'Panther and all them other Shimmery People was a'waiting for her and I said Arlon shot her Dead didn't he and Miz Choat said Yes he Did Yes he Did. Then they all went to crying bout it and me too, Papa said, and we couldn't stop it for a Long Long Time but when we did Miz Choat said Calley Pearsall and Wasskum Yancy the Artist and that o'Flop Eared Dog Possum went on off three days ago to go catch that Bad Boy Arlon Clavic and Hang him from a Tree for his Crime to Little Missey. I don't know why they didn't wait on me to go long with em, Papa said, and Marcellus said Cause didn't no body reckon you was even gonna Live after that whupping o'Arlon give you with his Gun that's why. And Mister Pearsall was fraid they'd lose that Murderer to the Distance if they didn't Go on and Go after him right now, Mister Choat said. So they just Went on and Went. Well I'm a'going after him too I said, Papa said, Ain't No Body can keep me from it. Well them Knots there on your Head can keep you from it, Miz Choat said, least for a'time. Here Mister Choat said Mister Pearsall said give you this Letter he wrote but, Papa said, Bird still had a'holt a'my Finger and wouldn't let go so I said Just read it to me would you please and Mister Choat said It says If you are reading this Letter you are a'Live and I am glad to hear it but I know you and I know you will want to Foller us but No don't Foller us we will get this Murderer for what he done to Little Missey and Others and I don't want him to do the same to you if I can help it. But I know you are a Hard Headed Boy some time and I worry bout that. Your Friend Calley Pearsall and Wasskum Yancy here with me.

I COULDN'T GET OUT THE BED
for my Head a'hurting so Bad that Day and not the Next Day neither, Papa said, but the next Day after that I come a'Live again and Ever Body walked me down to the end a'the Field where Gilbert Lee Choat and Miss Gusa and now Little Missey with the Bones a'her Little Son there in her Arms was all buried in the Ground up bove the Creek a'running so Pretty down below. I

reckon she and her Boy glad to be here, Mister Choat said, where they got some Company. Yes Sir and we glad to have em too, Miz Choat said, I didn't know Little Missey for long and didn't never understand a Word she ever said but I almost come to think a'her as the Little Daughter I never did have. I hope Don't no body try to dig her up outta here Marcellus said and then Miz Choat put her arm round him and said We wouldn't never let no body do that Marcellus and then he said, Papa said, No Ma'am but they's some People ain't gonna like it she's buried in White People Ground and gonna wanna come dig her up out a'it some Night when they ain't no body looking. Now just hold your Horses there a minute, Miz Choat said, I don't see where God put up a Sign any wheres round here says White People Ground only or Some Body Else Ground only or No Body Else's Ground only or nothing else. No but Marcellus got a Point there don't he, Mister Choat said, I mean they's People do such a thing like that and we might even know one or two of em our self but I ain't a'naming no Names. Your talking bout o'Lester What's His Name ain't you Mister Choat, Miz Choat said. I ain't saying for sure but I might be talking bout o'Lester What's His Name and I might be talking bout o'Buster What's His Name runs the Dry Goods Store both, Mister Choat said, if I was a'naming Names which I ain't. Well we can quit talking bout it any how, Papa said Miz Choat said, Cause they ain't no body ever digging Little Missey up outta this Ground here long as I'm a'Live and got my Bird Gun handy. If I was to up and die, Marcellus said, You wouldn't let no body dig me up outta here neither would you. Well your o'Granny Jeffey gonna want you next to her over yonder in the Colony Ground any how don't you reckon Marcellus, Miz Choat said, so I doubt the question ever even gonna come up. Well I wanna be next to my Granny Jeffey but I wanna be next to yall too, Marcellus said. Well Hon, Miz Choat said, that might be hard to do. Maybe yall could come over there to the Colony and get buried in the Ground next to me, Marcellus said. Well Yes Sir that's a Idea, Miz Choat said, but they's Black People over there in the Colony might not like it White People being buried in the same Ground with them. You don't think they'd try to dig you up outta there do you, Marcellus said. Well they might, Papa said Miz Choat said, You don't never know do you what with Black People and White People both being bout the same on the inside.

THAT NIGHT AT SUPPERS, Papa said, I ask Did any body know which way Mister Pearsall and Mister Yancy and o'Possum went off in to catch o'Arlon and Miz Choat said South. South to Where I said, Papa said, and Mister Choat said South to Where Ever Body goes that done some thing Bad North a'there. That sounds like Mexico to me, Miz Choat said, less they catch him short a'there. Well if they don't I will, Papa said, and I ain't gonna stop til I do. Yes Sir I'm a'feeling the same bout it my self, Marcellus said. I didn't know we was having Suppers here with the James Boys Frank and Jesse this evening did you Mister Choat, Miz Choat said. And here's another thing Marcellus, she said, You ain't a'going off no wheres whether you want to or not. Your o'Granny Jeffey'd skin you and me both a'Live and spit out the Seeds. Oh Marcellus was just bout to cry bout it, Papa said, and had to scrunch up his Face to keep from it and then Bird come over and took a'holt a'my Hand. Bird don't want you to go neither you know it, Miz Choat said. I think he probably got more sense bout it'n you do. I'm a'going any how, Papa said, They ain't no Other Way bout it. You wanna have a Mark on your Soul you killed some body when you meet you Maker, Miz Choat said, that the kind a'Mark you want on your Soul. I don't care if I do, Papa said, not after what he done to Little Missey. I don't care neither, Marcellus said. Well it don't matter if you care or not Marcellus, Miz Choat said, you ain't a'going no wheres any how. But this time, Papa said, Marcellus did start crying bout it and then Miz Choat did too and reached out both her Hands and took a'holt a'Marcellus in one and me in the other and then I looked over there, he said, and Why Mister Choat was just a'crying too and so was o'Fritz and then fore I knowed it I was too and Oh, Papa said, we just set there a'holding Hands and a'Crying like little Babies. I'm gonna count to Three, Miz Choat said, and when I get to Three I want all a'us to stop this Crying yall hear me But when she got to Three, Papa said, we just cried right on through it and kep a'going til I reckon we was at bout five hunderd and five and was just all wore out from it and couldn't Cry no more. Well all that Crying makes us feel better now don't it, Miz Choat said, then me and Marcellus went to warshing the Dishes but it was hard to do it cause Bird didn't want me to go neither and wouldn't let go my Hand. Don't Worry Bird, I said, I'll come back soons I can. Then, Papa said, he let go my Hand but now he wrapped both his little

Arms round my Leg tight as he could and set down on my Foot and I had to limp and stumble round everwheres with him just a'hanging on like that til it was time for ever body to go to Bed and get some sleep.

*D*IDN'T NO BODY KNOW IT, Papa said, but me and Sister and o'Fritz all sneaked out late that Night and was long gone down the Road by the time the Moon come up to light our Way on South. Well here we go Amigos I told em, he said, but Where To I ain't got no Idea in the World. All I know, I said, is we gonna find Bad Arlon One Way or the Other and when we do we gonna Fix him for what he done to Little Missey and it bout made me Cry to say it cause she ain't never done nothing to No Body but now she was Gone Forever. But just to show you how this Trip started out, Papa said, Why the First Thing we seen next morning when the Sun come up was three sets a'Tracks out there in the Middle a'the Road and one set was Firefoot and one was o'Pete the Donkey and the other One was o'Possum and what they was all Three a'saying was This Way This Way This Way so, he said, I just pointed my o'John B Stetson Hat in that same Direction and a'way we went with o'Fritz a'going Heh Heh Heh cause he didn't have no Idea the Danger we was maybe heading in and didn't know no better any how. Course I didn't neither, Papa said, or I might a'turned round my self and gone the other way too. But No I was set on getting o'Arlon for what he done and then it come to me they was some thing Different bout him when he come a'Jumping down out the Loff at me and that was His Eyes didn't close DOWN when he blinked like ever body else but closed UP from Bottom to Top in sted like some o'Lizert you might find under a Rock some wheres. Closed UP, Papa said, Why it was like o'Arlon wadn't even who he'd BEEN when I first come to know him no more but was Some Body ELSE now. Or some THING else, he said, and Oh it spooked me to think it cause What if I was Right and we was maybe even dealing with some o'Devil now and not o'Arlon Clavic no more at all and Oh, Papa said, I wished o'Calley'd been there to tell me which one it was fore it was too Late.

160

So WE JUST KEP A'GOING

in the Direction we was already a'going in, Papa said, and it wadn't long and we was in the Mesquites and Cactuses far as you could see and the World went just flat as some o'Board you might find out yonder behind the Barn or some wheres but they wadn't nothing to do bout it but just keep on a'going. Then bout two days later I reckon it was, Papa said, Why here come some o'Man a'wearing him a Navy Suit with a bunch of raggedy ribbons on it and a'carrying him a old rotten Flag on a Stick said Nothing Fancy It's A Yancy on it and Oh he was bout all give out from his Travels and couldn't barely keep from a'falling off his o'wore out Horse. You look like you could use you a Rest Mister I said, Papa said, and the Man said No I never felt no better in all my Life can you tell me where I am Please. Yes Sir, Papa said, you are in Texas same as me and this Horse and Little Dog here But I don't know I can tell you xactly where in Texas that is. Oh Thank God the Man said then stepped down off his Horse and curled up on the Ground and went right off to sleep like some Little Baby and it wadn't til Bright and Early next morning he come a'wake again and I give him a drink a'water and some Bread I had for Breakfast. I never xpected to find the Good Samaritan out here in the Wilderness, he said, but here you are. No Sir I ain't no Samaritan, Papa said, I don't even know the Samaritans less they that Bunch lives over yonder pass Buckner Store on Snake Creek. But, Papa said, your Flag there reminds me of a Artist goes round the Country painting Pitchurs by the name a'Wasskum Yancy. Oh Good God in the Starry Heavens, the Man said, You a'talking about my own Son. You his Daddy huh, Papa said. Yes Sir that's me, the Man said, Benton Yancy father of Wasskum Yancy. Can you tell me Where he is, he said. Him and my o'Amigo Calley Pearsall is off chasing a Murderer name a'Arlon Clavic, Papa said, and we are too. A Murderer, Mister Yancy said, Oh My God my Son Wasskum is off chasing a Murderer through the Wilds of Texas. Yes Sir I reckon he is, Papa said, less they done Caught and Hanged him from a Tree by now or he done shot em both Dead for trying one or the other. That Would Break his Mother's Heart, Mister Yancy said, And mine too. I didn't know to believe him or not bout that, Papa said, after what all Wasskum said bout him so I said What's your Flag mean. A Yancy, Mister Yancy said, is a suit a'Long Under Wear has both Arms and Legs in it to keep you warm and a Two Button Drop Down Trap Door in the Back. Nothing Fancy you understand, he said, It's a Yancy. But our Under Wears give you a lot a'Peace a'Mine when you in a Hurry if you take my meaning. Peace a'Mine that's what we built our Name on. Course they's another Company makes em too, Mister Yancy said, but they Buttons fall short cause they so hard to undo when you a'hurrying. You come to Philadelphia some time I'll have our Manager walk you through the Mill and you can see how we do it yourself, he said. Thank you, Papa said. Alright then, Mister Yancy said, now where's Wasskum. I don't have no idea in the World, Papa said, we just a'going cross the Country to see if we can find em fore it's too late and o'Arlon shoots em.

*T*ELL ME SOME MORE BOUT MY SON Mister Yancy said when we was riding on off later that Morning, Papa said. Well he's a'chasing Arlon Clavic the Thief and Murderer now but, I said, most a'the Time he's a Artist and paints Pitchurs a'what he makes up in his Head from what he sees. He'll have to leave such Notions behind when he goes to running the Mill, Mister Yancy said. He didn't never say nothing bout running no Mill, Papa said, You sure he knows its coming up. My Great Grandfather knowed it and my Grandfather knowed it and my Father and me both knowed it Mister Yancy said. I don't know why Wasskum wouldn't Know it too. Well then maybe he does know it, Papa said, but maybe he don't care nothing bout it and just wants to go round painting Pitchurs. You mean when he's not chasing Thieves and Murderers, Mister Yancy said, and looked like he was Glad to say it. Well that just come up here the other day, Papa said, not none a'us do it all the Time. Notions pass, Mister Yancy said, Why when I was his age I wanted my Father to buy me a Great Sailing Ship and sail cross the Seven Seas on it. I been thinking bout being a Horn Man my self, Papa said, and play in a Dance Band if I can find one to let me play in it. Well that's a Foolish Idea, Mister Yancy said, how ever would you make Money blowing a Horn. That never come to me to even think bout it, Papa said, I just want to do it cause it looks like Fun and I like the Sound comes out when ever bodys a'blowing they Horn all together. What does your Father have to say bout your Ambitions, he said. Nothing, Papa said, he's a setting on a Flat Rock down in Hell and don't get to talk much any more. And when I said that, he said, Why o'Fritz went to licking on his Behind and a'going Heh Heh Heh. Maybe when you come to visit the Mill, Mister Yancy said, we could have Mister Flaret create a uniform for your little Dog there. I doubt he'd wear it, Papa said, we put a Road Runner suit on him one time for the Bird Dance over at Fischer Hall and ever time he went to Lick his Hiney Why he poked it with his Beak and he ain't never got over it yet but I like that Outfit you a'wearing he said. Thank you, Mister Yancy said, Flaret took his Idea for it from the Great Admirals. Seems like you oughta have you a Boat if you gonna go round wearing clothes like that, Papa said. Oh I'd like that, Mister Yancy said. Maybe when Wasskum is running the Mill I'll live my Boyhood Dream and buy one. I had a Feeling o'Wasskum wadn't never gonna wanna run that Mill in his Life, Papa said, so I said Maybe you oughta go on and live your Dream now while you still a'Dreaming it Mister Yancy. But, Papa said, fore he could answer me back Why here come two Men and a Boy and a Dog at us from way off out yonder in the Cactuses somewheres and the Boy looked to me like they had him tied Hand to Foot to where they wadn't no way he was gonna get a'loose and run off on em and I knowed just xactly who it was too.

YES SIR IT WAS O'ARLON THEY HAD,

Papa said, and by the Look a'Wasskum he was the one catched him Why his Clothes and his face was so tore up you'd a'thought a Wild Cat been on him with all four Feets just a'going. But, he said, Mister Yancy just give me a Ugly Look bout it and said I thought you said my Son Wasskum was out after Thieves and Murderers but this ain't nothing but a Child they got here. Hello Father, Wasskum said, I am surprised to see you. Just look at you, Mister Yancy said, Just look at you. Yes Sir do look at him, Calley said, This is the Man just saved my Life here a while ago and you either talk better to him then you are now or take you a Good Whupping for it One or the Other. Oh and then, Papa said, Mister Yancy give o'Calley a little wave a'his Hand like he was shooing a Fly off a Cow Flop and said Don't interrupt me when I'm talking Mister Who Ever You Think You Are and Oh Calley come out the Saddle like a Duck on a June Bug and give that Man One Two Three quick Licks put him down to the Ground and said Calley Pearsall is who I think I am and now I reckon you know it too don't you Mister. Then Wasskum

tried to help his Daddy up on his Feet, Papa said, but No his Daddy wouldn't have it and pushed him back and the other thing I seen at the same time, he said, was how o'Arlon's Eye Lids was a'blinking Down Up Down Up cause I reckon he was thinking he might could turn this to his own use when the Time Come. Wash your Face and Pack your things, Mister Yancy said, and Let's be off. I have a Life here now Father, Wasskum said, and don't want no other. A Life doing What, his Father said, Painting Pitchurs. Yes Sir Painting Pitchurs or chasing Criminals or Sleeping out at Night under the stars or Skipping Rocks cross the Creek or What Ever the god dam Else I wanna do. You are a Yancy Young Sir, Mister Yancy hollered at him, a Yancy Yancy Yancy same as me. I don't wanna be a Yancy, Wasskum said, and I don't believe you wanna be a Yancy neither or you wouldn't be wearing that Sailor Suit. Oh Mister Yancy was mad bout him saying that and hollered I am Robert Charles Benton Yancy of Philadelphia Pennsylvania United States of America Sir and I will wear any thing I decide I want to wear and they ain't no body on this Earth got one thing to say bout it. I feel the same xact way Father, Wasskum said then went over there and started putting some Bee Honey on all them Scratches and Bruises he had on him and then, Papa said, I went over to o'Arlon and said Well you in a Fix now ain't you Arlon. I been in a Fix all my Whole Life he said. It don't mean nothing to me. They gonna Hang you and I'm gonna be a'Standing right there a'watching for what you done to Little Missey, I said. Watch all you want, Arlon said, I don't care a Lick. I hope they give me the Quirt when they ready, Papa said. Why I'll Quirt that Horse right out from under you then watch you Dance on the End a'the Rope til you can't Dance a'nother step. Oh I could taste that copper Taste in my mouth, he said, and meant ever word of it. I wouldn't go counting my Chickens fore they Hatch if I was you Mister, o'Arlon said then give me a'couple a'them Down Up Down Up Blinks and a Grin.

*F*RITZ AND O'POSSUM NEVER SAID NOTHING bout it to warn us that night, Papa said, but next morning Arlon and Mister Yancy was both gone and the Ropes that been a'holding Arlon tight was cut up and scattered all over the place. Your Daddy don't have no idea in the World what he got his self into a'letting that Boy go, Calley said. Wouldn't

s sir it was o'Arlon they had...

surprise me we find him out there somewheres in the Cactuses with a Knife in his Heart or a Hole in his Head. I know it, Wasskum said, but he's my Daddy and I gotta go find him. And us there right long with you Calley said ain't that Right and I said Yes Sir that is Right, Papa said. So we saddled up, he said, and a'way we did go and I could tell o'Wasskum was scared to Death a'what we might find when we did find him. You Daddy and my mean o'Daddy was a'lot a'like I reckon I said, Papa said, Both of em just wants us to go Home and work ain't that Right. Mine just wants me to be Him, Wasskum said. A Yancy always got some body else to do the Work and then the Yancy don't have to do much sides count the Money and stick it down they Pocket. Old Karl put his Money in a Hole under the Burn Pile out there by the Barn, Papa said, and I reckon it'd still be there if we hadn't a'found it after my Momma's Horse Precious bout bit his Head off and killed him. We never had nothing like that in my Family, o'Wasskum said. I guess closest we ever come to it was when o'Commodore our Dog bit Father one day when he was trying to keep him from eating his new Pair a'shoes from Mayweathers in London. Maybe you'll get you a pair a'Mayweathers some day you self, he said, even if they won't last you moren a day or two in this Country you got round here. You love your Daddy, Wasskum said. Mister Pearsall's my Daddy, Papa said. No I mean your real Daddy, he said. I never had no real Daddy, Papa said, Mister Pearsall's the only Daddy I ever had and he's good enough to last me I reckon. Do you love you Daddy I said, Papa said, and he said Yes Sir I do love my Daddy but all my Daddy knows in the World is how to be a Yancy and all I wanna know is How to be a Artist. What you gonna do when we find him, Papa said. Well if he's still a'live after that Boy gets through with him I'm gonna tell him to just Go on back Home and leave me a'lone, he said. And what if he ain't still a'Live, I said. O'Wasskum give it a good long thought then Oh his Eyes just went to shining and he said Well I reckon that'd just Break my Heart is What. And right then, Papa said, Calley hollered Yonder comes some body and Bessa my Coola look who it is.

WHY IT WAS O'PELO BLANCO

was who it was, Papa said, and he had Mister Benton Yancy a'hobbling long side a'him but didn't look like Mister Yancy could take but maybe just one more step fore he dropped down Dead on the ground. Father, o'Wasskum hollered, Father Father Father then run over there to him fast as he could and when me and Calley and Fritz and Possum got over there Why o'Wasskum was already a'holding his Daddy in his arms and just a'crying like a Baby. That Boy put his Knife in me and tried to Murder me, Mister Yancy said. You was right bout him being a Criminal and I'm sorry I said you wadn't. Yes Sir, Calley said, you oughta be Sorry a'talking like that to your own Son when you didn't know nothing bout it. I said I'm sorry Mister, Mister Yancy said, I take it all back and ever other Bad Thing I ever said to you in my Life. You go on and be a Artist if you want to and I won't say one Word against it, he said. I got all the time in the World to be a Artist, Wasskum said, only thing I got to do now is get you to a Doctor. Put some Bee Honey on it I said, Papa said, but they was Blood Bubbles just a'bubbling out his Chest where Arlon went and stabbed him. I don't think that Man is going to Live too much longer you know it, o'Pelo said. You want me to say some Words over him before he dies. We want you to just be Quiet you god dam o'Red Face Story Stealing Son of a Bitch, Calley said. Here let me Help You Mister Yancy he said and tried to wipe the Bubbles off with his Bandana but they still come a'Bubbling up. I'm taking you to a Doctor Daddy, Wasskum said. I don't wanna go to a Doctor, Mister Yancy said, I wanna stay here with you Son. He ain't staying here, Calley said, He just tole you he's a'taking you to a Doctor so get you self up on that Horse Mister or you ain't gonna make it in time. You're just Right as you can be Mister Pearsall, Mister Yancy said, Now if you'll just help me a'board we'll be a'way and a Pleasure to meet you Sir. He give Calley and me both a Hand Shake, Papa said, then we ooched him up on his Horse and o'Wasskum climbed up behind him and put his Arms round his Daddy to hold him on tight so he wouldn't fall off on they Trip. Good Luck, Calley said, Good Luck to you both. And I said the same thing, Papa said, then give em a salute like we was all in the Navy. Then here in a minute, he said, o'Wasskum turned round and blowed o'Possum a little Kiss Good Bye and o'Possum went to crying bout it then give each one a'us a Look Good Bye his self and went a'trotting off after o'Wasskum and his Daddy and now, Papa said, It was o'Fritz went to crying cause there went his o'Friend Possum and he didn't reckon he was ever gonna see him again in his Life.

*O*H AND THEN,
Papa said, Why o'Calley took a'holt a'o'Pelo and give him the Snake Eyes.
Where's Pela at, he said, you better not a'done nothing to her Mister then
o'Pelo give him his own Snake Eyes back and said Her and this other Girl
is a'Singing and Dancing for Coins in Senyora Garza's Place over in San Antoneya and they's both a'getting Rich at it. Where'd this Other Girl come
from, Calley said, I didn't even know Pela knowed one. Oh she just come
a'running down the Street one day cause her o'Granny up and died on her
and she needed a Friend. I don't know how I knowed it, Papa said, but I
knowed it was Annie he was a'talking bout and she was running down the
street cause she was a'looking for me. Was her name Annie I said, Papa said,
Annie Oster. I don't have no Idea was it or not, o'Pelo said. You'd need to go
ask her bout it you self. Then he put his Hand down his Pants and come out
with his Pistol to see he had some Bullets in it. I'm on the trail to find that
Bad Boy fore some body else does, he said. I figgur I do just one Great Big
Good Thing it's gonna be bettern doing all them Little Good Things I been
a'doing to keep from setting on that Flat Rock down there in Hell. What
bout Pela, Calley said, You didn't just run off and leave her Singing and
Dancing in San Antoneya did you. Yes Sir I did, o'Pelo said, I ain't got time
for no Woman. You mean you set Pela Free and give her Her Word back That
what you mean. Well what was I gonna do with it, o'Pelo said. Sides that, he
said, I figgur maybe they'll count it in my Favor when they go to counting
up all the Good Things I done. Then, Papa said, o'Pelo stuck his Pistol back
down his Pants and went a'walking off South and Mister Pearsall said Even
if he does catch that Boy I don't believe it's gonna be nough to make up for
all them Bad Things he done in his Life but I do admire the Ugly o'Son of a
Bitch for a'trying it don't you and I said Yes Sir I do, Papa said.

*A*IN'T YOU WORRIED
o'Pelo's gonna catch Arlon fore we do, Papa said, Maybe we oughta tied him
to a Rock or some thing to slow him down some. No I ain't worried, Calley
said, Why o'Pelo don't even know where to look. Mexico same as us, Papa
said, ain't that where o'Arlon's a'going. Calley shaked his head No and said
Not less he's looking for six seven Bullets in his cabeza for murdering that

Mexkin Family and they poor o'Dog that day out there in they Field. That's one thing you might wanna put in your Sack to remember bout Mexkins, he said. They ain't no body on Earth Loves they Family moren a'Mexkin does and if you do Bad Harm to One Why it's like you done Bad Harm to the Whole Bunch and Listen Here Senyor they gonna get you back for it just sures o'Bobby Lee's Momma whistles Dixie. Well if o'Arlon ain't a'going to Mexico, Papa said, Where you reckon he is a'going. I know xactly where he's a'going, Calley said, then pointed his Finger way out yonder in the Direction he was talking bout. Bout two three Days in that Direction yonder, he said, to where the o'Devil keeps all the Lost Souls they ever was in the World. The Devil's Sinkhole o'Calley said then took his John B off and fanned his self with it cause of a sudden it was getting Hot round here just talking bout it. And then, Papa said, Why o'Fritz scooted back on his Hiney and went Heh Heh Heh but they wadn't nothing Funny bout it this time. I think you went and scared o'Fritz with all this talk bout the Devil you know it I said, Papa said. Oh I don't reckon o'Fritz got any thing to worry bout, Calley said, Why I doubt the o'Devil'd want him even if we was to tie a Bow round his Tail and stick a Flower in his Ear. You always got a Joke ain't you Mister Pearsall, Papa said. The Devil's Sinkhole ain't no Joke if that's what you thinking, Calley said. It ain't just Some Place some body made up to scare the Little Chilrens with. No Sir, he said, it's a real Place all right and it will scare the Hairs right off the Top a'your Head to where they go a'running off down the Road and don't never even look back. You must a'been down in there you self huh Mister Pearsall, Papa said, to know so much bout it. No Sir, Calley said, ain't no body ever gone down in there that ever come back out again that I know of. Well how you know so much then, Papa said. Well when I run out a'what I do know I just make up some more to go long with it and pretty much ever time it turns out that's Right too. That don't make no Sense, Papa said, How you figgur that. I can't say I know, he said, I reckon I just know moren I know I know and then when I need to know some more why here it comes to me. It's like this here, Calley said, I know Pela Rosa is a'waiting for me back in San Antoneya but what I don't know is the Particulars of our Happy Life together after me and you put the Budge on that little Son of a Bitch Arlon Clavic for what he done to our Little Missey. So I just been making em up in my Head, he said. What Particulars tween you and Pela Rosa you talking bout, Papa said, but o'Calley said Oh No Sir not for you Mister.

169

WELL IT'S JUST YOU AND ME AGAIN

now ain't it Amigo, Calley said, when me and him and o'Fritz went a'riding on off next morning to go find Arlon and stop his Bad Deeds. How long we been a'riding together like this any how he said and I said, Papa said, I don't have no Idea how long Mister Pearsall but I'd reckon it is somewheres round seventeen twenty years if it's a Day. Why how can that be he said, Papa said, Hell you ain't even that Old you self yet are you. Well maybe I am and maybe I ain't, Papa said, I don't know. You don't know how Old you are, Calley said and I said, No Sir I don't know how Old I am. Well how Old was you on your last Birthday then, he said. When was that, Papa said. No body ever tole me it even come round. Maybe we just gonna have to give you a Birthday, Calley said, Tell me One you like bettern all them others. Well I don't know, Papa said. Why Hell just make one up then, Calley said, it ain't ever body in the World gets to name they own Birthday. When was o'Genral Lee's Birthday, I said. Oh I don't know, Calley said, I think it was in January some time but I wadn't there to know what Day. Well that's the One I want if I get to name one for my self, Papa said. Okay, Calley said, we'll just say your Birthday is January the Something til we know January the What how bout that. Okay, Papa said. So, Calley said, how old was you last January the Something and then went to laughing like I knowed more bout how old I was now'n I did a minute or two ago when it first come up. You always got a Joke ain't you Mister Pearsall I said, Papa said, but then when o'Calley got over laughing bout that one too he said This ain't no Joke what we're a'going to do now you know it. You mean going to the Devil's Sinkhole to catch o'Arlon. That is xactly what I mean, he said, you ain't scared are you. Oh No Sir, I ain't scared a'Lick I said, Papa said, but I had to reach down and give o'Fritz a'Pet so o'Calley wouldn't see I was shaking so Bad I was bout to cry. Well by god I am, he said. Fact is I'm so scared I'm bout to Dirty my Pants and have to go buy me a'new Pair back at the Joske Store in San Antoneya. You ain't scared, Papa said, you just Joking me again ain't you. Why you the Bravest Man I ever did see in all my Life Mister Pearsall, I said. Brave don't mean you ain't scared, Calley said, No Sir he said, Brave means it don't matter how god dam Scared you are you just gonna jump right over it and go do what you know in your Heart you gotta go do any how. Ain't that how you see it too, he said and I said, Well I'm a'trying to see it that way Mister Pearsall. Well you ain't turned round and gone Home have you, Calley said and I said, No

Sir not yet I ain't. O'Calley reached over and pulled o'Sister up and said You go on Home now if you want to I won't never say nothing bout it. Oh and I might a'done just that, Papa said, but of a sudden here come that Copper Taste up in my mouth for what o'Arlon done to Little Missey and it was like some o'German Black Smith took a'holt a'my Ear and wadn't never gonna let go til we put o'Arlon Clavic back down in Hell where he come from in the First Place. No Sir I ain't a'going Home, Papa said, and give Sister my heels then here in a minute o'Calley and Firefoot catched up and Calley said Oh I do like to travel round with my Brave Friends. Then, Papa said, he give me a Smile and tipped his John B Stetson Hat like I was one a'them Brave Friends he been a'talking bout so I tipped my John B back at my o'Amigo and give him a Smile a'my own.

AFTER BOUT A'NOTHER DAY AND A HALF, Papa said, Sister tole me she didn't wanna go no further by jumping round all the time and trying to go back Home. Sister don't wanna go no more I said, Papa said. Maybe you got your Momma's Saddle on wrong and its a'pinching her, Calley said. No Sir I don't never get my Saddle on wrong, Papa said, I think maybe she just don't wanna go to the Devil's Sinkhole is all. No Sir and not me neither, Calley said, but that's Where we a'going any how ain't it if we wanna catch that Boy and we dam sure do wanna catch him don't we. Yes Sir we do, Papa said, I don't see why o'Arlon had to go and do all them Bad Things any how do you. No Sir and I don't reckon he could tell you neither, Calley said, even if we was all setting down at the table drinking us a glass a'Grape Juice together. Maybe he was just borned that way huh, Papa said, Maybe he didn't never have no Choice bout it. Course I don't claim to know for sure, Calley said, but No Sir I don't believe the Big Lord God a'Mighty'd ever say You gonna be a Bad Man to one Fella and You gonna be a Good Man to another. No Sir, he said, I think he just says You Choose Mister then cuts us all a'loose in the World and gets out the Way. And then what happens, Papa said, after the Big Lord God All Mighty cuts us all a'loose. Why then we got to make up our own Mine and Choose what kind a'Life we gonna Live from then on out. Like for xample, he said, One Man might Choose him a Life a'setting out there on his Front Porch a'smoking his Pipe and Another

One might Choose him a Life where he's a'working on his Farm ever day and a'making some thing of his self. Where'd he get that Farm he's a'working on, Papa said. Well I reckon he just Choosed it when the Big Lord God a'Mighty tole him It's Your Turn to Choose Mister, Calley said. Just like that and he got him a Farm huh I said, Papa said, and o'Calley snapped his Finger and said Yes Sir just like that I reckon. So what'd you Choose when it come Your Turn to Choose Mister Pearsall, Papa said. Well, Calley said, First Thing was I wanted to be borned here in Texas like all my People was fore me and next thing was I wanted to have me a Good Horse and a Good Dog and I got o'Firefoot here the Best Horse they ever was in the World but the Tonks et my Little Dog that Night remember I tole you that Sad Story bout it. Yes Sir, Papa said, I do remember you did. After they got him out from under the Porch where he was a'sleeping ain't that Right. And a'course, Calley said, I wanted all the Girls to like me but that wadn't never no Problem that I could tell and still ain't is it. How'd you go bout Choosing, Papa said. Oh best I recall I just made Pitchurs a'what I wanted in my Head, Calley said, and then all them things I made Pitchurs of in my Head just come to me Simple as Pie I reckon. Even fore you was borned you was already making up Pitchurs in you Head a'what you wanted in your Life huh, Papa said. Yes Sir I reckon I was, Calley said, how else you figgur I could a'done it. I don't have no idea How Else, Papa said, I reckon you'd be the one to know bout that cause you was the one a'doing the Choosing wadn't you. Well I just done it I reckon, Calley said. That was so Long ago I can't hardly even remember it no more.

*T*HE CLOSER WE GOT to the Devil's Sinkhole, Papa said, the more Hard it was to get Sister and o'Firefoot to go. And, he said, o'Fritz wadn't Happy bout it neither. Our Amigos here is a'getting Persnickety bout our Trip ain't they, Calley said, Maybe we oughta just left em at Home. Where's that at, Papa said. It ain't nowhere, Calley said, It's just some thing Funny I said, he said. You got a Bad Habit a'listening too close you know it. I just meant we ain't got no Home is all, Papa said. I know what you meant, Calley said, That's what's Funny bout what I just said. We ain't got no Pet Buffalo neither but I didn't say nothing bout that cause it don't Pertain does it. Let's just be quiet bout it here for a'minute okay, he said. Okay I said, Papa said, and then we didn't none a'us talk no more and it was like we was a bunch a'little Mices a'riding cross the Country with our Mouth tied shut. Oh but then, he said, we all heared this Door Squeek and it bout scared us out our Pants. Who's that Squeeking that Door, Papa said, but fore o'Calley could answer me back why they was a'nother hunderd Doors started a'Squeeking and then Oh the whole World went a'Squeeking like it was about to come off the Hinge. What is that I hollered, Papa said, and o'Calley put his Hands round his Mouth and hollered back It's either all them poor lost Souls a'Crying cause they can't get out the Devil's Sinkhole or It's bout nine hundered million and six Bats a'wanting to go catch they Suppers fore they go back to bed. Then of a sudden, Papa said, we looked and Way Way Way off out yonder come this Big Black Whirled Wind a'Bats just a'Squeeking and a'Screeching and a'Screaming up out the Ground and Calley said See what I told you Mister. Oh I didn't like it worth a Lick, Papa said. They ain't gonna try and eat us too are they I said. No you too Skinny and I'm too Pretty and I don't reckon they'd want o'Fritz there even if we was to serve him on a plate with a big Red Apple a'sticking out his Mouth like them Romes usted to do back in the Olden Days. I don't believe our Horse gonna go another step with all them Bats a'flying round out here, Papa said. Well we gonna have to go on without em then ain't we, Calley said. So, Papa said, We grabbed our Ropes off our Saddle and went a'walking through the Cactuses and Mesquites toward where all them Bats was still a'Squeeking up out a'the Ground to go find they Suppers and Oh when we got to there, he said, Why the Devil's Sinkhole was so big round you could just barely see the other side but Calley said You think it's some thing how Wide it is just come over here and lookee how Deep. So we crawled up to the Edge a'the Sinkhole and looked down in it and Oh it was so Deep you couldn't no way see the Bottom and when o'Calley dropped a Rock in Why you almost never heared it hit the Bottom neither. Oh that's Deep ain't it Mister Pearsall, Papa said. Yes Sir Deep Deep Deep, Calley said, and they say if you listen real close some time you can hear all them Lost Souls at the Bottom just a'Hollering and a'Crying bout it. I don't hear no Lost Soul a'Hollering and a'Crying, Papa said. Might help some if you'd just Hush and Listen a minute then, Calley said, Why don't you try that. So, Papa said, I cupped my Hand round my Ear and me and o'Fritz leaned way out over the Sinkhole to listen but I didn't hear no body. I don't hear no Lost Soul down there Mister Pearsall, Papa said, I don't know where you got that Story. Then, he said, I dropped another Rock down the Hole just for the Fun of it and grabbed o'Fritz to go but then Oh some body way down there Hollered STOP throwing them ROCKS on Me or I'm gonna come up there and wring your SKINNY NECK for You.

*Y*OU KNOW WHO THAT IS DON'T YOU, Calley said. No Sir I don't have no Idea, Papa said. Why that's the Lostest god dam Soul they ever was in the World that's who that is, o'Calley said, And bout the ugliest one too he said then pitched a'nother three four Rocks down the Hole and hollered Better look out down there Senyor Blanco the Skys bout to Fall in on you. Oh and then, Papa said, they was a BOOM from down there in the Hole and a Bullet come a'whistling up pass our Ear and scared some more Bats off the Wall. You better stop that shooting Mister fore I come down there and talk to you bout it, Calley hollered, you hear me. That wadn't me Mister, o'Pelo hollered back. I'm just setting out here on this rock in the middle a'all this Bat Quache a'bleeding to death. I'm Sorry, Calley hollered, I didn't know that til you tole me just now. Where'd he shoot you any how. Here in my arm, o'Pelo hollered. Well I hope you shot him back for it didn't you, Calley said. I will when I get the chancet but right now I ain't even got no idea where he is. Oh and then they was a'nother BOOM down there, Papa said, and o'Pelo hollered THERE HE IS THERE HE IS and then they was a'nother BOOM BOOM BOOM and then another BOOM and then Nothing. You get him or not, o'Calley hollered down the Hole but didn't no Holler come back. You don't reckon that Boy got the ugly o'SonofaBitch in sted do you Calley said and I said, Papa said, wouldn't Surprise me a'Lick if he did I reckon. No me neither, Calley said then set back and twirled his Spur Ching e Ching e ChingChingChing. Well ain't nothing to do but go down there and See I reckon, he said, If o'Pelo ain't Dead we wouldn't want him to lose that Arm would we. You just stay here and keep your Ear tucked in okay. Oh that did sound Good to me, Papa said, but No Sir I said I'm a'going down there with you Mister Pearsall you might could use a Hand. You ain't scared that Boy down there might Murder you like he been a'Murdering ever body else round here, he said. Yes Sir I am scared a'that, Papa said, but

...Oh it was so Deep you couldr.
no way see the Bottom

I'm just gonna have to jump over it for Little Missey and see whether he does or not. Well may be you oughta go First then, o'Calley said, I ain't sure I'm that Brave my self.

SO WE TIED OUR ROPES TOGETHER over a Stump and threw the Other End down the Hole, Papa said, but it didn't come no wheres near reaching Bottom so I said You ain't planning on us a'jumping the last Mile or two off this Rope to the Bottom are you Mister Pearsall but o'Calley was already a'sliding on down the Rope and said When I get to the end a'this Rope you just slide on down and set you self down on my shoulder til we see What we do after that. So, Papa said, I went a'sliding on down the Rope til I was a'setting there on his shoulder like he said and Oh now I seen the inside a'the Sinkhole curved way back in there like the inside a'some o'Jug and they wadn't no Wall you could reach out and grab holt of to pull youself over on. Oh and poor o'Fritz was up there at the top just a'whining cause we couldn't do no moren just dangle out there in the empty Air. Fritz ain't so sure bout this I said, Papa said, but Calley just went to pumping his legs To and Fro To and Fro and then I did too and then here in a minute, he said, we was just a'swinging Back and Forth Back and Forth out over the Bottom a'the Hole with all them Bats a'flapping by so close you could a'reached out and grabbed you one if you'd a'knowed what to do with it oncet you did. Pump, o'Calley hollered, PUMP PUMP PUMP. And Oh we did Pump, Papa said, but ever time we reached out to grab a'holt a'the Wall to pull our self over on Why the Rock give way and went a'falling to the Bottom and they wadn't nothing to do but just keep a'pumping Back and Forth Back and Forth out over that Hole to where Mister Pearsall finally said I think maybe we in some Trouble here don't you and I was bout to say Yes Sir I do believe we in some Trouble here When of a sudden I looked over there to the Wall when we come a'Pumping close by and Why there was my o'Amigo Mister Pegleg just a'Shining and a'Shimmering on this little Rock Ledge and I hollered Over There Over There so, Papa said, we Pumped and we Pumped and we Pumped and next thing you knowed we grabbed a'holt a'the Wall and stepped out on this little Rock Ledge Mister Pegleg a'showed me. Then, Papa said, o'Calley hanged our Rope over a Rock to where we

176

could find it again and went to scattering Bugs and Rats and some Critters I didn't even know nothing bout and went to climbing on down in the Sinkhole. How you reckon we ever gonna get back out a'this Hole again in our Life I said, Papa said. I ain't got no Idea, Calley said, but Listen here Mister I'm sure gonna be Glad when that's all we got to worry bout ain't you.

OH WE CLIMBED DOWN DOWN DOWN, Papa said, then just bout when we got to thinking they wadn't no more Down we could climb Why there we was at the Bottom a'the Hole and Oh the Rats and Scorpins just went a'scattering ever which way and all kind a'other little Critters did too but the Thing got my Eye, he said, was the Floor was just a'Twisting and a'Turning and a'Going this Way and That Way like a Big o'River and it didn't smell so good neither. What is this here I said, Papa said. That's that Bat Quache o'Pelo was talking bout here a minute or so ago, Calley said. You ain't a'telling me that's Bat Do come a'Live and gone running round like this are you, Papa said. No what you a'seeing is bout a hunderd Million and three Little o'Bat Bugs Skating round in there on the Quache, Calley said. If you was to step off Bare Foot in it Why they'd eat you toes right off you Feet fore you could even holler Whoopsees, he said. Just take a Look over yonder you don't believe me and when I looked, Papa said, Why they was Bones scattered all over big as Trees and some of em Two Three times biggern that. I reckon they from them Olden Times same as that o'Antique Rock Aligater Head we found that time in Landa's Pasture was, Calley said, Remember that. I said Yes Sir I do remember that, Papa said, that's when me and you and my Brother Herman first met. Oh and then of a sudden o'Pelo hollered from some wheres way out there in the Dark There He Is There He Is and then they was a BOOM BOOM BOOM and a Bullet come a'flying and took o'Calley's John B right off his Head and then they was a'nother BOOM BOOM BOOM from some wheres else over there in the Dark and o'Calley pulled his big o'Pistola out his Pants and let go a BOOM BOOM BOOM up in the Air his self. You see some thing I said, Papa said, but Calley said No I'm just shooting my Gun off cause ever body else is that's all. Oh and then, Papa said, o'Pelo hollered WATCH OUT WATCH OUT then here come a'nother BOOM and a Bullet blowed some

Quache up on us then next thing they was a big OOOOH OH OOOOH and a big CAPLONK CAPLONK and Calley said That sounds to me like One of em knocked the Other One in the Quache but I can't tell which one just by the sound a'it. No Sir me neither, Papa said. So we rooted round and made us some Fire Sticks to see in the Dark and went a'looking round in there to see but No we couldn't find em neither one but we did find the Rock where o'Pelo been a'setting cause they was Blood all over on it from when o'Arlon shot him in his Arm and maybe some other place too.

OH WE LOOKED AND WE LOOKED, Papa said, but we couldn't find o'Arlon or o'Pelo neither one no wheres down there in the Devil's Sinkhole. Well they just Up and Disappeard on us like a Ghost didn't they, Calley said. But then, Papa said, I looked over yonder hind one a'them Big o'Antique Rock Bones and they was a Water Hole back there and I said Mister Pearsall I think I might know where they maybe went. So o'Calley come over there and said Where's that and I said Why down in this Water Hole here is Where and then Calley studied it a minute and said Yes Sir you might just be Right then kicked his Boots off and shed his pants and ever thing else too cep his underwears and said You stay here I'll write you a Letter first chance I get if I find em then jumped on in and wadn't nothing left but Bubbles where he went. And then Oh Boy Hidy I got scared What if my o'Amigo Calley Pearsall drowns down under there and don't never come back again then I started counting off the seconds he was gone and when I got to Twenty Six I went to a'shucking my Pants off cause by Thirty I decided I was a'going in to save my Friend if I could but at Twenty Nine Why o'Calley come up out a'the water again just a'Spitting and a'Blowing and said They's a'nother Hole down there in the Bottom a'this Hole just a little too Little for me to go a'swimming through. But just bout right for a Boy a'Arlon's size huh, Papa said. Yes Sir, o'Calley said, just bout that size. Well it's just bout my size too then ain't it, Papa said. What difference it make, o'Calley said, You ain't a'going down there any how. Yes Sir I am I am, Papa said. Don't worry I'll write you a Letter first chance I get. Oh he give me a Look then and squeezed my shoulder. I'm gonna miss you if you don't come back Mister, Calley said, you know that don't you. Yes Sir I do know it, Papa said, and I'm gonna miss you too Mister Pearsall. You a'wasting Time, he said, Now get a'going.

*L*AST THING I DONE, Papa said, was give o'Fritz a wave Goodbye up there at the top a'the Sinkhole then set my John B down on a Rock to keep it Dry and jumped on in. Oh the Fish down there under the Water wadn't nothing like any Fish I ever seen fore in my Life Why they had Thorns on em like Cactuses and Horns like some o'Billy Goat and some thing tole me Don't Touch em Don't Touch em then here in a minute I seen that Hole in the Bottom a'the Hole o'Calley been a'talking bout and I was just the right size to go a'swimming right on through without no trouble and Oh they was Big Antique Rock Animal Heads and Feet just bout everwheres you looked and more Arra Heads'n you could shake a stick at and then of a sudden the Water grapped a'holt a'me and next thing, Papa said, I was a'Spinning and a'Going down this long Tunnel like I been caught in a Whirled Wind somewheres but No Sir it was Whirled Water I was caught in this time and that Tunnel started a'getting Littler and Littler til I was a'Bumping and a'Bouncing off the side and what I was thinking now was Oh Boy Hidy I wish I'd a'never jumped in here but then when I was bout to go Loonie from it that Whirled Water throwed me up on this Shore somewheres and I looked up and there was the Sky and up in the Sky Why there was the World just a'spinning round and then, Papa said, I looked over there and yonder was my o'Amigo Mister Pegleg just a'Shimmering in front a'this Dark o'Cave went way back in there some where and I give him a Hug to say Hidy and he give me a Lick to say Hidy back like that other time I come down here in my Dream and seen my mean o'Daddy a'setting on that Flat Rock. Oh and then, he said, I follered Mister Pegleg on in the Cave and they was other Caves run off from this One in ever which Direction and Oh they was neckid People in ever one of em and they was all a'Crying and a'Moaning and a'Hollering and a'Pulling they Hair out and a'Bugging they Eyes like the End a'the World just like that first Time and they was the Saddest People I ever did see in all my Life. But, Papa said, o'Mister Pegleg just went a'Hobbling right on pass and I had to trot to keep up and Oh we went Deeper Deeper Deeper down in the Cave til here in a minute Why there was my o'Daddy still a'setting on his Flat Rock and a'Crying in his Hands and a'Hollering Oh Poor Me Oh Poor Me O Poor Me but this time, he said, I seen bout ten hundered and nine other People a'setting on they own Flat Rock all over the Place and most of em was Men but some of em was Womens too and they was all colors White Black Brown Red Yeller kind a'Purply and they was Black Dominoes piled all round they Feet ever one of em And course, Papa said, they was all Crying bout it just like my poor o'Daddy was. Then some body hollered, What you a'doing in here Mister, and I looked over there and Why there was them same Seven Old Men a'setting at that Table had them stacks a'Black and White Dominoes on it. No Sir I ain't doing nothing, Papa said, just looking round. Wadn't you in here one time before, the o'Mexkin Man said, but we had to run you off cause you wadn't on our Lista yet ain't that Right. Yes Sir that's me I reckon, I said. So what you want now, the o'China Man said, we ain't got Time to fool with you Mister. I'm just looking round a'little is all, Papa said, I ain't hurting nothing. Well you like what you see, the o'Black Man said. You got any Question while we waiting for our next Job to start. Well, Papa said, I seen all them Womens a'setting out there on a Flat Rock long with all them Men but I don't see no Womens a'setting here at the Table with you and I's just wondering Why's that. Cause they ain't no such thing as a Woman that's Why, the o'White Man said. Course, the o'Black Man said, they ain't no such thing as a Man neither. In the Beginning, he said, They was just this One got broke in Two and Half a'it come out a Woman and the other Half come out a Man and ever since then them Two Halfs been a'trying to get back together again and when they do Why that's where Ever Body Else come from. Oh and then, Papa said, All them Seven Old Men just went to wiggling they Eye Brows up and down and bout fell out they chairs on the Floor a'laughing. Yall got a Funny Bone bout it ain't you, Papa said. Well it's Funny all them Halfs jumping on Top a'each other to make a new Whole One again. And not only that, the Old China Man said, but all the Hollering and Wiggling they do when they at it is Funny too.

OH THEN HERE COME TWO SHIMMERY PEOPLE, Papa said, and one of em was o'Arlon Clavic and the other one was Pelo Blanco and, he said, o'Pelo looked bout scared to Death even if he was already Dead but o'Arlon was just a'Grinning Ear to Ear like some little o'Possum found him a piece a'Watermelon to eat out there in the Road. Then the Old Inyin Man pointed at Arlon and said Come on over here a minute and set down We wanna hear what you got to say for you self. So, Papa said, o'Arlon went over there and set down in the Chair had all them Black and White Dominoes on the Table in front a'it. I hope this ain't gonna take long, Arlon said, I got other Fish to Fry here in a minute. Oh them Old Men did laugh bout that, Papa said, then the Old China Man said You got to tell us bout all the Good Things you done in your Life and then you got to tell us bout all the Bad Things you done in your Life and it's our Job to see how they stack up one a'gainst the other fore we can turn you a'Loose for a'nother Try. Or not the Old Black Man said and then, Papa said, all them other Old Men nodded they Head Yes Sir that is xactly Right Mister. So o'Arlon said some thing bout some thing Good he done and grabbed him a White Domino for it and then said some thing else bout some thing he done but this time them Old Men wouldn't let him have a White Domino for it but give him a Black Domino for it in sted and then, Papa said, when o'Arlon thought they wadn't looking he tried to sneak him another White Domino but the Old Mexkin Man seen it and slapped his Hand for him and took it back. Oh and then, Papa said, o'Arlon just went to grabbing at them White Dominoes but them Old Men wouldn't have it and grabbed em back ever time and give him a Black Domino in sted and wadn't long and o'Arlon had this great big Stack a'Black Dominoes in front a'him for all the Bad Things he done in his Life but not hardly no White Ones for the Good Things he done and I thought Well I reckon that's Fair ain't it but then o'Arlon give me a Look his Eyes just a'blinking Down Up Down Up like that o'Lizert and said Ain't you gonna help me Amigo but that o'Copper Taste come up in my Mouth like a Flood for what he done to Little Missey and all them other People and I said Oh No Sir Not Any at all No Sir. But when I said it, Papa said, Why I could tell my Eyes was starting to blink Down to Up Down to Up just like his was and Oh it come to me then I better shed my Hate Quicks I can fore it turns me into One a'him and I can't never turn it back round to who I was in the First Place. Oh and then, he said, them Old Men pointed over there to the Corner where they was a big pile a'Flat Rocks and told o'Arlon to go over there and pick him out one he liked cause he was gonna be a'setting on it from here to

Kingdom Come but o'Arlon just went to laughing bout it like some o'Loonie then looked over at me his Eye Lids just a'going Down Up Down Up Down Up and said I'm gonna come back up There one a'these Days and get you for being a False Friend to me cause that's the Worsted Crime they ever was in the World and that's what you done to me. Oh and then he went over there and picked him out a Flat Rock he liked and went over there and set down on it beside my Mean o'Daddy. And when he did, Papa said, that Old China Man waved at poor o'Pelo Blanco a'standing there to come on over and set down at the Table and tell em bout all the Good Things and all the Bad Things he done in his Life so they could see how they stacked up one against the other and tell him if he needed to go pick him out a Flat Rock to set on or not. Then, he said, all them Old Men looked over at me and said Good Bye Mister we don't never wanna see you down here again til it's your Time you hear. And I said Yes Sir I do hear, Papa said, and then me and o'Mister Pegleg went on off and in a minute we was back at that Water Hole where I come from.

I GIVE MISTER PEGLEG SOME HUGS
to say Good Bye to my o'Amigo, Papa said, and he give me some Licks back for it and it bout made me cry to leave him but I jumped back in the Hole and Oh that Whirled Water grabbed a'holt a'me again but this time it was a'Whirling the other Direction and now the Fish I seen didn't have no Thorns on em and no Billy Goat Horns neither. Oh and then, he said, I seen all them People o'Arlon Murdered a'swimming long side me I reckon to make sure I got back to Calley safe. O'Superintendent Shettles and Mister Medcalf and that Man Arlon Murdered over in Kendalia long time ago and then that Mexkin Family and they poor o'Dog he Murdered out there in they Field and then some other Ones I reckon he Murdered when wadn't no body else looking and then Oh, Papa said, Oh and then here come Little Missey and her o'Pet Panther a'swimming right up close but not only them, he said, but now her Little Boy Bomonee was with em too and Little Missey reached out her Hand to me and I reached out my Hand to her and when we touched Why of a sudden it wadn't her Hand no more but was o'Calley's Hand in sted and he pulled me right back up out the water to where I started out from.

...I seen all them People o'Arlon Murdered
a'swimming long side...

They dead I said, Papa said, o'Arlon and Pelo Blanco both. You ain't telling me nothing I don't already know, o'Calley said then handed me my John B and pointed his Finger out cross that River a'Bat Do to where bout ten million and seven o'Bat Bugs was just a'eating away on o'Pelo's Bones while he was a'hugging o'Arlon's Bones tight to his self. I figgur what happened, Calley said, was o'Pelo grabbed him when o'Arlon went to shooting at us and took him on down under the Quache with his self to save our Life. And may be his own Soul too while he was at it huh, he said. I don't know did he or not, Papa said, o'Pelo was just a'setting down at the Table with them Old Men to talk bout it when they tole me I had to go on and go. I wish I'd a'been there with you, Calley said. Me and o'Pelo had our Differences but I'd a'tried to put in a Good Word for the Ugly o'SonofaBitch if I could a'come up with one he said then reached over and wiped the Quache off his Hat. Our o'John B's is starting to get em a History ain't they he said, Papa said.

WELL THEY AIN'T NOTHING LEFT TO DO,

o'Calley said, cep go back and get my Pela Rosa in San Antoneya and start our Happy Life together. And Annie too I said, Papa said. We ain't a'leaving her in Senyora Garza's Place to Sing and Dance for her suppers neither. No we ain't, o'Calley said, you don't have to worry bout that. Course we gotta get out a'here first I reckon don't you, he said. So, Papa said, I hollered We's a'coming Amigo at o'Fritz so he'd hush his crying up at the Top and we went to climbing the wall to where o'Calley left our Rope to climb back out the Devil's Sinkhole on but Oh No, Papa said, when we got up there Why our Rope wadn't there no more but was a'dangling out over the Hole bout six miles out our Reach. Well this is a piece a'Bad Luck ain't it, Calley said, I reckon them Hungry Bats knocked it a'loose on the way to get they Suppers. Maybe I can jump for it, Papa said. No Sir you ain't a Grass Hopper and I don't wanna have to climb down there again and fish you out the Bat Poot. Well what you reckon we gonna do then, Papa said. I don't have no Idea in the World what, Calley said. You tell me if you come up with some thing and I'll listen to ever word you say. No Sir, I don't have no Idea neither, Papa said. So we just set there bout a hour and then I said I don't wanna hurt your Feelings Mister Pearsall but wadn't you the one said Whatever you a'looking for in this World is some wheres out there in the World a'looking for you too. I ain't sure I ever said that or not, o'Calley said, I'm just trying to concentrate on the Future right now and not the Pass if you please Sir. Well the reason I ask it, Papa said, is we just setting here on this Rock a'looking for a way to get holt a'our Rope so we can climb on out the Sinkhole on it ain't that Right. I couldn't a'put it no Better my self, Calley said. Well I said, Papa said, Here it comes. Oh and then o'Calley looked where I was pointing at and our Rope started a'swinging Back and Forth Back and Forth out over the Hole and ever time it did Why it come closer and closer to where we could reach out and Grab it but not Quite. Oh and then Some body hollered up there at the Top a'the Hole Yall better grab that Rope I'm bout all wore out up here a'swinging it and Oh, Papa said, it was o'Marcellus a'doing the Hollering and the Rope Swinging both and next time the Rope come a'Swinging in close Why o'Calley jumped for it and grabbed a'holt but Oh went a'sliding on down the Rope and only thing saved him was the knot at the End broke his slide and then here in a minute he had a good Holt on the Rope and was a'pumping Back and Forth Back and Forth then come a'Swinging over to get me but Right then, Papa said, here come all them Bats back in the Sinkhole after they All Night Suppers and they was so many a'em I total lost o'Calley to sight but then I heared him a'hollering When I say Jump you Jump you hear me and then fore I could say Yes Sir I do hear you he hollered JUMP and Oh Boy Hidy, Papa said, I jumped just when o'Calley come to view through all them Bats.

*B*UT I JUMPED A LITTLE LOW, Papa said, and all I got holt of was o'Calley's Spurs and Oh now they really did go Ching e Ching e ChingChingChing and I all but lost my holt cause they was Twirling in my Hands but o'Calley reached down with one hand and pulled me up then squeezed me tight to him. You might wanna jump a'little Higher next time Mister he said and I said Yes Sir I will, Papa said, then we just hanged on tight as we could to each other with them screeching Bats bout to beat us to Death with they Wings just a'Flapping to get on back Home fore the Sun come up in the Morning. Oh and then, he said, of a sudden they was a little shake on the Rope and then next thing it started a'pulling us Up Up Up through all them Flapping Bats and Calley hollered Hang On Hang On and Oh I did Hang On for my Life and in just bout a year why we was up and out the Devil's Sinkhole and back in Texas again and now o'Fritz went to jumping on me and a'going Heh Heh Heh and then I seen o'Marcellus pulled us up out the Hole by tying our Rope on his Saddle Horn and o'Edward a'walking off with it. How'd you ever find us, Mister Pearsall said. O'Jeffey tole me to just keep a'going South til I seen this big o'Whirled Wind a'Bats and that'd be yall at the bottom of it and here you are. I'm surprised Miz Choat even let you go, Papa said. No she never, Marcellus said, I just up and went on my own. Well may be you better get on back fore she comes a'looking for you with her Bird Gun, Papa said, I wouldn't put it pass her. Ain't yall coming long with me, Marcellus said. It's hard to talk to just o'Edward all day. We headed up to San Antoneya first, Calley said, They's a'couple a'Ladies waiting for us there. O'Jeffey tole me she better not never catch me a'going in a Place like that or she gonna skin me a'live and throw the rest a'me to the Piggies. It ain't a Place like that Mister, o'Calley said, And Shame on you for ever a'thinking it. I wadn't thinking nothing Mister Pearsall, Marcellus said, if that's what you was a'thinking. No I didn't think you was, Calley said. But it don't never hurt to make sure does it. So, Papa said, we walked on back over there to where we left o'Firefoot and Sister yesterday when they wouldn't go no more and best we could tell they was glad to see us and we was them too. Well let's get a'going, o'Calley said, they's many the mile tween here and Senyora Garza's Place back in San Antoneya ain't they. So o'Fritz jumped up on Sister with me and a'way we all did go and then, Papa said, o'Marcellus said Mister Pearsall if Senyora Garza's Place ain't the kind a'Place I wadn't thinking it was then what kind a'Place is it. Well you gonna see for you self what kind a'Place it is here in a bit, Calley said, so stop worrying bout it so much okay. You mean they gonna let me in there Mister Pearsall, Marcellus said. No I mean if they won't let you in there, Calley said, why then by god I'm gonna let you in there my self.

WE COME A'RIDING INTO SAN ANTONEYA next day by where they Mexkin Market is, Papa said, and when we went a'riding by the Man a'selling the Sombreros I could tell o'Marcellus wanted him one cause there me and o'Calley was wearing our John Bs and him with just some o'Hand Me Down on his Head. Marcellus, Mister Pearsall said, I been wanting to treat you with some thing for a'getting us out the Sinkhole and it just come to me I might could do it by getting you a new Hat. You reckon that'd be okay with you. Oh Yes Sir, Marcellus said. You talking bout one like yall got huh. Well I reckon I could be if you don't like any a'them Fancy Dan Straw Sombreros that Mexkin got right over there. I usted to wear one just like that my self, Calley said, but the Pretty Girls wouldn't let me a'lone and I had to give it a'way almost fore it got broke in good. So we went over there, Papa said, and Marcellus picked him out one so big you couldn't hardly even tell they was some body under it. I like this one here, he said and o'Calley said, Yes Sir and it's gonna look a'lot better when you get a new pair a'Boots on your Feet to go long with it ain't it. And then, Papa said, we went over to a'nother Mexkin and o'Calley treated Marcellus to a pair a'Boots and Why o'Marcellus throwed his shoulders back and went to strutting round like o'Genral Lee just give him a Medal. I wish I had me some Spurs to put on these Boots here like you got Mister Pearsall, he said. Well Marcellus you work hard and save your money like I did and maybe one day you can go buy you self a Pair fore you get too old to wear em, o'Calley said. Course they ain't cheap, he said, and it may take you a'while but it'll give you some thing to do with your Life won't it. Yes Sir less you give me that pair you got when they wear out and you go buy you a new pair. Well now Marcellus I'm fraid that ain't never gonna happen, Calley said, cause I wouldn't have a pair a'Spurs that'd ever wear out on me in the First Place. You understand what I'm saying. Yes Sir I believe I do, Marcellus said, You a'saying I ain't getting no Spurs today am I. We ain't got time to talk bout it no more any how, Calley said, we got to get on down to Senyora Garza's Place and surprise the Ladies. So, Papa said, a'way we went on down the Street then here in a minute me and o'Calley put our John B's over our Heart cause we was bout to go pass the Alamo cause it was the Holiest Place in Texas and then Marcellus did his too but Oh then, he said, o'Fritz let out a Yelp and jumped off o'Sister and run over there behind a Bush and when he come back out a'gain, Papa said, Why he had o'Possum with him and Oh Boy Hidy we was glad to see him and he was us.

WELL POSSUM YOU A SURPRISE AIN'T YOU

I said, Papa said, Where's o'Wasskum and his Daddy a'keeping they self these days. But No, he said, o'Possum just set there while him and o'Fritz was a'sniffing round on each others Behind to say Hidy. I hope some thing ain't happened to em, Calley said. You don't never know do you. Well I don't believe o'Wasskum'd just run off and leave o'Possum to his self do you, Papa said. Not the o'Wasskum I know he wouldn't, Marcellus said, No Sir. So, Papa said, we looked all round for em but didn't have no Luck and figgured they went on back Home to Philadelphia but o'Possum didn't wanna go and just stayed here at Home. Well Calley said nothing left to do but get on over to Senyora Garza's Place and watch Pela Rosa fall down Dead when she sees me come a'walking in the Door and then, Papa said, we went a'riding on down the street o'Calley just a'grinning at the Future and I reckon me and o'Marcellus was too. What's the First Thing you gonna say when you see her Mister Pearsall, Marcellus said, You been planning on some thing. I'm probably gonna say Why Pela you a sight for sore Eyes ain't you, Calley said, you know some thing Sweet like that I reckon. Then o'Calley looked over at me, Papa said, and said How bout you Mister what you gonna say to you own little Sweet Heart. I don't know I might not say nothing, Papa said, I might wanna see what Annie got to say First. Oh No you don't never want a Woman to get the First Word in on you or you gonna be standing there til next Tuesday a'chewing on your Tongue cause they won't be nothing else to do with it, Calley said and Why o'Marcellus just went to laughing bout it. What you laughing bout, Papa said, you don't know nothing bout no Womens. Well I do now, Marcellus said, and I ain't gonna forget it neither. Oh and then, Papa said, o'Calley pulled o'Firefoot up short and said Why Lookee yonder by god and when we looked what we seen was that Little Bear tied to that Hitching Rail again like the first time me and o'Wasskum ever seen him but now he had some kind a'Iron contraption round his Head so he couldn't bite no body and one a'his Eyes was put out and that same Man a'wearing that High Hat was a'Poking him with his Pointy Stick again and laughing bout it and Calley reached out with his Foot and give that Man a little Kick on his Butt to get his attention and said I bet that little Bear don't like it you a'Poking him with that Stick like that but the Man just laughed and said Well how bout you mine your own Bidness Mister Fancy John B Stetson Hat. Course, Papa said, they was Men a'standing all round and they went to laughing at what that Man called Calley but o'Calley just stepped down off o'Firefoot easy as you please and said Any Body ever Poked you with a Sharp Stick like that Mister and the Man laughed like it was the funniest thing he ever did hear in his Life and said Nope and won't Never and then, Papa said, o'Calley said Well here's what it feels like Mister and Oh, Papa said, Why then o'Calley's Hand flew out like a Rattlesnake Bite and grapped that Pointy Stick right out the Man's Hand and give him a good Poke with it and Oh then a'nother and a'nother and a'nother and Oh Listen here, he said, that Man took off a'running down the Street to get a'way from all them Pokes but o'Calley run right after him just a'Poking and a'Poking him on his Butt til the Man slipped and fell down in some Horse Do and then went to crying bout it like some body's little Baby Boy and course, Papa said, all them other Men went to laughing at him all up and down the street to where you couldn't hardly keep from laughing at him you self. Oh I never seen nothing like it in all my Life, Papa said, and Marcellus hadn't neither cause him and Fritz and o'Possum all three was over there a'laughing too. And then, Papa said, Calley went over there and took that Contraption off from round that Little Bear's Head and undid the knot to set him Free but No that Little One Eyed Bear didn't wanna go Free cause he had him a Friend now and he wadn't bout to run off and leave him. You sure give that Man a whupping gonna last him a time didn't you Mister Pearsall, Papa said. Well, Calley said, they say First Thing o'Saint Peter asks you when you get up to the Gate is How was you with the Animals Mister and I didn't want that Bear Poking Son of a Bitch to slip by.

SO NOW, Papa said, we was a Man and two Boys and three Horses and two Dogs and one little o'One Eyed Bear a'going down the Street there in San Antoneya to Senyora Garza's Place and when we got there, he said, Why they was People all lined up to get in and that poor o'Loonie with his twisted up Face was a'setting out there on the Board Walk a'Wiggling his little fat Fingers at the end a'his Fins but wadn't no body a'dropping any Coins in his Tin Pan no moren they was that First Time we ever seen him over by the Joske Brothers Store. But course o'Calley dropped some Coins in his Pan, Papa said,

189

and said Good to see you again Mister. Been a'while ain't it. Oh and then, Papa said, Why that little o'One Eyed Bear crawled up on the Board Walk and set down right there side that Loonie and then o'Possum set his self down on the other side and they both went to giving his o'Twisted up Face some Licks and when they did, he said, Why that o'Fella started a'wiggling his Fingers and tried to hug em he liked it so much and then all Three of em started Howling bout it like they was Singers in the Choir and Oh then People went to clapping and dropping they Coins in his Tin Pan cause they ain't never heared nothing like it in all they Life and didn't never want it to stop. Well he got him some Friends now ain't he, Calley said, even if one of em's a One Eyed Bear and the other one's a Flop Eared Dog. Then, Papa said, we pushed our way on in Senyora Garza's Place and when we did Why o'Fritz took off a'Running and Jumped up on the Bar where Pela Rosa and Annie was a'Dancing to and Fro just pretty as you please and a'singing Beautiful Dreamer and I bout fell over it was so good to see Annie on top a'the World like this. But then, he said, some Man drunk on some thing or other reached his Hand out and took a'holt a'Pela's Foot when she danced by then give it a little Shake and said You come Home with me Darling I'll show you a'nother Dance you ain't never gonna forget But Oh fore he could say it o'Calley give him a good knock on his Head that put him down on the Floor then tipped his John B and give Pela that big Smile. Hidy Pela, he said, I been a'waiting for you all my whole Life and now Here I am. Then, Papa said, o'Calley reached out his arms to her but No she just went a'Singing and a'Dancing on down the Bar and a'scooping up the Coins and didn't even look back. I thought she was gonna be your Wife Mister Pearsall, Marcellus said, Ain't that what you thought. Yes Sir I said, Papa said, but Pela Rosa just danced on off down the Bar and then I seen o'Calley a'going out the Front Door in the other Direction and I knowed we was both Wrong.

*W*E FOUND O'CALLEY A'SETTING

out there in front a'the Alamo on a Bench with his Heart Broke in two, Papa said, and I never seen no body look no Sadder. She picked her a'nother Life over me didn't she, he said and I said, Yes Sir I believe she did, and then Mar-

190   *...o'Calley give him a good knock on his Head*
                                               that put him down on the Floor..

cellus said, Yes Sir I believe she did too. And then, Papa said, of a sudden this big o'Dark Cloud come a'rolling over my own Heart and I said Well I reckon o'Annie picked her a'nother Life too didn't she but right then, he said, here come o'Fritz just a'running out the Dark and wadn't but a second and Why here come Annie too and I was so glad to see her I didn't know what to do. I was fraid I was gonna find you gone a'gain, she said, like you was that other time then she put her Hands to her Face and went to crying bout it and I stepped over and give her a Hug cause I felt the same way bout her. Oh Annie, I said, Oh Annie I am so glad to see you here. I thought you was Lost to me For Ever. No, she said, I won't never be Lost to you For Ever. What bout the Singing and Dancing, Papa said, it ain't gonna take you a'way like it did Pela Rosa is it. I love to Sing and Dance moren any thing in the World, Annie said, but it don't own me. Well what you reckon we gonna do next then Annie, Papa said. I just want be with you is all, Annie said. Yes me too Annie, Papa said, then I looked over there and seen o'Calley a'watching us. Dam if the Door don't shut on one Man but what it opens on a'nother just down the Hall, he said. Oh and then here come Senyora Garza out the Dark and stepped up to o'Calley a'setting there on the Bench. You a'looking for a Job Mister or you just passing through Town like most other Men I ever knowed in my Life, she said. I don't know what I'm a'doing any more, Calley said. I reckon the Good Days is all behind me now. Well why don't you come work for me then, Senyora Garza said. I could use a Hand with the Rowdys when they go to Drinking and a'Whooping it up. Well I don't know what Pela'd have to say bout that, Calley said, she hardly even give me a Look. Why she's the one tole me to come ask you, Senyora Garza said. It ain't that she don't Love you, she said, she just don't wanna go traipsing round the Country like a Gipsy no more is all. Oh it was like the Sun come up on o'Calley then, Papa said, and he was so Happy he just couldn't get out from under it. I'll take the Job Senyora, he said, Yes Ma'am and be glad of it. Oh and then, Papa said, here come Pela Rosa a'stepping out the Dark and she give o'Calley a Look and he give her a Look back and then they hugged one another and went off in the Night together back behind the Alamo some wheres and we didn't hear another Peep out of em.

$\mathcal{S}$ENYORA GARZA WENT AND GOT US
some blankets, Papa said, and me and Annie and Marcellus and o'Fritz all leaned up a'gainst one another and went on off to sleep on that Bench even if they was People a'walking round all over the place but then, he said, I closed my Eyes and Why they was Shimmery People ever wheres you looked too and they was all going round whispering in all them Real People's ear. Oh they was Mexkin Shimmerys and White Shimmerys and Black Shimmerys and Baby Shimmerys and Old Man and Old Woman Shimmerys and it was like they had a Secret they was trying to get over to ever body else but No ever body else was too busy with what they was already a'doing and didn't wanna listen. But, Papa said, I wanted to hear what they got to say so I waved one a'them Old Shimmery Men over and said What's that yall a'whispering in ever bodys Ear but don't no body wanna hear it. Oh we just going round trying to give Good Advice is all. Well I might like to hear some my self, Papa said, if you got any for me. Okay, the Old Shimmery Man said, Here's some You listening. Yes Sir I am, Papa said. Do Right and Risk the Consequences, the Old Shimmery Man said, Good Advice don't get no bettern that does it. My o'Amigo Calley Pearsall says o'Sam Houston said that first, Papa said. Well Yes, the Old Man said, o'Sam Houston did say it First but he got it from us one Night. Who are yall any how, Papa said, I been here two three times and ain't never seen yall before. Yes Sir we always here cause this is a Holy Place and People come here to talk to they self bout some Problem or other. Yes Sir that's xactly what my o'Amigo Calley Pearsall says too, Papa said. Yes Sir but it's us a'doing the Answering even if they think they just talking to they Self. That's our Job, he said. And it ain't easy. Like just fore the War we went round whispering A House Divided Can Not Stand Mister but No Sir didn't no body wanna hear it and you seen what happened next when they went to warring bout it. Some time you just wanna shake em til they Head falls off on the Ground don't you, he said. Was it o'Robert Lee said that bout the House, Papa said, but the Old Shimmery Man said No Sir it was o'Abe Lincoln said it but I been tole he got it out the Good Book one day when he was a'looking for something to say to the People. I made up one my self one time, Papa said. I'd like to hear it, the Old Shimmery Man said, I bet it's a good one ain't it. Don't Never Just Set There Mister, Papa said. That's it. Don't Never Just Set There Mister huh, the Old

Man said. You sure you didn't take that one off a'some body else. No Sir it come to me just like that out the sky one night, Papa said, and I grabbed it for my Family Motto. Well it's a good one, the man said. You don't mine I might pass it on to some body else round here needs to hear it. Maybe you got a'nother one for me you wanna whisper in my Ear fore I wake up, Papa said. How bout that. Okay here's One just specially for you, the Old Shimmery Man said then cupped his Hands round my Ear and whispered some thing in it but then I waked up and couldn't remember a Word he said.

*N*EXT MORNING, Papa said, we went back down the street to have some Eggs and Beans at Senyora Garza's Place and Why that o'Loonie and Possum and that little One-Eyed Bear was already a'having em some thing to Eat out there on the Board Walk and Annie said Well I ain't surprised. Senyora Garza'd feed a Frog if it hopped up and stuck out it's tongue. Then we went on in and there was o'Calley a'setting at the Bar with Senyora Garza a'bringing him Pan Cakes and Pela Rosa a'pouring on the Molasses. Well yall up Bright and Early this morning ain't you, he said, I didn't spect to see you til some time round Christmas. You reckon they's one a'them Pan Cakes for me, Marcellus said. I wouldn't ask cep I'm hungry. Well you and that little Dog set you self down, Senyora Garza said. Yall come to the right place if you hungry and got Forty Dollars on you to pay for it. She's just joking you, Annie said, Why I never seen her charge moren Ten Dollars in my Life. Oh ever body laughed at that, Papa said, But not me cause I knowed my o'Amigo Calley Pearsall was a'Staying and I was a'Going. I'm gonna miss you Mister Pearsall I said, Papa said, I hope you ain't gonna forget me. No Sir, o'Calley said, you already got your Roots in so deep I don't believe I could pull you out with both Hands and a Mule. Oh and then, Papa said, we just naturally give each other a big Hug and wadn't Shy bout it one bit neither. You ever need me Why I'll come a'running, he said, you remember that. Yes Sir I will, Papa said, And I will too. Course we may come a'running any how just to say Hidy he said then Pela Rosa give Annie a Hug a'her own and they both went to crying bout Parting. They ain't nothing bettern having a Friend is they,

Senyora Garza said, then give o'Marcellus a Hug cause they wadn't no body else a'Hugging on him. Oh and then, Papa said, o'Marcellus give her a good long Hug back and all but went to crying his self. I can't help it, he said, I been a'missing my o'Granny Jeffey and Miz Choat both. But after that, Papa said, couldn't no body eat they Pan Cakes no more cep o'Fritz cause we was all so Sad bout leaving and I reckon just wanted to go on and get it over with quicks we could. So, he said, we went on out the Door to where Sister and o'Edward was a'waiting and got on. How far we going, Annie said and I said, Not far as you might think Annie but far enough you gonna know you been on a Trip when we get there. I don't care how far it is, Annie said and give me a squeeze round my middle. Then me and o'Calley give each other a little Tip a'our John B's Adios and we Bumped on off down the Street but not fore we passed that o'Loonie and Possum and that little One Eyed Bear all a'setting out there on the Board Walk a'Crying and a'Howling they Good Byes like it was the End a'the World.

‸IFE'S A FUNNY O'DOG

ain't it Marcellus said when we went a'riding on out a'San Antoneya, Papa said. Started out, Marcellus said, o'Pelo Blanco wanted to Hang you Dead from a Tree but then turned round and saved your Life in the Devil's Sinkhole when he took o'Arlon down under the Quache with his self. Well I hope o'Pelo saved his own Soul a'doing it, Papa said, Be a shame if he don't get some thing out a'it his self. We can ask my o'Granny Jeffey bout it, Marcellus said. She always a'talking Back and Forth to Dead People any how. I reckon some body gonna know. Your o'Granny talks to Dead People, Annie said. Why I never heared such a thing. Yes she does, Papa said, They ain't nothing to it for o'Jeffey. I'd like to hear what o'Arlon got to say for his self after what all he done, Marcellus said, I'd like to hear that. I don't care if I don't never hear nothing more bout o'Arlon the whole rest a'my Life, Papa said, I already heared all I wanna hear. What you reckon made him so Bad, Marcellus said, Maybe he just come in the World like that huh. Some People do, Annie said, like them two Men come up on my Mother that day and done her Bad. Now Annie, Papa said, I thought you wadn't supposed to talk bout that no more. Some time I can't help it, she said. My Daddy didn't never get over it neither and hanged his self off that Oak Tree down there by the Creek. You talk bout it all you want then Annie, Papa said, we got time. No I'll quit it now, she said, I don't wanna hear it no more my self. So, Papa said, we just rode long not no body hardly saying nothing for a good long while but then, he said, we started seeing other People a'going long in the same Direction we was a'going in and some of em was a'going on Horseback and some of em was a'going on Foot but they was all a'going the same Direction we was so, Papa said, I hollered at a Old Man and his Wife a'riding pass on they o'Horse Where yall a'going Mister and the Man hollered back We wanna say Hello to our Little Son one more time fore it's too late. Is he a'going off on a Trip today, Annie said, Is that Why. He went off on his Trip bout forty seven years ago, the Old Man said, and been Dead in the Ground ever since. Oh I'm sorry, Annie said, I didn't know you was talking bout a Long Time a'go. No you didn't know that or nothing else neither, the Old Woman said, but you gonna know it soon nough you ever lose one a'your own like I did mine. Yes Ma'am you gonna know it then. She just talking, the Old Man said, she don't mean nothing by it. Hadn't a'been for o'Jeffey a'talking back and forth tween Her and our Dead Boy she'd a'lost her mine over it long time ago. O'Jeffey, Marcellus said, Why that's my o'Granny you a'talking bout there Mister. Well I don't know bout that, the Old Man said, but what I hear is o'Jeffey's Sick and Dying and most likely won't last the Day out. Oh and when o'Marcellus heared that water come up in his Eye and he said Granny Granny Granny then give o'Edward his heels and run on off down the Road fast as he could go and so did me and Annie and o'Fritz on Sister.

*A*ND WHEN WE GOT THERE, Papa said, Why there was o'Jeffey in her Bed out there under the Shade Tree in her Front Yard where some body'd a'took her and Oh, he said, they was People all lined up and a'crying to get a Last Word from some body or other on the Other Side fore o'Jeffey passed on over her self and couldn't do it no more. Come on Marcellus said and we run over there to o'Jeffey in her Bed but her Eyes was shut down tight and she wadn't hardly breathing no more. Granny, Marcellus said. Granny Granny Granny. Then of a sudden, Papa said, Why o'Jeffey opened one Eye to a little crack and give us a Squint. Shhhh, she said. Oh and o'Marcellus bout went to pieces cause his o'Granny was still a'live and breathing. Oh Granny I thought you was Dead, he said, but you was just playing Possum wadn't you but she put her hand up to Marcellus' cheek and give him a little Pet. No Hon, she said, I ain't playing Possum. Why I already got one Foot over on the other side and bout to slide the other one on over too. Ain't gonna be but just a minute or two more, she said. You scared Granny, Marcellus said. I reckon I'd be scared. Oh Lawd no I ain't scared, o'Jeffey said. Why that's where we all come when we was borned ain't it. Course, she said, they gonna wanna see what all Bad Habits I put in my Sack when I was over here fore they let me back in. But Don't Worry they's always some body to help you climb up the Ladder if you ain't been too Bad, she said, You ain't never just all by you self here or there neither one. The Ladder, Papa said, now where'd this Ladder come from you talking bout. The one goes up to the Big Mister's House, o'Jeffey said, that Ladder. Why Granny you ain't never said nothing bout no Big Mister before, Marcellus said. Well I guess it's just the closer I get the more I remember is all, o'Jeffey said. The Big Mister ain't nobody but all the Good People they ever was all rolled up into One any how, she said, and only way to get rolled up into One with em is to climb up that Ladder you self and Jump in but the only way you ever gonna climb up that Ladder is to help some body else climb up it too and for ever Step you don't help some body else climb up it Why you gonna lose a Step back you self. Oh and then of a sudden, Papa said, o'Jeffey raised her self up on her bed and pointed her Finger out cross all them other People to where Mister and Miz Choat was a'coming with Little Bird and Oh he was a'pointing his Finger straight back at o'Jeffey same as she was at him.

FIRST THING MIZ CHOAT DONE,

Papa said, was bend down and give o'Jeffey a Kiss on her Head. Oh Jeffey, she said, Oh Jeffey Oh Jeffey what we ever gonna do with out you. Don't

197

worry, o'Jeffey said, Don't one Door close shut but what a'nother one opens up down the Hall, then she give me a look and said, Ain't that what your o'Amigo Calley says. And then, Papa said, Why o'Jeffey reached up and took a'holt a'Bird's Finger and give it a little Squeeze and then he took a'holt a'her Finger and give it a little Squeeze back. They talking, Marcellus said, They just a'talking back and forth ain't they. Then, Papa said, ever body come in close to catch a Word or two a'what they was saying but No they wadn't using no Words tween em you could hear cause Bird hadn't never said not even one Word in all his whole Life. But then, he said, o'Jeffey give Bird one last Squeeze on his Finger and closed her Eyes down tight For Ever and when she did, Papa said, Why of a sudden Bird opened his Eyes first time he ever did in his Life and looked round at all the People a'standing there Crying and then he turned his little sideways Face to me and said the first words he ever did say in the World. They's some body over here wants to talk to you he said and Oh when them words come out his mouth Why ever body drawed way back cause it wadn't no little Boy Voice said em. Who's that a'doing the talking out Bird's mouth, Mister Choat said and Marcellus said, Why that's my o'Granny Jeffey her self a'doing the talking. I knowed it was o'Jeffey too, Papa said, so I said Who you a'talking to over there wants to talk to me and she said I never seen him before but he's a'holding up one White Domino and says to tell you That's just how close he come. Oh it was o'Pelo Blanco was who it was, Papa said, and it bout made me cry I was so Happy to know he wadn't gonna have to set on no Flat Rock down in Hell from now til Kingdom Come. Tell him Hidy, Papa said, and tell him I'm glad to hear from him again. Well you ain't gonna be so glad when you hear what he got to say to you, o'Jeffey said out from Little Bird's mouth. Yes Ma'am I'm listening, Papa said. Go on and tell me. He says they building a'Hanging Stand out there in front a'the Alamo over in San Antoneya cause they gonna hang a Man from it Saturday Noon when ever bodys in town to watch. What'd that Man do they gonna hang him for it, Papa said. This Man I'm talking to here, o'Jeffey said, says that Man lost his temper and Killed a'nother man out there in the street where ever body seen it and now he's setting in the Jail House a'twirling his spur Ching e Ching e ChingChing-Ching cause they ain't nothing he can do to take it back and wouldn't never any how even if he could. Oh I bout fell down Dead from the Surprise, Papa

...o'Jeffey give Bird one last Squeeze on h
Finger and closed her Eyes down tight For Ever.

said, cause now I knowed it was my o'Friend Calley Pearsall they was gonna hang and not no other. I gotta get back to San Antoneya I said, Papa said, and jumped up on Sister like I had Bed Springs in my Feet and so did Annie and Fritz behind me. Let's go Annie said and throwed her arms round my middle and squeezed tight to hang on and Oh, Papa said, I give Sister my heels and Lit a Shuck on out a'there like a Ball a'Greeced Lighting. Don't worry Mister Pearsall, I hollered, I'm Coming I'm Coming I'm Coming . . .

And thus ends

THE DEVIL'S SINKHOLE

Book Two of The Papa Stories

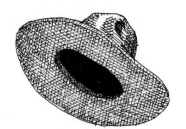

ACKNOWLEDGMENTS

Once again (as they did on *The Devil's Backbone*) my pals Steve Harrigan and Bill Broyles set their own work aside to read an early draft of this book and give good and perceptive advice. So did my longtime friend Connie Todd, and I am hugely grateful to all three for their wise counsel and friendship. That is true of other friends as well: George and Bonnie Siddons . . . Pat and Keith Carter . . . Julie Speed . . . Barbara Morgan . . . Van Ramsey . . . Dyson Lovell . . . Rolf Larson . . . and Jack Watson.

And thank you most kindly to my publisher Dave Hamrick who has championed these Papa Stories from the very beginning—as has my editor Casey Kittrell, who looks after Papa as if he were a member of his own family. Thank you, Dave. Thank you, Casey.

And thanks also to all the other good people over there at UT Press who have made the publishing of this book such a fun and congenial journey: Ellen McKie . . . Lynne Chapman . . . Jan McInroy . . . Colleen Ellis . . . Brian Contine . . . Brenda Jo Hoggatt . . . and Dawn Bishop.

Eternal thanks also to Joe Ciardiello for his fine illustrations that add life to these stories as well as information. Thank you, Joe.

I've always been blessed with bright and spunky office mates, none more so than Kate Bowie (now Carruth). Kate has that rare ability to make you feel good about what you're writing. Nothing was ever too silly or too odd or too sad for her, and her enthusiasm for these stories was a daily inspiration. That's true of Joe Pat Davis too, who took Kate's place when she moved on and quickly became an indispensable part of all things Papa, just as Kate had been. Thank you, Kate. Thank you, Joe Pat.

And certainly—and always—I thank my dear wife, Sally, for being such a treasured part of this and all my other pursuits. I'm a lucky boy. Thank you, Sally. And love . . .

Bill Wittliff
Austin, Texas
November 16, 2015